An Idol Killing

Edinburgh • London • San Francisco

An Idol Killing

mark j. white

Edinburgh • London • San Francisco

First published in 1997
by AK Press

P. O. Box 12766
Edinburgh, Scotland
EH8 9YE
UK

P. O. Box 40682
San Francisco, CA
94140-0682
USA

British Library Cataloguing-in-Publication Data
A CIP catalogue record for this book is available
from the British Library

Library of Congress Cataloging-in-Publication Data
A catalog record for this title is available
from the Library of Congress

ISBN 1 873176 89 9

Printed in USA.

Cover and interior design by Bruce Grant.

To
SW, JC, OSH and DLeC
for all the fun we've had

Special thanks to Phil for the encouragement and a few conversations; Gina for the proofreading; Kate; and everyone at AK, especially Dean for being interested in the first place.

———————————————————————— Sixteen lanes of ConGrip™ curved off into the distance. Sixteen lanes heading clockwise. And to their right, another sixteen lanes heading anticlockwise. More than just a roadway, it provides a multitude of services for the City's residents. Most of them call it the Ring, and it gives them a place to sit and fume in their own metal worlds during rush time. It also provides a playground for the City's youth, the children that grew up with it as an everyday reality in their lives. Somewhere they, the Surfers and Bikers and Joyriders, could come and compete; in full view of their peers and the Cams. The Ring's main service to the residents of the City, and the principal reason for its construction, wasn't to aid commuters and the transporters getting from one side of the vast metropolis to the other; it was designed to totally separate the vast city-centre it constrained from everyone else. The Government called it the Restricted Zone, and referred to its residents as either refugees or illegal aliens. Everyone else, including the decent people in the neon-lit, super-clean, air-filtered, UV-shielded, taxed cars that crawled around it, called it Edge Central. The people in the cars didn't live there, they lived on the outside of the thirty-two lanes, on the side known as the City, and most wanted to forget Edge Central existed. They couldn't even see Edge Central as they drove around the Ring because the inside wall rose far into the air; a vast, pulsating, ever changing billboard advertising fantasy, concealing a different reality beyond. The only people who could see into Edge Central on a daily basis were those rich and lucky enough to live or work in one of the towering offices or apartment blocks that surrounded the Ring. Or unless you watched the news on either Sat or Net, that is; Edge Central was featured quite a lot these days.

The reasons behind the Ring's construction were of little concern to the occupants of the jet black van with the jet black windows, cutting radically across the anticlockwise lanes. They were more concerned about whether they were going to make the correct exit tube in one piece; the driver had nearly overshot.

'Jus' cause you embarrassed yourself big time today ain't no reason to try an' impress us with your drivin' technique,' laughed one of the passengers.

The driver didn't reply, he was too busy overcompensating the van's hypersensitive steering.

'Dwain! Cut that shit out this instant!' snapped another. 'Everyone makes mistakes sometimes. Or do you want me to remind you of that messy little incident in Mexico when someone's gun jammed? No one wanted to sit next to you on the flight home now did they?' he laughed sourly.

The third passenger started to laugh.

'You can shut the fuck up! . . . It was the slop they call food over there, anyways . . .' Dwain stated, indignantly.

'Enough! You're supposed to be professionals so act fuckin' professional!'

The van shuddered as it rapidly reduced speed to join the queue of traffic leaving the Ring down the nearest exit tube. It was a fairly nondescript vehicle based on the Naguki LoadStar, a very common production model. Normally it wouldn't have merited a second glance from anyone. The driver of the vehicle in front, however, caught a brief glimpse of it in his rear monitor, and was more than eager to immediately pull into one of the slower lanes of the descending tube, even if this meant forcing the vehicles already in that lane to take evasive action to avoid colliding. Horns blared. He sat facing rigidly ahead as the black van accelerated past, as if refusing to acknowledge it even existed, or that he was ever in front of it. He only became animated again when the large coach that was now in front of the black van, began to cut in front of him.

Not all the exits from the Ring were through exit tubes. Some were above ground ramps that swept, spaghetti like, off the ring, and down into the overburdened terra-level road system, or up and onto one of the many raised hyperways that could take you directly to the suburbs. Exit tubes normally took the drivers into buildings surrounding the Ring, or into private toll tunnels, and they all curved away from Edge Central. Except this tube. It was the newest exit to date, only completed two years earlier and the only one to curve underneath the Ring, into Edge Central. It took the vehicles that travelled through it to the only nonrestricted building in the zone: the highly exclusive and very expensive Pyramid Plaza. The Plaza was the first, and only, building so far completed in the Government's much publicised Restricted Zone regeneration plan.

Overhead signs pulsed directions to the vehicles as they passed beneath them, informing the drivers of possible destinations and which lane they should be in to get to them. The signs were generated by the Plaza's Guidance/Surveillance system, which also interrogated all the vehicles that entered the complex on auto, then generated directions for their onboard ice to follow.

'Take the first on the left, I'm not walking all the way from the car park.'

'Hey, Max, don't you know they have walkways an' stuff nowadays?' asked Dwain.

Max looked up from the bag at his feet, ignoring the last comment directly, 'Now remember what I said, all of you,' he looked first at the two men opposite him, then at the one driving. 'We're professionals; this is going to be done in a professional manner. We're going to cause as little disturbance as possible doing this, I don't want to receive no unwanted attention from anywhere. Do you hear me?' he asked sternly. The two men opposite him nodded, but didn't respond verbally.

'Well?' he snapped.

'Yes, sir!' they chorused, with just a hint of sarcasm.

Max chose to ignore it. 'I want everything on this job to be done quick and quietly with a minimum of fuss. I trust you boys will be showing our, er . . . trainee, how professionals work, won't you?' he nodded towards the driver frantically struggling with the controls up front.

The van veered across the lanes of traffic, causing the vehicles nearest it to brake and swerve sharply out of its unpredictable path, and towards the empty emergency slip lane on the left side of the tube. Surprisingly, none of the inconvenienced drivers used their horns as retribution for the act. The road branched apart, and changed from a gentle incline into a much steeper upwards spiral. The van driver broke sharply as he was bombarded with REDUCE SPEED NOW messages from the Guidance/Surveillance system, then the tunnel opened out and disappeared. The van did not emerge at ground level, but into a large, magnificently lit cavern, perhaps twenty metres high. The tunnel road joined a curved two lane white highway, running along its edge. Neither end was visible because the cavern, along with the road, curved away in both directions. The centre of the cavern looked to be full of marble and chrome tubes or pillars, rising to the vaulted ceiling from a maze of smaller pillars and walls. Slip roads, also white and spotlessly clean, radiated inwards from the highway, and led to the vast maze. A virtual map popped up before the driver, explaining visually that the cavern was actually a huge subterranean doughnut, and he should pull off to the right and park if he wanted to enter the building above. The van swerved right and headed down the nearest one of the ridiculously clean roads, towards the nearest pillars. Eventually the road led past one of the many entrances and the van slid to a halt.

'Hey, Boy,' Max turned to the driver, 'we're getting out here. I want you to go and park the van somewhere, not too far away mind, then come and find us.'

'Uh, okay, er, Max.' The driver, even under the large goggles he wore, looked nervous. 'Where, er, I mean how, er . . .'

'We'll be having a cup of coffee.' He leaned a bit closer to the boy, as if seeing him for he first time, 'You can use your glasses to find us, remember? Just the way they showed you in the academy.'

The driver nodded sheepishly.

'If you have any problems, ask Frank. He'll be watching you.' Max shook his head as he turned away, a weary half smile on his face, then opened the rear door of the van. As he climbed out, he turned back to the driver, 'So don't forget that bag over there,' he nodded to a black holdall on the floor of the van before stepping out.

Three men climbed out of the jet black van. They were each dressed identically, in large dark glasses and knee length, leather-look, black coats. The first shooed the nervously advancing doorman away and led the other two towards the entrance in front of him. He was about thirty five, maybe forty, years old, with a wide, square head, no neck to speak of, and extensive shoulders that stretched his old and battered coat to its limits. He was known as Max. The second man, Dwain, was altogether much smaller, and perhaps fifteen or twenty years younger. He had no real distinguishing features save for a small, twisted mouth that, when opened, exposed a pair of large bucked teeth. The man bringing up the rear, Dillon, was the same build as Max, but even taller, black, and sporting dreadlocks and piercings. He was also the only one of the trio who looked happy. Behind him the van squealed noisily away from the curb, leaving a portion of its tires behind to mar the super clean road.

The trio walked to the nearest entrance along a thick red carpet, lined with small, gnarled Bonsai trees. It led up to an exquisitely carved piece of marble-look wall and an entervator. As the men walked up the carpet they could see that it was only one of about twenty entervators in the immediate area. It hung on the wall, at floor level, a glass and metal cylinder, about twelve feet high with an equal diameter, sitting in a small groove amongst the carvings. Above it was a sign welcoming them to the Pyramid Plaza. Not a pulsating, three-dimensional ice-driven logo, but a tasteful, slightly curved, hand-crafted plaque of rosewood, with golden letters etched into it. The door of the entervator slid silently open as the three approached, and crossed its proximity threshold.

'Welcome to the PYRAMID PLAZA! Please select your internal destination from the hologramatic U-Choose™ three-dimensional representation before you.' The voice emphasized the name of the building as if it were a game show host plugging its latest show. The entervator's interior was attempting to be plush but tasteful; red, artificially aged, leather-look seats, finished in brass, wrapped around its glass wall, a thick shag carpet covered the floor and more leather the ceiling. The only overt sign of modernity was the brightly opaque holo-map of the building floating in the centre of the lift.

'Max?' The large black man stepped inside first, and up to the map. The Plaza, according to the image, was a three-sided pyramid. The cutaway view had a 'U ARE HERE' arrow positioned towards the bottom, and a series of highlighted tracks leading from it; indicating the possible routes the entervator could take.

Max shrugged, 'How high can we go before we have to change?'

Dillon studied the map as Max and Dwain sat down. 'The lobby of the hotel section on the second stage I think . . .' he answered absently, and touched the end of the highest highlighted route with a gloved finger.

The doors closed and the entervator rose up the groove behind the welcome sign, disappearing through an impossibly smooth ellipse in the cavern's dramatically lit ceiling. The entervator's ice, linked to the Plaza's SecCam system, began its scan cycle and started sending information about its present occupants to the central ice of the Pyramid Plaza, which in turn passed the information on to the various security firms responsible for the Plaza's internal well being. Its first scan would be of their ID cards, specifically their credit rating; the entervator they rode in was VIP only designated, and not for use by the general public, unless they could afford to pay for the privilege.

'Would you look at this then; un-fuckin' believable, it's huge man, fuckin' huge! Those walls must be a mile long at least!' whistled Dwain as the lift rose into the lowest above-ground part of the Plaza.

All three men stared.

The lift had brought them up near the middle of a huge, enclosed, triangular park, its walls tapering upwards towards a smaller triangular ceiling a quarter of a mile above their heads. The park was landscaped, and full of exotic plants, trees and animals. There was a three-sided waterfall in the centre that supplied a number of the streams that snaked through the vegetation. Almost hidden by the subtropical chaos of the park were perhaps a hundred other entervators, identical to the one they were in and thousands of steps and spindly walkways joining it to the enclosing building. The walkways cut through the lower vegetation and rose upwards to join one of the three walls, at various levels. The entervators hung on thin tubes that passed through only a few inches of one side of each cylinder so they appeared, from a distance at least, to rise magically unaided through the branches and vines of the trees. Dancing around the tubes and trees, competing with the birds, were a number of Surfers, employed by the Plaza Corporation to entertain those users not overawed by the atrium itself. And if that didn't impress, it was even possible to rent a balloon and harness to join them.

'Been 'ere previous, Boss Man?' Dillon asked Max.

'No I haven't and I don't like it. Shit, we still don't have a recent plan for this place on our ice yet. I'm telling you, this is feeling sloppy, y'know what I mean?' Max leaned towards Dillon, as if to say something further, but Dwain interrupted.

'I don't see what your problem is, we ain't gonna be doin' nothin' tonight anyway, 'cept sittin' aroun' while someone else has all the fun.' He sounded belligerent, and looked annoyed.

'Do that upset you, Redneck?' asked Dillon, grinning.

Dwain sat up at Dillon's tone, and glared at the man, 'This is a chicken shit waste of time 'cause it ain't never gonna happen, so there ain't no point in us bein' here. So yeah, I'm upset 'cause I don't like wastin' my time,' argued Dwain. 'Besides,' he added, rising from the seat, 'who're you callin' Redneck? You shouldn't be callin' no one nothin' 'till you learn to speak properly,' he emphasized the LY with a sneer.

'Do you know what a double negative is, Redneck?' Dillon grinned, adopting a strained upper class accent.

Dwain opened and closed his mouth a couple of times, as if about to respond, but caught the look on Max's face and lapsed back into a sullen silence.

The entervator informed them they were approaching their destination by chiming once, then the park's ceiling obscured their view and they slid to a halt. The trio turned to face the door, waiting for it and the lobby door beyond, to open. Dwain was still grumbling under his breath and being ignored by the smiling Dillon and stern Max.

The doors parted and someone poked a wide bore, very offensive looking gun muzzle into the lift. The security guard on the end of it didn't even have time to say "Freeze" before Dillon stepped forward, caught the muzzle and twisted it, wrenching the weapon from her grasp. He then jabbed it back the way it had come, smashing the plastic butt into her stunned face. Blood spurting from her shattered nose, she collapsed backwards. As she dropped, Dillon moved out of the entervator and swung the weapon in a wide arc, aiming a second blow towards her cranium. A nano second before the gun butt would have made contact her head exploded, spraying blood, bone and brains unevenly across the white, marble-look floor of the lobby. And over the advancing Dillon. Her body flipped backwards and slumped clumsily into its own gore, twitching.

Dillon turned around slowly, away from the dead woman in front of him, and the horrified faces of shoppers unlucky enough to have witnessed the scene, and stared at the demented expression on Dwain's face. Dwain relaxed, and smiled back at him, then blew the smoke away from the muzzle of his recently used hand-cannon, before re-holstering it.

'Unnecessary, Redneck, very unnecessary . . .' Dillon sighed, extremely calmly for a man with grey matter splattered all over him.

Max just stood there with a look of utter disbelief on his face.

Johnny pointed the van in the direction he hoped he'd find the car park and once more tried to cope with the hypersensitive controls of the van. He was having a hard time. Today wasn't turning out to be the best day of his life. In fact, it was rapidly turning into the worst day of his life, which he found hard to believe considering recent history.

'I could just drive off now, get lost, just disappear . . .' he spoke out loud, without even realising it.

'No you couldn't!'

Johnny nearly crashed the van into the row of bonsai trees lining the slip road. It was Frank.

Frank unfolded in the seat next to him, and looked at the boy, 'You're one of us now, in the firm so to speak, so you best get used to the idea quickly: it'll make life a whole lot easier for everyone.'

Johnny quickly looked at Frank, then back to the road. He knew that the man wasn't really there; he was somewhere else, perhaps at the academy or on one of the mobile platforms. It was the glasses he was wearing that made it look like he was sitting next to him. If

An Idol

he didn't have them on he wouldn't be able to see him. He'd been told that he shouldn't even think of the glasses as glasses really; they were solid, totally opaque plastic with circuits that digitally reproduced the scene their user would see, as if they really were glasses. With, of course, any adjustments that his personal ice, or anyone on the same wavelength with the right decoder signal, thought necessary or useful. In this instance Frank, the fifth member of the team, was instructing his own ice to tell Johnny's ice to generate a virtual image of himself, as if he were really in the van with him.

'I was, ere, just . . .' Johnny sheepishly began.

'Well don't do it out loud!' said Frank, fading out of sight.

There were no spaces on the first level of parking Johnny came to, according to the Plaza's guidance system, so he continued heading downwards. The next tube dropped him three floors, then opened into another large subterranean cavern. Noticeably shabbier than the uppermost level, its open expanses were being used as a huge parking area. Spread evenly amongst the parked vehicles were large entervators, at least twice the size of those on the higher, VIP level. Around them were clusters of vendors and hawkers, attempting to pre-empt the lures of the classier shops higher up. There was no valet parking here; this was where the modestly well off and the coach loads of tourists parked.

Johnny swung the van into the nearest space, clipping the back of the car in the next bay.

'Hey, you! Asshole . . .' the internal speaker in the van amplified an angry voice from outside. Johnny realised that the car he had clipped, a large, almost new, Neo-Caddie, must only just have arrived as well and that the occupant was still in it. He opened the door of the van, picked up the bag with Frank's amplifier in it and turned to see a fat man, standing beside the Caddie, staring at him with his mouth open.

'I bet you wish you'd looked at who you were about to slag off before you opened your mouth, don't you, fatty?' Johnny asked menacingly, jumping down from the raised door. In the academy he'd been taught that the correct (the quickest) way for an IS agent to deal with members of the public that are not targets in any ongoing operation was to immediately intimidate them into blind compliance with the wishes of the afore-mentioned agent. The van's door silently shut behind Johnny as he stared at the ashen-faced man.

'See this? It says IS.' Johnny held up his ID laminate. 'That means that the government, who I'm sure you voted for, say I can do whatever I like.' He walked around the large, ostentatious car, towards the man. The rear lights on the left side were shattered, and the bumper pushed, unnaturally, into its recess.

'Now, who the fuck are you?' he asked menacingly.

The fat man had frozen, totally unable to speak. He was about fifty, with short, untidy hair. He appeared to be in a state of partial undress; beneath his Agushi lawn jacket his shirt was untucked and buttoned up wrong and his flies were undone. Johnny noticed the passenger for the first time and revised his opinion of how long the man had been parked there.

'Weaver, Adrian Weaver,' the man finally blurted.

'And is this Mrs. Weaver?' asked Johnny, peering at the woman unsteadily putting her lipstick on in the passenger seat.

'Ere, no . . . she's not.'

'There is a Mrs. Weaver though, isn't there?' Johnny straightened his back and was grinning openly at the man's discomfort.

'Ere, yes, but it really isn't . . .' Mr. Weaver began, unconvincingly.

'Leave!' commanded Johnny, as per academy instructions on terminating an interview with a member of the public who was of no use to the ongoing operation. Mr. Weaver couldn't get his car door open fast enough.

Johnny began walking towards the entervator, his step and mood much lighter now; he was beginning to enjoy himself.

An Idol

'That was a complete waste of time!' Frank appeared, walking next to him. 'You should have told him to get lost and just ignored him, boy, we've got work to do!' he added.

They walked up to the nearest entervator dock, passed a small crowd of shoppers and stalls. The dock was empty, but indicated the entervator would land within seconds.

'Where are the others?' Johnny decided he should just ignore Frank's comments because it was obvious he wasn't going to be able to do anything right by him. He watched as Frank walked, ghostlike, through a tourist taking a photograph.

'Use your glasses, Johnny.'

The entervator arrived, and its doors opened, allowing its passengers to disembark. Its ice then proceeded to welcome its new passengers and, unlike the entervators in the upper levels, embarked on a list of the currently available discounts on goods and services provided by the wide range of stores inside the Plaza. Johnny, and Frank after a fashion, stepped into the entervator, but the people nearest them, who had been waiting for the entervator to arrive, suddenly found other things to look at and drifted away, leaving Johnny as its only passenger.

Frank watched as Johnny ignored the entervators holo-map and fumbled awkwardly with his own virtual controls. They had popped up, invisible to anyone not wearing IS issue goggles, near the boy's left hand. As Johnny moved his arm from the elbow, the virtual controls moved as well, always being just out of reach.

'Don't move your arm, just your hand, from the wrist,' helped Frank, tersely.

Johnny did as he was told and his finger "touched" the node linked to the telepresence mode. Tactile feedback was provided by a reactor pad in the tip of his glove. The controls evaporated and reappeared in another configuration, enabling Johnny to select, from a translucent menu hanging in the air in front of him, whose view he was going to see. The choices were Max (greyed out and unavailable), Dwain or Dillon. He chose Dillon.

Killing

'Ah, Johnny Boy, payin' I a visit, I see,' greeted Dillon. The system was designed to warn the user that they had company.

'Where are you?' asked Johnny, after a moment's pause. He had been momentarily confused to find himself face to face with Dillon, until he realised the man was looking in a mirror. The telepresence image was floating in a virtual window in front of him, its three-dimensional representation of Dillon's view spilling out towards him whenever he focused directly onto it.

'Jus' havin' a wash.' Johnny watched Dillon turn around, and saw he was in a large, opulent-looking lavatory.

His location appeared on a holo-map, overlaid over the window, as he spoke. Johnny compared it to the holo-map of the Plaza inside the entervator and realised he'd have to walk the last section; the entervator he was in only went up to the lower levels of the park atrium. He selected the destination and the doors silently closed.

'You been missin' the fun, Johnny Boy. Dwain got himself exited an' blew the head off one of the Plaza security. Max's pissed off, as you can imagine. Seems someone ain't been communicating, know what I mean?'

Johnny's mouth dropped open and he watched as Dillon walked out into the lobby. There were orange suited Plaza guards everywhere and a gawping crowd had built up around one of the entervator tubes. The orange suited guards were setting up a blur screen around it and trying to disperse the onlookers. Johnny could see Max standing next to Dwain, arguing with an angry, yet nervous looking security guard with gold epaulets. That guard was flanked by three ashen faced security guards and an older woman in a pin-striped smock. As Dillon approached the group Johnny could make out a crumpled orange jumpsuit lying on the floor behind the screen and a fan of red staining the floor where the head should have been.

'What happened?' Johnny asked.

'Not sure. The lift must've scanned our hardware and notified the guard, although why she didn't know we were IS is beyond me. She should have been informed by the building's ice,' Dillon explained, puzzled.

Johnny watched Max turn away from the security chief and touch his left ear with his left forefinger. He started speaking rapidly to the air in front of him and kept gesturing towards Dwain. Johnny couldn't hear what was being said, but saw a look of immense discomfort cross Dwain's face. The security chief began walking away, talking to the woman. As Dillon got nearer to the group Johnny could hear her response: '. . . Nothing I can do, you heard him; they are IS. What do you want me to do? Have you arrest them?' she snapped at the man in the epaulets. 'Look, I've been told to fuck off and that's what I'm going to do, now get that body moved before it ends up on the news . . .'

Johnny's entervator arrived at its destination, drawing his attention away from the macabre scene in the floating box. Its ice informed him he must change to reach his final destination and provided him with a printout detailing the most direct route.

'I'll see you there, I've got to walk,' he informed Dillon, terminating the link.

Frank had disappeared again, so Johnny stepped into the Plaza alone, ignoring the printout that the entervator had thoughtfully provided, and activated the internal map of the Plaza stored on the goggles' ice.

The doors had opened onto a small shopping arcade in one of the external walls. The arcade was halfway up the wall and overlooked the park below, but Johnny didn't immediately notice the inside of the building, not until he reached the walkway that would take him to the lobby; he was too busy trying to follow the virtual map in the air in front of him, and not trip over anything in the process. He looked up and whistled, stopping in his tracks. He'd seen Vid clips of the interior of the Plaza, it was famous worldwide, but he'd never appreciated the sheer scale of the place. He'd never seen so much vegetation in one place before either, at least not the well kept riot of colours that greeted his gaze; the parks in the City were just parched grasslands with a few stunted and misshapen trees and bushes for fauna. He turned around on the spot, letting his gaze drift upwards and across the tiered wall stretching up above him. Almost obscured behind the hanging trellises were the shops and cafes that overlooked the colossal garden. The second thing that struck him about the place was how uncrowded it was; Johnny, like most people brought up in the City, had grown used to crowds. So much so, he had never really noticed them until they were absent. The Plaza certainly wasn't empty, but due to its size, gave the impression of an excess of space and room he wasn't at all used to.

He stood for an instant, taking in the incredible scene in front of him, then stepped onto the walkway. It started as a powered ramp that took him out over the vast garden, then turned into shallow steps that spiralled up, towards the ceiling.

Johnny didn't see the surfers until he was halfway across the void, when three passed by, both above and below the walkway. A look of longing crossed his face and he whirled to follow their progress. They all cut back in unison, then dived towards the waterfall below, pulling up at the last second to arc majestically upwards again and disappear behind a clump of tall trees in the middle distance. A few seconds later they reappeared, zig-zagging slowly towards the roof of the atrium. Instead of the baggy UV street wear most surfers used, "designed to keep the rays off and your skin on", these surfers wore either brightly coloured, tightly fitting body suits that would be no good at stopping road rash, or were naked and painted; Johnny couldn't tell. His expression hardened, 'Nah, that looks boring.'

He turned away, looking for the thermal generators he knew must be around somewhere. They produced the thermals that the surfers needed to get the altitude and stay fast. He only managed to spot a couple before disappearing into the lobby of the hotel.

The scene appeared to have changed somewhat in the short time it had taken him to get there. The Plaza security guards didn't seem quite as unhappy as they had before; in fact a couple of them, especially the security chief, seem to be trying to stop themselves from laughing openly. Johnny walked up to Dillon.

'What's happened now?' he asked. The man looked up, and grinned.

'Seems the reason the security guard Dwain offed didn't know we was IS was that the building's ice didn't tell her. You wanna know why?' He didn't wait for an answer before continuing, 'Because the dumb bitch had bypassed it and was plugged directly into the entervator system.' He shrugged. 'She didn't want the building's ice to know what information she was accessing or what software she was running, so she was jacked directly into the entervators, bypassing it. All she saw was three heavily armed dudes. She had her own ice set to weapons an' outlines mode only; so it didn't read our identity codes.' Dillon shook his head at her folly then, seeing Johnny's uncomprehending expression, carried on, 'She was not a hundred percent Plaza Sec, see . . . I mean she was employed by them, sure, but was an undercover operative for someone else.'

Johnny nodded, unconvincingly. Then after a pause asked, 'Who was she working for?'

'Us,' Dillon answered.

The girl squeezed through the small gap between two of the speaker stacks, away from the wall of the building, and moved towards the open ground in front of her. She paused, still in the shadows, and quickly bent to adjust her shoe fastenings. She was about five feet tall, slim bordering on skinny, and wearing a short black PuffaMac, black leggings and black trainers. The hood of the girl's coat was up, concealing her hair and most of her face. She raised her head, and looked around; the remainder of her face, not already obscured by the hood, was hidden behind a pair of large green sunnies and an OzFilter. There were perhaps only twenty or thirty people in the area directly in front of her, mainly technicians making final adjustments to the sound system or RaveWall behind her. And a handful of HappySec bouncers, just standing around, looking hard. Past them, the moshing fence had been set up: a fifteen-foot high Synthnet tube pinned into the ground. It encircled what was being laughingly referred to as "the stage". The moshing fence separated the technicians and the bouncers from a seething hoard of excited, stoned, drunk, screaming, dirty, but generally happy, individuals on the other side. The girl inside the moshing fence stood and stared for several moments, as if looking for someone or something in particular on the other side, then walked out into the sunshine.

She turned to her right and began walking towards where she knew there would be an exit through the fence. The HappySec bouncer manning the gate, if surprised to see someone leaving the "stage area", didn't show it. He opened the fence quickly, then efficiently moved the nearest people out of her way so she could leave. He used a Serbian cattle prod, so they moved promptly. She slipped away from the rapidly shutting fence and protesting dancers, and into the crowd, heading east. The nearest buildings, other than the one that loomed up behind her, were about half a mile away. Two men had watched her leave the enclosed area; and they began to follow. It was busy, the crowd was making progress very slow. Consisting of mainly over excited juves or twenty-somethings of both sexes, it writhed around her to the deafening beat of the late afternoon music. Mixed amongst the revellers were many Cam ops, struggling to find the definitive clip of the evening, and make their fortune.

After speaking briefly together, the fatter one of the two men following the girl, the one in the sweat stained straw hat, sped up and pushed his way past her, so that he was positioned in front of her. He kept his back towards her and continued to walk a few feet in front of her, moving the crowd out of his, and by default of his ample bulk, her way as well. The girl didn't appear to notice. The man behind her, the one with no hair and a big grin, grinned even more. They made their way towards the distant buildings.

When the crowd began to noticeably thin out, and it was possible to walk without having to push past someone every step, the two men drifted away from her and were eventually lost from sight. She was amongst the buildings now. They stretched up towards the red evening clouds, but as only a shadow of their former glory; they were now broken, jagged, or fallen. Their lower levels were brightly daubed however, despite their ill health, and many supported various, more recent if as decrepit, tarpaulin and card-covered shacks. And they were all playing host to thousands of people. All the still intact roofs and balconies had been turned into temporary platforms, allowing the party people to gather and prepare for the evening; they were the royal boxes and the front row seats for the night's forthcoming festivities. The girl didn't stop and look around, but carried on purposefully down the cracked tarmac between the old buildings. Some of the people around her were just milling around or dancing, trying to find people up on the buildings and arrange their vantage points for the show, or trying to buy things from the dealers who were out in force. Most of the people were moving though, making in the direction she had come from. Some of them were on their own, obviously looking for friends or maybe customers, while others were in groups of up to thirty or forty people. The girl watched their faces as they trooped past. A wide selection of the City's subgroups were present, mixing freely without any sign of the tensions normally caused by differences in skin, clothes or washing habits. All of them appeared to be a having a wild time. Mixed amongst the City inhabitants were small pockets of tourists, clinging tightly to their Cams and each other, their eyes wide and questioning. And more reporters recording and broadcasting it all:

'There are so many of them, so soon; it isn't even dark yet. I can't even estimate the volume of people building up around me! This is totally incredible, Brian . . .'

A couple of Technicals, souped-up Edge-built off-roaders, were attempting to nose their way down the shattered, overcrowded street. They appeared to be stuck by the sheer volume of people around them. As the girl got nearer to them she could see that both of the brightly painted vehicles were flying the One Tribe colours. One of them had a bright pink and green striped anti-tank cannon on the roof, and the man sitting behind it appeared to be threatening the people in front of his vehicle with it. They were just laughing at him, the way only totally wrecked people can laugh. The man with the big gun threw his arms into the air and gave up. Above all of the chaos around her was the noise caused by the competing sound systems on every street corner. The girl walked on, from one shattered street to the next. The buildings gradually became smaller, turning from abandoned offices and shops into abandoned, once suburban, homes. The one constant was the crowd; the ever changing mass showed no signs of thinning out.

A while later the broken buildings ended suddenly, as if some momentous hand had descended and swept away everything beyond an invisible marker. She had reached the 'cleared' area just before the Ring, half a mile away. From ground level the Ring rose to between twenty five and seventy five metres into the air, depending on where you were. The girl was heading for a low section, just visible above the jutting waste and debris before her. Beyond the Ring, the shining, complete towers of the City shimmered through the haze. Other people were also heading out of Edge Central, but nowhere near as many as were coming in. Some of those leaving were obviously families; mothers and fathers and children. Other were on their own. They were all laden down with ill-wrapped baggages, as much as they could carry; the meagre possessions of an uncomfortably hard life. She passed along the column of very ragged figures roped together, also shuffling in the direction of the City. Some of them were crying and screaming, flaying their hands about as if warding off invisible flies, others seemed quite happy and contented, some babbling incoherently at the crowds around them, while others seemed oblivious to them. They were all quite insane. The girl watched as the revellers, flocking the other way, shouted and jeered at the ragged column, but didn't hinder it in any way.

It was like rushtime on a Monday morning under the Ring when she got there. The smaller, heavily burdened column of those leaving Edge Central, to which she belonged, were pushed to one side of the tunnel by the mass of bodies coming the other way. The two men that had been walking with the girl earlier, reappeared at her side and, without any exchange of words or a glance, resumed their earlier positions.

Killing

This tunnel under the ring was not designed for pedestrians, or even vehicles. There were no official entrances to Edge Central other than the Plaza tunnel and that didn't count; no paths or bridges, steps or ladders, off-ramps or tunnels of any description. They had all been sealed up years ago. The tunnel the girl was walking through was really a half-tube, part of the Ring's superstructure. The thirty-two lane roadway sat on the top of tens of thousands of half-tubes. The radius of each tube varied, depending upon how high the roadway was to be above the ground, but each tube spanned all thirty-two lanes of the Ring, forming a tunnel underneath it.

To stop people walking through the tubes, from one side of the Ring to the other, the construction companies that built the Ring decided to fill each end of each tube with concrete. However, the Government was concerned that this would not be sufficient to stop access to Edge Central from the City, or vice versa; concrete is easily drilled through.

But it is cheap; so to discourage people from attempting to drill through them, the Government released nuclear waste in fist-sized blister balls to the construction companies. While the waste was confined inside the balls it was within the limits of the World Nuke Treaty, if not totally safe. Should a ball be ruptured, anyone up to fifty feet away would receive a bad rad burn, unless suitably protected, and those within about twenty feet would die. The immediate area around the spillage would then become radioactive and would contaminate anyone who returned to the spot. The Government ordered these to be mixed into the concrete used to cap the tubes.

It didn't work. Holes started to be made almost immediately. Some were refilled, others expanded. The larger ones became unofficial checkpoints, manned by the police or IS on the City side and the dealers, religious groups and, later, the One Tribe, on the Edge Central side. Officially this was denied, the Government maintaining that no one was going in or out, but the checkpoints remained and everyone using them got a small dose of radiation each time.

The Ring breach the girl had made for was a recent one. It brought her out into a multistorey carport, twenty feet above the ground. She scrambled down the cargo netting and onto the car deck, then made for the exit. The cars that had been left in the carport when the hole had been made were just smoking shells now; first they had been stripped of anything saleable or recyclable, then smashed, then finally torched. Outside, the streets were chaotic, packed almost solid with people and vehicles, all trying to get somewhere, but mainly getting in each others way. Fighting had broken out in a few places, but they were isolated incidents and it wasn't spreading. Even here the crowd were being remarkably good humoured; everyone seemed to be treating it as a public holiday or something. The girl ran across the road, dodging the slow moving vehicles easily. She was on her own now; the grinning skinhead and the fat man with the hat had disappeared again. She moved away from the Ring and down a side street. The street was still crowded with vehicles but they were moving faster here, there were less people walking in the middle of the road. The sun was yet to set, but the street lights were already on in this section; the tall buildings meant that very little sunlight ever reached street level here, at any time other than midday. The girl walked to the next intersection and stopped at the first taxi rank she came to, joining a man already waiting.

'Excuse me, have you been waiting long?' The girl had a slight, almost breathless voice and spoke very quietly. The man she spoke to wore a suit, and was disdainfully eyeing up the people walking past him. He didn't respond, so she asked the question again in a louder voice.

'Yes I bloody well have!' he sounded extremely unhappy and was anxiously standing on tip toe, trying to look farther down the street. He didn't even look at her when he answered. He was regretting working late, and wished he was a long way away from the disgusting spectacle unfolding before his very eyes.

As they waited, the girl watched the people going past her. They were heading, mostly, towards the Ring. Many seemed typical of those that went to Edge Central normally, or hung out in the pubs and clubs near it on the City side. The usual motley mixture of techno crusties, punks, ravers, bikers and surfers were represented, but there were also many others as well; students and militants (with Socialist Worker placards), News crews and Sat show hosts, even religious orders. Not all were happy, though. Some, such as the right-wing Neo-Christians, were out protesting; they seemed to have buried their differences with the Catholic church and were mounting a joint Christian opposition to what was going on. There were also packs of young yuppies heading towards the Ring as well, although they definitely wouldn't cross, instead they would go to any one of a number of parties being held in buildings that overlooked Edge Central; a number of booking agents had been advertising "very reasonably priced" tickets for parties in these select locations, as had a number of people to their friends.

The girl hadn't seen any police units since entering the City.

'. . . Joey'll be pissed he missed this, Wow, this is brilliant, look at all these people, all together like, it's like . . . like . . . well, I dunno, but it's good, y'know what I'm sayin'? It's like it's meant to be, y'know what I'm sayin'? Hey! You changed up a level yet? I think I've just changed up a level! Oh Wow, this is greaaaaat, what a day we're havin', boy, Joey'll be pissed he missed the. . . Hey! Nice swing!'

The rapid voice stopped suddenly and the man waiting next to the girl began to slip quietly away from her, trying not to make anything look too obvious or turn around. The girl turned around slowly. There were five juves standing in a semicircle around her, trapping her from moving in any direction other than backwards

An Idol

into the speeding traffic. The man in the queue next to her vanished.

The boy who had been talking was obviously the leader of this little gang, and probably the oldest, maybe ten or eleven. 'Burb insignia on the inverted sun-visor he wore indicated that they were from the Midlands agri-belt, or somewhere close, and not local to the Ring or surrounding areas. He stood with his arms folded across his chest and had been staring at her arse and legs. He now stood staring openly at her crotch. His mates hung around him, sniggering. They were unmistakably all out of their faces.

'Yeah Dean, go on, do her, one for the 'burb.' Encouraged one of his friends.

'Hey, Sister, how's it goin'? What say you an me an' Jules here,' he put his arm around the boy on his left, 'go and play somewhere, huh?'

His friend nodded his head, knowingly. Dean finally looked up at her face, to see what her reaction was. It was impossible to tell her expression because of the glasses and OzFilter she wore. Dean, not to be perturbed, emphasized his question by clutching his crotch and shaking it towards her in what he thought was a good imitation of shagging. He could see his own saucer-like pupils reflected in the girl's glasses as one of her gloved hands reached up to her face. She pulled the air filter away from her mouth, then smiled at him. A frown crossed Dean's face; she wasn't supposed to be acting like this. The girl started to laugh.

'Hey, you might not have a choice in this, Sister!' Dean straightened, an edge coming into his young voice; he wasn't going to let her show him up like this, especially in front of the lads! He opened his mouth. Whatever it was that he was going to say next, didn't come out; he was distracted by a low-pitched whumping noise and Jules jerking backwards. Dean turned around and stared at his friend, lying on the pavement behind him. He watched as a red stain began to spread across Jules' chest. The boy jerked spasmodically, appearing to be fighting for his breath. Dean stood speechless, his mouth open; somewhere inside, through the euphoria of the drugs he was on, he realised that things were getting, for no visible reason, totally out of control. He turned back to the girl; she hadn't moved, just stood there smiling at him.

Dean's three other friends bolted, leaving him on his own with her. Dean looked back at Jules, who had stopped jerking and was lying, quite dead, in a spreading pool of blood. Dean felt his bowels empty.

'Why are you still here? You can go if you want,' the girl said helpfully, still smiling.

Dean looked up at her, his mouth opened again, as if he wanted to ask something, but didn't know quite how to say it.

'I guess you're a bit out of your depth, aren't you?' she teased, raising a gloved finger at the boy, and cocked her thumb like the hammer of a revolver. Dean turned and fled.

'Kid givin' you shit, love? Wadda ya do, mace 'im?' The cabbie's low grade features leered at the girl from the ComScreen in the front wall of the taxi's passenger compartment. The girl ignored him as she settled back into the seat harness and waited until the door had shut. She unzipped the hood of her coat, pushing it back to expose short cropped red hair, and stared back at the screen. The image kept cracking up and the colour balance seemed to be adjusting itself at random; at the moment the cabbie was green, with purple hair.

PLEASE STATE YOUR DESTINATION CLEARLY was flashing, beneath him.

'So where you going then?' he asked the red head.

She watched him shift the parking restrainer and disengage the clutch as he spoke, then pull smartly out into the traffic, still looking at her. Most cabbies seemed to drive that way, not bothering to check who else was on the same road as them; there was nothing on the road that could possibly do much damage to a cab. The squeal of something braking heavily was caught by the cab's outside 'phones, and the girl watched as the cabbie's face broke into a wide, purple grin. She reached into a pocket on the sleeve of her jacket and pulled out a small gold card. Leaning forward, she waved it in front of the ComScreen. Information flashed up on the cabbie's old terminal, she could see him squint briefly at it before glancing sharply up at her. The wide angle camera that filmed the cabbie was mounted above his natural line of vision, so that it didn't obscure too much of his view of the road. This distorted his image, making him look as if he was stuffed into a fishbowl, as if he wasn't grotesque enough already.

'Well well well, what are you then? Mixing in some rather high an' mighty circles ain't ya?' The cabbie looked back to the road, grinning even more now. 'You look a bit young to be hooker, but you don't look rich enough not to be, if you don't mind me sayin' so, but you might be; fuckin' impossible to tell, these days.' His image began changing colour again, finally settling on a yellow version of normal.

The card she had held up, for the screen to read, was an invitation card inviting its bearer to a party. The cab's CS had scanned the thin sliver of ice embossed onto the card. The invitation's ice provided the taxi's CS with not only the destination the girl wished to be taken to, but also the credit account to which the fare was to be charged to. The cabbie was impressed with the credit account code; the account was with an extremely exclusive old firm that only dealt with multinationals or very wealthy individuals. The code, under closer scrutiny, indicated that the type of account the fare was being charged to was a private, not corporate, account. He thought the name looked familiar, but wasn't sure; what did he care, so long as there was credit in the account. He started whistling and turned right at the next junction without signalling, then right again, cutting in front of a queue of vehicles that had been waiting for the lights to change.

'Like I was sayin', you never can tell with people, not these days anyway. One time, sure, you could just look at someone, tell 'em

Killing

instantly; you knew what they were an' who they were, whether they had values or not, whether you should let 'em into your cab or not. Not now though! Shit! Not with the fuckin' Only Tribe an' the rest of those loony fuckers about! People are bein' tol' all sorts o' shit an' they're fuckin' well believin' it, behavin' all fuckin' weird; jus' giving up and lettin' themselves go all to pieces.' His smile had disappeared and he looked as if he was just getting into his stride.

'Shit, last week I picked up some geezer, he seems to be nicely turned out, you know, in a suit an' all that, so's I don't pay 'im much attention, like. He's payin' for the ride with a gold Amex y'know, I mean, he's fuckin' rich. Anyway, he's been inside for a few minutes when the air purity alarm goes off, an' I think he's chucked up or somethin', but no, he's just sittin' there, all happy like. I zoom the picture an' realise that it's the bloke 'imself who's set the alarm off; he hasn't washed or changed his clothes for what must be months. He's all covered in lice an' scabies, an' a load of shit and dirt. I thought it was some pattern on his suit at first, but no; he was a complete nutter.' The cabbie suddenly stamped on the brakes, pressing the horn at the same time.

'Get off the fuckin' road, shit head!' he screamed, then looked up at the girl again, 'Did you see that? Nearly run one of those freaks over, the kid was jus' in the road, starin' up like he didn't have a care in the world!' His expression had changed and the girl thought he looked slightly melancholy.

'This is what I mean!' the cabbie pointed absently out of the window, forgetting his passenger couldn't see what he was pointing at, 'I mean, look at it out there! It's fuckin' chaos! Tell me why this is bein' allowed to go on? Why isn't anythin' being done about it? Huh? I'll be fucked if I know! Somethin' should be done about it, every last fuckin' one of the fuckers should be sterilized or somethin'! It's that fuckin' namby pamby government we're lumbered with, you know that? Call themselves the party of law and order . . .'

An Idol

The girl leant forward towards the ComLink screen, the taxi driver had obviously had quite a lot of Go and wasn't about to stop talking; she flicked the taxi's Satdish on, and replaced his image with the Australian soap Chunda Valley. While Jodie discovered Alan in bed with the blond from Brunswick Street, the girl surfed the preview window up to the nearest news broadcast, then flipped over.

'. . . were prevented from getting any closer by ten thousand police in pacification gear. The march was able to continue after a two hour delay. A spokesman for the right-wing Democratic Social Alliance made this address . . .' The postage stamp image of a fat man, in the corner of the screen, expanded and became animated.

'. . . This is the sort of thing we were marching for to prevent; I urge every moral, God-fearing, freethinking, drug-free citizen in this great city of ours to join with us in our stand against the decline of moral and economic values promoted, in a most vile and insipid manner, by Vee and his terrorist supporters. This man must not be given a platform to freely express his repugnant, morally reprehensible opinions, for the sake of our nation and the free-market values that have made us great, I implore you . . .'

The image froze, then changed, as the voice faded out. The aging, red faced politician was replaced by a younger, tanned woman. She picked up the pieces of paper in front of her and deftly shuffled them into a stack.

'Strong words indeed, however the protest would appear to have failed, in the short term at least, with no sign of the Government changing its present position on tonight's free concert.' She frowned dramatically for the camera before continuing.

'And, once again, the main story tonight, the concert by the wanted terrorist media personality, Empti Vee, appears to be going ahead as planned. Conservative estimates suggest that up to as many as three million people are, as we speak, illegally crossing into the Restricted Zone and heading towards the so-called

"Ministry of Truth" tower, rumoured to be the headquarters of the One Tribe terrorist group. Various Right-wing and religious organizations have failed in their attempts to force the Government to take measures to prevent the concert taking place. The Government, once more, has elected not to intervene or even comment at this stage in time, except asking us to remind our viewers that trespassing into the Restricted Zone is a criminal offence and that anyone doing so would be liable for prosecution and psychological readjustment.

'As yet there have been no confirmed sightings of Vee, but keep tuned for SatSix news updates throughout the night.

'This is Sal Daley wishing you a good weekend from everyone on SatSix afternoon news, see you all on Monday in the PM, good night.'

The news credits flew past and were replaced by the network's own advertisements for programs later that evening. The next programme scheduled was to be a repeat showing of the award winning SatSix documentary on the alleged link between Empti Vee and the One Tribe ecological protest movement, apparently featuring real additional-never-been-seen-before footage. The trailer for the documentary used some old, classic footage of eight years earlier.

'Hey, yeah! That's the little shit himself!'

It was the taxi driver. He'd noticed the girl had turned into the Sat and decided to watch what she was watching. His head appeared in a small box on the corner of the larger image, his face animated.

'He's the one to blame for the fuckin' mess this country's in, startin' all that Only Family crap,' the cabbie got their name wrong again, 'I mean, who does he think he is? Tellin' everyone who'll listen that they can do whatever they want, so long as it feels right! Christ! What a load of old bollocks! That sort of talk is dangerous, you can't have people walkin' aroun' thinkin' they can do or be whatever they want. Am I right or am I right? I mean, where will it end? Eh?'

The girl gave no indication that she saw or heard the driver. She sat very still, facing the screen and the image on it. It showed a young man . . .

. . . dance erratically across a stage in front of a frenzied group of inept but enthusiastic musicians. The man paused by a monitor, glaring directly at the Cam that filmed him, then threw himself off the stage and into the moshpit below. The Cam panned back to record his plunge and landing. This clip was replaced by a still of the same young man, taken at another time. He was smiling and looked almost angelic.

A young girl, perhaps ten years old, with a mass of unruly red hair, sat up and took proper notice of the image on tube. Someone else wolf whistled.

'He could have my cherry any time!' a girl's voice screeched. Mary turned around to see who had called out, the spell broken.

'He's a bit late ain't he?' another girl called out. The school transporter erupted into laughter. Turning back to the screen above the driver Mary was disappointed to see the man's picture replaced by the morning newscaster reading the weather.

'What happened?' she asked the girl next to her. Lizzie, always the swot, had actually been listening to the broadcast, plugged into the bus' comm system. Mary hadn't been listening. She never did; news was boring so she just watched the pictures and listened to her mini 'phones, like everyone else.

Lizzie looked at her friend, and grinned mysteriously, 'Do you want the good news or the bad news?' she asked.

Mary cocked her head on one side and stared at her, 'Don't push it or you'll never make nine!' she warned.

'He's not dead, or even injured or anything,' Lizzie watched the look of relief cross her friend's face and, inwardly, smiled as she added, 'but he is going to prison for about fifteen years.'

Mary sat there, shocked, as Lizzie proceeded to repeat the same piece of information to the other children on the bus who also never bothered to listen to the news. Mary's seven year old mind tried to make sense of what she was hearing; it just wasn't right! The Police had raided a so-called illegal gig and managed to kill most of the band playing at the time by landing a troop carrier on the stage before they had finished their set. The one surviving member of the band, the singer Empti Vee, had survived because he had stage-dived only seconds earlier. According to Lizzie, the news says that the Police have decided to prosecute him for leading "antisocial activities".

Mary didn't think it was fair at all; what was so "antisocial" about singing anyway? It wasn't as antisocial as landing a six ton troop lifter on someone. She was also a bit annoyed because she'd been into the Vee and his band, Drunkadelic, way before anyone else had even heard of them and now, because of all the publicity, everyone at school was going to be into him. It just wasn't fair.

At lunch time the protesting Lizzie was forced to stand lookout as Mary confused the fence gate lock into opening. It was simple. Lizzie's older sister, Madonna, had shown them how. The lock LED clicked green and Mary was out, pulling the other girl with her.

'We'll get caught Mary, and you know what'll happen again . . .' Lizzie began to whine.

'Stay here if you want to, see if I care!' Mary wasn't in any mood for it today; she was on a mission and nothing was going to stop her.

The ground level entrance to Shoppers Universe was only a block from the school, but the two girls walked past it another block to use the entrance on Sub Level One; the mall was off limits to students during term time, unless accompanied by an adult. The main entrance was too well guarded but the Sub levels were always breachable. Mary and Lizzie walked into the mall, following a group of tourists. The security guards would be unsure whether they were with the group or not, so long as they stayed close to them, and no one challenged them.

'Where we going?' hissed Lizzie nervously.

'SonicBoy, I want to get a disc,' Mary responded, pushing Lizzie towards the nearest walkway heading up. 'I think they've moved to the third level now,' she added.

A short time later, Mary looked up at Lizzie and saw she was about to start crying again.

'Wha. . . wha. . . wha. . . what's going to ha. . . ha. . . happen . . ?' she blubbered to the security guard standing next to her.

'Well, I'm afraid that's for the authorities to decide, young lady,' he began piously. 'We at Shoppers Universe always press for the maximum penalties possible under the law. You could be sent to a Young Offenders Correctional Facility daycare centre for shoplifting,' he waved a small, flat plastic case at her, the security tag obviously still on it, 'Or you could possibly be expelled from your school, d'you know that?' the guard answered, seemingly oblivious to the stress the young girl was already under.

'But as for your friend there,' they both looked down at Mary, the guard shook his head at the severity of her predicament, 'she'll probably be put into care for doing that to Billy.'

'I think the little bitch broke it!' said the man, Billy. He was an undercover store detective and was sitting on top of Mary; his latest arrest. Blood was still streaming out of his shattered nose, despite his best attempts to stem the flow. 'Oh, she's in trouble alright, but not as much as her parents will be by the time I've finished suing them!' he added.

Mary lay there silently, arms pinned by the man's knees, staring malevolently at the ceiling above.

It was Lizzie's mum who came to the holding pen to pick them both up; the police clerk hadn't been able to contact Mary's yet, and they needed the space in the cells so they'd told Lizzie's mother they'd only release her daughter if she accepted responsibility for

Mary as well. Lizzie, it seemed, had yet to convince her mother of Mary's complete responsibility, but was valiantly trying. Her mother wasn't listening, and barely looked at Mary; she remained tight lipped and stern faced the whole time, listening intently to the police clerk as he outlined for her what would be happening to her daughter and herself in the coming months. She thanked him when he handed her a large stack of forms that she had to complete and return within seven days or face yet more criminal and civil charges, and smartly left the building, herding her two charges in front of her. Once outside, she crammed the forms into her handbag, then, with her now free hand, smacked her still sobbing daughter across the back of her head. Lizzie stopped crying and began wailing. A smart family station wagon pulled up to the curb near the group, and its door swung up. Mary could see Lizzie's dad behind the wheel, waiting for them.

'Get her in quickly, Jean, I don't want anyone to see us here. We can talk to her properly later, when we get her home.' He turned to look at them as they climbed in, 'And I'm going to want to talk to your mother as well, young lady,' he glared at Mary. 'And I don't think she's going to like what I'm going to say!' He turned to his wife, 'Now do you see what happens when you start letting unmarried mothers into our 'hood?'

As far as Mary was concerned, everything had been going to plan; breaking the undercover guard's nose had been unexpected, but these things happen and you have to learn to live with them. Mostly it had all been going well; that was, until her mum came back from the talk with Lizzie's father. Lizzie's family lived opposite Mary's flat, not in a conversion, but a proper house; they were quite a bit richer. They were also very active on the Neighbourhood Community Control Group, and had convinced the required majority of the Housing Committee Board that, since Mary's mother was obviously not capable of controlling the actions of her daughter and, because her daughter's actions were proving to have a disruptive and antisocial influence on her peers, she should therefore have her housing permit revoked and be expelled from the neighbourhood as soon as was practicable. Mary's mother was in tears as she told her they had until the end of the month to find somewhere else to live. She was so distressed Mary was just sent to bed, without even harsh words to take the edge off the shame and guilt she felt for the position she'd put her mother in.

After Mary had undressed and climbed into bed she pulled out her mini 'phones and flipped the disc already inside it onto the floor. She then tipped one of her trainers up, and watched a small, flat plastic case fall to the floor. The picture of Empti Vee on the case was partially obscured by the squashed security tag that was still attached to it.

Mary listened to the disc almost constantly over the next three weeks; she had nothing else to do because she had been expelled from school, not for stealing but because she was technically no longer a resident in one of the schools catchment blocks and therefore not eligible for a place there.

She was listening to the disc when a Relocation Coordinator from the Child Welfare Agency came to see her mother. Because they were facing imminent eviction and Mary's mother hadn't been able to find anywhere else to live yet, Mary was to be taken into custody immediately, pending review of the case or a change in her mother's circumstances. She was allowed just enough time to pack a small holdall of personal belongings, and was hurried out of the building after a brief, but very tearful farewell from her distressed mother.

She listened to the disc on the way to the Pre-Teen Transition Home, clutching the small unit to her as she listened, as if her sanity and well being depended on it, and refused to answer any of the Relocation Coordinator's banal questions.

One hour after arriving at the transition home, the mini 'phones and disc were stolen from her by some older girls; she was never to get them back again.

Killing

The cab pulled up at the girl's destination, and its door slid up, allowing her to step out. The black clad girl with the short cropped red hair didn't look back as the cab squealed away. She walked up to the nearest entervator, along a plush red carpet, fiddling absently with a silver pad sewn into the lining of her jacket. The jacket and trousers she wore shimmered, then turned a violent green.

'Welcome to the PYRAMID PLAZA, please select your internal destination from the U-Choose™ three-dimensional representation of the PYRAMID PLAZA before you,' the entervator welcomed her.

The girl, now dressed all in green, pulled the gold invite from the arm pocket of her jacket and waved it absently around as she stepped over its threshold. The doors shut and she was sucked up, into the building. She didn't look out of the window at the park and the surfers or study the map of the interior of the building; she used her reflection in the glass to put on the hat she'd pulled out of her small clutch-bag. It was a pillbox affair with a mesh veil falling down around her face, towards her shoulders. And it was green, just like the rest of her clothes. Then she pulled out a small tube and ran that over her lips, darkening their colour slightly. She puckered them and blew her reflection a kiss as the doors opened, then walked out into the lobby before her, without bothering to collect the entervator's thoughtfully provided direction slip as she passed.

There was a Net newsman directly in front of her, attempting to set up for a broadcast. He was arguing with a group of security men, while his remote Cam buzzed around behind them. The source of the argument appeared to be a dark stain on the floor and the security guards' reluctance to let him film it. The girl ignored them and walked across the lobby towards a sign that stated RESIDENTIAL/PENTHOUSE AREA ENTERVATORS – ACCESS BY PRIOR ARRANGEMENT ONLY. She smiled; she herself was a prior arrangement.

Before leading his team out of the hotel lobby, which by now had been totally cleared of the general public, Max stopped to have a few final words with the smirking Security Chief and the pin-striped woman. Their expressions quickly changed from subdued mirth to anxious appeasement as Max talked. Johnny couldn't hear exactly what was being said, but could guess the general gist of it; Max was doing his level best to put the fear of god into the two people, ensuring they would cooperate with him in the way they reported the "incident". Once satisfied, he strode out of the lobby in the direction of the roof terrace and the shops at this level.

'So, are you enjoying yourself, rookie?'

Johnny looked up, saw Dwain grinning at him. 'Huh?'

'You don't look as if you are, boy.'

Johnny bridled at being referred to as "boy" by Dwain. He didn't think Dwain could be much more than three or four years older than him, perhaps twenty two or three at the most.

'Yeah, I'm alright,' he answered, with more conviction than he really felt.

'Yeah, sure,' snorted Dwain. 'So how comes you're a rookie then, rookie? You ain't exactly here by choice, are you?'

'Er . . . I . . . I was sectioned, then drafted.' Johnny hesitantly responded.

Dwain started laughing, loudly at first, then quietly after Max turned around and stared at him.

'Sucks, don't it!' Dillon slapped Johnny on the back. ' 'Cept there ain't no way out, so you just gotta accept it!' he added, helpfully. Johnny looked at him, expecting more, but Dillon didn't expand upon his statement, just grinned.

'Well, all I've got to say on the subject is don't lose Frank, whatever you do or you'll be fuck all use to anyone!' Dwain gestured to the bag over Johnny's shoulder, without even trying to disguise the animosity he felt for the new recruit.

The roof terrace went around all three sides of the top of the Plaza's second section and was predominantly covered by transparent UV reflective plastic; no one sat directly in the sun any more, the Government had made it illegal because of the huge drain on Medical resources caused by the massive increase in skin cancer cases over the last decade. The terrace was split into hundreds of separate businesses, mainly restaurants and coffee shops, with a meandering pathway leading between them. Max wanted a cup of coffee but decided he wanted to overlook Edge Central while he was drinking it. They had come out of the exit on the opposite side of the building, facing the City, so Max decided they should walk around the terrace to the other side. Although not crowded, it was busy, with most of the bars and restaurants filling up; the offices inside the Plaza were now closing for the weekend and the Plaza seemed to be a good spot for others to come and watch the evening's show. As they walked, Johnny noticed that the other people walking around the terrace gave him, and the three men he was with, a wide berth, without even appearing to notice them. Dwain had given up baiting Johnny, and Max and Dillon were talking quietly amongst themselves, so he was left to his own, uneasy thoughts.

Ahead of him he could see the Ring, far below, sweep past the building he was standing on. The lights of the cars and transporters were already on, making the massive road appear to be writhing in optic cables. To his right Johnny could see the City spread out, on the other side of the Ring, cupping the roadway with its many buildings. He thought about the Plaza itself, and what he knew about it, mainly to keep his mind off his present predicament.

The Plaza hadn't been open for very long, and up until this year it was the first building to be constructed in Edge Central for years, and was still the only building on the Restricted Zone side of the Ring that was still linked to the City. As part of the Government/ Corporate 'Fight Back' campaign, the Plaza had been built as the vanguard of the Restricted Zone re-population programme. The City couldn't grow any more in any other direction due to the massive Eco-parks and farm land that surrounded it to the North and South. Expansion was impossible either East or West because the City already reached the sea in both directions; but space was still needed for new developments, so the Government had decided to allow and promote new building projects on the inside of the Ring.

To show prospective developers the advantages of building in the Restricted Zone, the Plaza had been built without the usual space conscious considerations necessary in the overcrowded City. In fact, part of the architects' brief was to exploit this and waste as much space as possible; give the rich the room they could afford. Hence the three-sided Pyramid Plaza.

The group rounded the corner of the Pyramid and the Restricted Zone dramatically spread out before them. It was a dark, almost featureless void, festering beneath the very distant neon lights of City south. Unbidden, the last few hours of Johnny's life muscled their way into his consciousness, demanding a replay. He struggled against them briefly, not really wanting to consider the position he found himself in, but finally they overwhelmed him and flooded through like a vast, totally realistic, hi-res nightmare. He looked up, through the plastic roof above him, past the sloping side of the main Pyramid and its weirdly overhanging penthouse, up to the dark gathering clouds above.

'I think I'm going to die . . .' he said quietly to himself.

Killing

'Get a move on son, we haven't got all day!' The short-haired man with the dark glasses held the door frame with one hand and reached out with the other, pulling the young man into the van. Johnny glanced around the interior of the van. There were two other men inside, one black, the other white, both lounging in travel harnesses in the back. Johnny couldn't see their eyes because of the dark glasses they wore but he assumed that they were looking at him. He nodded to them. Other than the glasses, he was dressed identically to them: all in black with a leather coat – the standard uniform of Internal Security. The black man smiled a welcome, but didn't speak. The other scowled and looked questioningly at the older man who had opened the door and let Johnny in.

'What the fuck's happening, Max? This ain't no training exercise!' He didn't seem too happy about Johnny being in the van with him.

'You know the situation, Dwain; put up an' shut up.' The older man, Max, dismissed the complaint, then went on, 'This is Johnny, he will be with us on tonight's operation.' Then to Johnny, 'Put these on.' He handed him a pair of solid dark glasses, more like goggles than sunnies; they were standard IS issue Virtualwear, and went with his gloves.

'Now, before you start complaining again, Dwain, you should know that he'll be under the supervision of Frank O'Reilly, from his deck in the Virtual Lab. Does that cheer you up?'

Dwain nodded, pacified, then turned to the man next to him, 'Nice to have Frank along again; always admired the way that man worked.' The man next to him didn't answer.

Max tapped Johnny on the shoulder, then gestured to a small bag on the floor of the van, next to three larger bags. 'That's the booster link Frank'll use. It's your responsibility to have it with you at all times, understand?'

'Yes sir.'

'Right, now let's go, Johnny Boy. You drive; I always evaluate new team members by watchin' em drive. Take us to the Ring, then head north.'

'Yes sir.'
'Oh, Johnny?'
'Yes sir?'
'Don't call me sir, call me Max, okay?'
'Yes sir, er . . . Max . . .'

Johnny found himself in the driver's harness of the IS van, attempting to control the heavily modified vehicle. He decided not to tell Max he'd never learned to drive; sure, he knew a bit, but only enough to steal them when he was younger and even then he wasn't very good at it. The jet black van lurched out of the parking bay and erratically past the identical jet black vans that filled the underground garage. Johnny over-braked before the exit cones, then over-accelerated up the exit ramp which joined the academy's main road. The van fishtailed slightly as Johnny turned onto it, then shot past the razor wire fences, gun towers and small, squat concrete entrances that were the only indication that there was anything else here other than trees. The south gate opened automatically as the van approached it and they left the compound. He turned left, on instructions from the van's Nav-ice, and headed east, towards the City.

Max leant towards the men sitting in the back of the van. 'While Johnny drives us to the Ring, I want you boys to check your toys. Dillon, could you do Johnny's as well?'
'Okay, Boss Man.'
Both Dillon and Dwain started opening the bags at their feet; they contained several tubed sections, some irregular shaped cubes and some asymmetrical joining sections. There was also an instruction manual and shoulder holster in each. Dwain let out a low whistle.
'Would you look at these,' he eagerly started assembling one without referring to the instruction book. 'Oooo, self calibrating lead-n-laser assault rifle with sight. This is a state-of-the-art military

pop gun. Shit, even the boy there could hit a gnat's arse at five clicks with this!' He extended the gun's mini barrel and butt to their maximum positions, checked its balance was evenly distributed, then folded it back down before fixing the larger tubed front section and laser port onto the stock. Dwain repeated the balance check again, then slammed the big-bore ammo clip into the hand grip and slipped the ungainly looking weapon into its Y-shaped holster. He clipped the holster to the inside of his coat, next to his standard IS issue hand-cannon and sat back to watch Dillon finish his own weapon, then start on Johnny's.

Somehow Johnny had managed to reach Hyper-Route Two without hitting anything with the van. The raised roadway would take them directly to the Ring, missing much of the terra-level suburban traffic that the West End was famous for.

'Put the van onto the road's guidance system and settle back Johnny, it's time for the briefing.' Max indicated the autopilot icon on the vehicle's dashboard. 'You should relax more when you drive,' he added, absently.

Johnny flipped the switch and settled back in his seat, relieved not to be trying to control the ultra sensitive vehicle any more. A small virtual-window appeared in the air in front of him, containing a spinning, three-dimensional "IS". It, and the window, expanded in size until most of the roadway was obscured, although he could still see Max out of the corner of one eye and the passing buildings out of the other.

The others, he knew, would be experiencing the same optical illusion whichever way they were facing, courtesy of the goggles they were all wearing. The spinning logo split, and the screen shifted into a head and shoulders image of Control. In Johnny's case, Control was a young girl with a severe expression and slicked back hair. Unknown to Johnny, Max saw an older woman, of approximately fifty years of age, Dillon saw a middle aged black man wearing a dark suit and Dwain saw his old Sergeant Major.

An Idol

They all saw different individuals because Control was really a psychologically designed construct, digitally generated by a CS at Operations Control, with the purpose of invoking the maximum response potential from each IS operative. Each operative was individually assessed to ascertain which gender/age/race type variable they would respond best to. Operations Control then provided each operative with a tailor-made Control figure to receive their orders from; it allegedly increased the operatives willingness to comply with their orders.

'We have a most urgent situation on our hands,' Control began without any preliminaries. 'All team leaders are to provide the operatives under them with enough ORANGE capsules for a seventy two hour period . . .' Johnny could see Max get up and move to the storage rack on the side wall of the van. He pulled out four pump tubes, like Nesbury Smartysweet dispensers, and began handing them out.

'Your team is part of a multi-force operation that is currently running at the moment; strict compliance with your instructions is necessary if you are to successfully integrate with the overall plan. Un-sanctioned actions are not to be undertaken under any circumstances, unless your mission parameters are threatened. There will be a fifth member of your team tonight . . .' A smaller frame popped up next to Control, with a man inside.

'Hi!' the man waved.

'Hullo Frank, nice to see you again,' Max greeted him, sitting down. He dropped one of the pump dispensers into Johnny's lap. Johnny looked down at it but the frame of Control moved down as well, obscuring them from his view. He moved his head back up, then looked down again, only moving his eyes this time, and began to study the tube.

'Frank will be looking after you tonight, Johnny.'

Johnny looked back up quickly, at Control, then Frank. Frank was looking at him, a strange smile on his face that made him feel slightly uneasy.

'Uh, hi,' he managed to say.

'Now listen up, as I said, this is a multi-force operation, not only are we working with the Police and private security forces on this one; we are also working with the Army . . .' Max sat up in his seat, shocked, '. . . so that should impress on you all the seriousness of what's occurring. If you haven't guessed already, this is the man we are most concerned with tonight.'

Control's frame reduced in size and joined Frank at the edge of the expanding window beneath. It was a piece of Vid footage showing a group of people surrounded by a host of paparazzi, Vid-News crews and journalists. The shot zoomed in on a man at the centre of the group; he was shouting at one of the journalists. A couple of the women around him appeared to be holding him back. The footage froze.

'I'm sure I hardly need to introduce him,' continued Control. 'Our politicians and their corporate masters have been very concerned about this man's activities over the last few years, so they've had us take an active interest in his affairs. We've infiltrated several of his organizations and "converted" some of his people to our side. Recently they've been reporting that it's all coming apart; there are massive internal divisions between his advisors, and a high level of corruption is appearing in many of his companies' management structures. It seems Vee is losing control of his empire. As you can imagine, we've been taking advantage of the situation and using these divisions to undermine his overall power and influence, with some level of success. However, our informants close to him are now saying he has a little, but very unpleasant, last minute surprise in store for us.' The face of Control loomed closer to each of the operatives.

'That's why you boys are here now. You know that, tonight, Vee and the One Tribe terrorist organization have planned to stage a Rock concert . . .' Johnny, forgetting where he was, involuntarily groaned at the practically obsolete term, '. . . on top of the illegal structure recently built at the centre of the Restricted Zone.' The main image changed to an aerial view, perhaps even a real-time satellite shot, of an extremely high building standing on its own in the midst of a shanty town.

'The structure, referred to by the media as the "Ministry of Truth", is too far inside the perimeter of the Restricted Zone to make an incursion by a large armed force practical. For this reason, Vee feels he is safe from capture and, therefore, able to perform to members and supporters of the One Tribe. Not only is he doing this in full view of the City, the rest of the world can watch too, live and totally free, courtesy of his own personal media empire.'

'Someone should have sorted that little shit out a long time ago . . .' Johnny could hear Max mumbling under his breath. The man hadn't smiled since he had found out that he was working with the army.

'Your team will be one of one hundred and twenty six IS teams positioned in the one hundred and twenty six areas of the City that can overlook this illegal structure. Once in position you are to stand by for further instructions. Any information concerning your location and tonight's operation has, or will be, transmitted to your personal ice; it can be accessed in the usual manner.

'If you encounter any resistance taking up your allocated positions, or when carrying out any future orders, you are authorized to take any action necessary to ensure that the resistance ceases immediately, including individual, un-sanctioned terminations.'

Johnny sat there, stunned. This wasn't happening. Individual un-sanctioned what's?

'Our informants tell us that Vee is going to use this opportunity to create drug induced mayhem, in an attempt to cause as much damage to the structure of our City, as well as our society, as he possibly can. IS has been given the task of preventing this from happening, and unlimited authority to do it.'

Johnny's pulse began racing, blood pounding through his veins.

Everything clicked into place. He totally forgot where he was and leapt from the driving seat of the vehicle, striking the air with his fist, 'Yes! We're gonna waste him!' he exclaimed jubilantly.

'Johnny Boy, are you with us?' Dillon's voice broke through Johnny's reverie. They were in a coffee shop that overlooked Edge Central, just as Max had wanted.

'Huh . . . oh no,' he answered to the man waving the whitener sachet at him. His coffee cup sat untouched on the table in front of him. The coffee shop was small compared to most of the businesses in the Plaza and right on the edge of the terrace, near one of the corners. Its few customers were protected from the just starting rain by a temporary glass wall that was designed to spring up in bad weather. Max had chosen a table in the far corner.

'Right, now listen up . . .' Max lent forward, leaning on the table to emphasise what he was going to say.

'Hey, this isn't regular coffee . . .' Dwain interrupted, rising from his seat.

Max caught Dwain by the sleeve of his coat and pulled him back into his chair.

'Now you listen to me carefully Dwain, cause I'm only going to say this once: I am totally, one hundred percent fuckin' pissed off with you already. To get back into me good books you're going to remain in that chair and not move. You will not get up, or talk to anyone else until I say it's okay. If you do, I will shoot you. Do I make my self understood?' Max spoke slowly and deliberately, leaning right into Dwain's face.

Dwain faced Max for several moments without answering, as if trying to gauge how serious the man was. 'Um, yeah, sure Max,' he eventually answered, grinning sheepishly.

Max turned to Dillon. 'Go have a look around in person, Dillon. Just get the feel of the place. I've got to go an' talk to Control, then have a look around the building's ice.' Dillon nodded, finished his coffee and left.

An Idol

'Um, what about me, Max?' Johnny asked quietly. Dwain snorted.

'You just keep quiet and out of the way until we need you, okay?' Max answered, as the edges of his glasses folded down and he jacked into another reality.

Johnny sat there, wondering if it would be alright if he went to find the toilet when a man in IS garb walked into the shop and up to their table. It was Frank. No one else seemed to notice him, not even Dwain, so Johnny concluded he was going to get Frank's undivided attention. He absently wondered why Frank had bothered to act 'real' and walk into the coffee shop as if he had substance.

'So, how're you doing?' Frank sat down on the air, just above the pot plants next to Johnny, in front of the window, 'Been looking at your data, see who I'm getting. You're a fit boy; that's good . . . very good. I don't like to see young, healthy people wasting what they've got.'

Johnny didn't like the way Frank was looking at him and his body again; it was making him really uncomfortable. He looked over at Max; Max was now pushing invisible keys on some virtual desktop. It seemed he was either going to have to talk to Dwain, the psychopath, or talk to Frank. Great. He looked at Dwain, who had taken one of his gloves off and was picking his nose with a naked finger.

'I can't remember what it felt like to be seventeen, it gets difficult, y'see, when you get older . . . and things happen . . . ' Frank continued, slightly morosely.

Johnny nodded, not sure what to say.

'Things that aren't really your fault . . . but can't be forgotten about. And because you done them, or just because they happened, everything changes . . . and time goes so quickly . . . so quickly . . . ' Frank had partially turned away from him, and was staring absently into the middle distance, not really seeing anything or anyone,

Killing

except whatever phantoms haunted him from the past.

Johnny glanced at Max, then, as if inspired, switched his goggles' virtual controls on and accessed its ice bank. A window appeared in front of him, with various options on it and verbal instructions overrode Frank's voice input. Johnny expanded the frame to maximum and Frank, Max, Dwain and the rest of reality were thankfully replaced by a virtual, near empty, blackness, with himself at the centre of it. He faced a small selection frame, floating in the air. Control nodes drifted up to his fingers. He double clicked the cursor node, not bothering to check on which topic was currently primed, and settled back to watch the show.

The ice generated entity that was Control strode out into a square of light and faced the seated figure.

'This is a brief synopsis of the personal history of the subversive activist know as Empti Vee.' A large two-dimensional picture of Vee's face, taken from a Vid broadcast, appeared beside the speaking girl, dwarfing her. It then stretched into a three-dimensional head and span around, showing his features to Johnny from every angle.

'Vee's real name is William McVeigh.' Statistics joined the image: date of birth, time and place, parents' names, and so on. Johnny was surprised to see he was only twenty six years old; he'd always assumed the man was older.

'Please select which part of McVeigh's life you wish to study.' A group of hyper-node options sprang up, listing various stages in the man's life, and other, related topics. Johnny selected the first, PERSONALITY SHAPING EVENTS IN PRE-TEENAGE YEARS, by accident, before he had time to read the list; he'd raised his finger to run it along the titles as he read them and the first node had jumped onto his outstretched finger.

'The only child of self-employed, lower middle class parents, there was nothing abnormal about the young boy . . .' another frame blipped into existence beside the spinning head. It contained an old Vid clip of a group of school children performing a nativity play. The frame panned in then enlarged to a grinning, scruffy dressed shepherd in the back row.

'. . . McVeigh was an intelligent underachiever who "could do better", according to school records accessed from the national data 'chives.'

A small hyper-node, marked SCHOOL DATA: McVEIGH, WILLIAM, appeared next to Johnny, and flashed. If selected, he could look at the actual reports. He carefully kept his hands still until it disappeared.

The images faded and were replaced by the start of another home Vid. It was a funeral.

'The first event of major importance in the life of the young McVeigh occurred at the age of twelve with the death of both of his parents.' The accompanying clip showed a large, sombre gathering in a modern crematorium. Two coffins sat side by side on a large, red velvet conveyor belt. The couple were being talked about by the vicar in-residence in the halting fashion of a bad actor who doesn't know his lines properly; he'd obviously never met the two individuals he was "laying to rest". The boy McVeigh stood in the front pew, next to two adults and three older children. He was staring directly at the two coffins, without a trace of emotion on his face. Johnny was wondering how to fast forward the morbid scene; the coffins had reminded him of his own situation.

'They died, along with seventy six other couples in a fish restaurant in the New-Chinatown district. The couple were out celebrating McVeigh senior's new contract at the Cannox Corporation. Apparently, the fish served that evening had not been Rad scanned correctly by the restaurant's chef. It shouldn't have mattered but the Spanish Trawler, El Disastro, that had supplied the fish originally, had been supplementing its quota by fishing in the North Sea from contaminated fish stocks. The catch was so toxic that samples retrieved from the restaurant had to be handled using protective clothing.'

Another hyper-node appeared, marked POLLUTION OF

Killing

NATURAL RESOURCES No. 5471/F4; FISH. Johnny ignored it.

'McVeigh went to live with his paternal uncle and his family.' Three frames replaced the one of the funeral footage, each one was primed to run a different clip. Johnny could see from the dates displayed on each that they were all within the same year.

'It would seem that the transition between guardians did not go well for the juve. Within three months he had committed his first property offence: he burned down a warehouse owned by a Mr. Jose Balzola.' One of the clips started to run; it was a SecCam image shot of a warehouse from high up on a building opposite. The virtual programme his glasses were running grabbed the image, expanded it and wrapped it around the area Johnny sat in. He found himself standing in a dark alleyway, next to the warehouse, watching McVeigh pouring petrol through one of its air vents. The boy turned and ran past him, just before the vent exploded out of the wall. The image froze, the vent in mid air, then swam into a court room. Johnny found himself staring at the young McVeigh sitting in the dock.

He raised his right hand, to scratch his nose, and a small right pointing double arrow appeared. Johnny tentatively pushed it, and the clip sped up; he'd found the fast forward. He stopped at the summary at the end; William McVeigh was given a course of psychiatric behavioural therapy and his uncle given the bill for the damages his nephew had caused, and another for the court costs. The figures froze and Control walked into the room as it faded around her.

'The bill for the damage took most of the meagre inheritance McVeigh senior had left behind. You can imagine that this didn't please McVeigh junior's uncle much. He had probably been looking forward to benefiting, as William and the money's guardian, from his brother's untimely demise. It would be fair to assume that the loss of this credit contributed, in part at least, to an increasingly unsatisfactory domestic life with his new guardians.

'McVeigh's psychiatric therapy didn't help much, either, and may even have hindered the juve's rehabilitation. The junior doctor in charge of the his case used an experimental form of indulgence/aversion/shock therapy, that encouraged patients to overindulge in their sickness until they were sated, then compelled them into doing it more and more, until they came to loath doing it. The patient is compelled to overindulge by the administration of synaptic shocks. This form of treatment has since been banned in the City, although is still common in the Eastern states.'

As Control spoke a hyper-node marked RECENT PROGRESSIVE TRENDS IN PSYCHIATRIC THERAPY: A LAYMAN'S PERSPECTIVE appeared and winked at Johnny. He ignored it and the second Vid clip started. Johnny found himself in, what was unmistakably, a room in a hospital. The boy, McVeigh, was sitting on one side of a table, with a therapist, dressed in a neon pink and blue jogging suit, on the other. The boy was staring at a small plastic disposable lighter on the table in front of him. Next to that was a box of plastic toy buildings. A floating time log indicated he'd been in the room, undergoing therapy, for over six hours without a break.

'Look, I keep telling you, I don't want to start any fires, not here or anywhere else. I didn't set fire to that building because I like to look at the pretty flames, alright?' The boy was beginning to lose his temper, not, it seemed, for the first time.

'Hey, look Billy, you know I'm only here for your own good.' The therapist reinforced his statement by pressing the trigger he held. The boy went rigid in his seat, teeth clenched.

'Everyone loves you and wants you to get better, but you have to admit to me, and to yourself, that you've got a problem. Denying it isn't helping anyone.' The psychiatrist sounded very reasonable, but adamant; the boy was wrong and he was going to receive help whether he liked it or not. He pressed the trigger again.

'Why aren't you listening to me? I've told you already, I didn't burn down the warehouse because I like fires: I burned it down because the bastard that ran it killed my fucking parents!' The young boy stated the sentence slowly and clearly so there could be no misunderstanding.

'We've discussed this already, Billy. He didn't kill your parents [shock], he didn't even know who they were. That's just an excuse; a justification or rationalization [shock]. Why must you look for excuses in the outside world, Billy? The problems are inside you. You just have to come to terms with them.

'Now, please, pick up that lighter, the sooner you start, the quicker this will all be over.'

The clip sped up, the timer flicked through another six hours, then slowed to real speed again.

'Christ! We've been here all day [shock], and you haven't set fire to one of the buildings yet! Pick up the fucking lighter [shock] you little shit and set fire to something [shock] before you make me really angry! You are a repressed pyromaniac [shock] and I will cure you [shock] whether you like it or not . . .' The therapist was standing over the boy, screaming at the rigidly shaking boy. Spittle sprayed into the upturned face before him.

Johnny watched as McVeigh bent down and picked up the lighter; it had fallen onto the floor during one of his spasms. The therapist turned his back on his patient and ran his fingers through his hair, exhaling. He'd obviously had more responsive patients in the past. He didn't notice the boy, still on the floor, stretch under the table and flick the lighter on, holding it next to the leg of his therapist's jogging suit. The fabric took all of two seconds to ignite into an inferno that rapidly engulfed the oblivious man. The virtual clip froze then faded away, leaving Control and Johnny in the black void again.

'This was his second offence: ABH. Once again, his uncle was forced to bear the brunt of the juve's antisocial tendencies and had to pay the therapist's not inconsiderable medical costs. He pleaded with the magistrate to permanently institutionalize his charge, on the grounds that the juve was out of control and would not listen to reason. The magistrate refused, instead sentencing McVeigh to only three months Juve detention. He didn't enjoy his stay much . . .'

A frantic lo-fi security clip of an anal rape scene popped up in a window next to Control. Several uniformed men were surrounding a smaller figure while another assaulted him from behind. Johnny quickly double clicked the fast forward and jumped that section of Vee's life.

Another virtual clip started. At first it was grainy and poor quality, like the previous scene, then several filters flicked over it and the picture became clearer. It showed a young person climbing a rope ladder, up a concrete wall, towards a ragged hole half way up. When the figure reached the hole, it turned around and looked back, as if knowing the clip was being shot. The image stuttered in onto the figure's face; Johnny could see it was the young McVeigh.

'Three weeks after being released from the detention facility, William McVeigh's oldest cousin, Darren, was admitted to the casualty wing of their apartment block's hospital section. At first the nurses thought he'd been involved in a road accident, but when he regained consciousness the sixteen year old stated that he had been the victim of a totally unprovoked attack by his cousin. William McVeigh fled into the Restricted Zone, aged thirteen.'

More hyper-node options sprang up. Johnny ignored the first section, which appeared to consist of interviews with citizens who had known or come into contact with the pre-teen McVeigh. Instead, he chose the more impressive looking section entitled THE RISE OF THE EMPTI VEE PERSONALITY CULT AND RELATED TOPICS. He selected the first option in the sub-menu; EMPTI VEE AND PERFECTPERFECT/ALEXANDER. M [INITIAL MEDIA EXPOSURE/BACKGROUND]. A window appeared, then expanded to the size of a multiplex screen. A Vid began to play: a young man glared in the direction of the Cam before throwing himself off the stage. Seconds later, the thrashing musicians left on the stage were flattened by a landing Police Pacification Vehicle, that had crudely dropped through the brightly coloured marquee above them.

Killing

Control continued the narrative, 'This piece of footage shows the event that propelled McVeigh, under the pseudonym of Empti Vee, into the world media spotlight eight years ago. The concert was an illegal gathering, allegedly in aid of the nonexistent starving children in the Restricted Zone. The police raid would have gone unreported, but because of the visual impact of the clip you've just seen, it was featured on most of the major Sat and Net channels across the globe.

'The Police raid rounded up several thousand suspects, many of whom were charged with a mixture of drug-related offences or illegal gathering offences. Vee, the only member of his band to survive, was among them. He was charged with the usual offences, and also for the assault on his cousin five years earlier.'

Johnny watched as Vee, now sporting blond dreadlocks and a wispy goatee, is escorted past a wall of cameras, into a government type building.

'The attention he received, under normal circumstances, would have died down almost immediately. The abnormality in Vee's case was this man.' Control raised one of her arms and a frame scrolled down to the floor, leaving a tall, thirtyish man, standing next to her. Johnny recognized him. A hyper-node emerged, providing access to the man's own history, but Johnny sat still and allowed Control to continue.

'This is Mr. Milton Alexander, the multi-billionaire entertainment tycoon. Two weeks prior to the accident with the Pacification vehicle, Vee and his band had recorded a demo for an independent disc label that was operating illegally in the Restricted Zone. The label was indirectly owned by another company, Ranson's own PerfectPerfect label. Neither company had planned to do anything with the recording, except analyse it to help make a more "user friendly" band or singer look and sound that little bit more authentic.

'This plan changed when Vee hit the headlines as the surviving star, now facing assault charges. Alexander had his huge organization go into overdrive and had a reproduced, re-mastered, fully packaged "Empti Vee" product on the shelves within thirty six hours. The promotion for the disc, and subsequent album that followed it, is, apparently, considered a work of genius amongst marketing consultants and was run on the back of a media campaign to have Vee released. Vee, the product, was advertised heavily on the news broadcasts because of the "news angle" associated with it; Milton Alexander had created an overnight sensation that eclipsed all his past success and everything he has attempted since.'

Samples of the news broadcasts, adverts, interviews with witnesses, etc., overlapped and spiralled in front of Johnny: there was so much of it! Hyper-nodes began popping up everywhere, but he ignored them.

'Alexander was in an ideal situation; there had never been a contract drawn up between himself and Vee or the rest of the band. The band were dead and Vee was in prison where he wasn't allowed to involve himself in any business deals or moneymaking endeavours whatsoever. Vee wasn't in any position to object to any "selling out" because, legally, he had no rights to the demo and no control over what Alexander did with it.

'Alexander was able to do whatever he liked with the material he had; produce it in any way he wanted to and market it however he pleased. He turned Vee into the biggest thing in the pre-teens/ teenage category the world had ever seen; he toned it all down, but kept some of the content and twisted it to appeal to a much wider audience. Using remixes, ice-generated resamples, synthesized vocal patterns and the like, Milton Alexander's producers could have kept up the output of "Vee" product indefinitely.'

A news clip sprung in front of the images before him and Johnny watched as a group of perhaps two thousand juves, predominantly female, cried or chanted abuse outside City Court One. He recognized the clip immediately. It was the day Vee was sentenced.

Killing

He remembered because he'd bet on the outcome, and lost.

'Alexander's lawyers had managed to drag out the pre-trial preparations for three years, costing billions in taxpayer's money and wasting as much time as possible. Although supposedly acting on Vee's behalf, Vee had remained inside for the whole time; they had never asked for him to be granted bail.'

The images around Johnny shifted again and he found himself overlooking a stretch of roadway. Control stood next to him.

'Eventually the trial collapsed because of this piece of footage; Vee's alleged assault on his cousin, was leaked to, then broadcast on, one of the pirate Net channels, then picked up by the majors. It was shot from a traffic surveillance Cam on the night of the alleged offence. The police had been sitting on the evidence for years and it is suspected that Alexander was partly responsible for its suppression. It is almost certain that his lawyers knew about its existence, but didn't want to use it.'

The clip showed Vee's cousin attempting to drag the smaller boy, by his legs, across a narrow path and onto a concrete slope. The boy was struggling violently, but to no avail; he couldn't find anything to hang on to. Johnny could see that the slope ran down to EastWestway 75. A group of onlookers drunkenly cheered Vee's cousin on. At the lip of the drop, Vee's cousin slipped and partially released one of the boy's legs. Vee pushed himself away from the older boy, back onto the path. His cousin went over the edge. Johnny watched as the tumbling boy fell into the path of an oncoming dispatch rider.

The virtual reproduction shifted into another court room. Control continued.

'Vee's lawyers were unable to deny the existence of this piece of evidence after it had been shown worldwide and had to present it in their client's defence. The judge ruled accidental misadventure on Vee's cousin's part and Vee was released immediately.'

The Vid footage changed to after the ruling had been announced; the juves outside, in tears only moments before, went crazy. Control turned the volume down on the clip as Johnny winced as the screaming drilled through his head.

'Vee, not surprisingly, wasn't happy with the way PerfectPerfect had exploited his situation and the way he had been turned into a product. He went public in holding Milton Alexander personally responsible.' The relevant clip was duly shown.

'It is believed he returned to the Restricted Zone shortly after this was shot. Nothing was heard from him for six months after that, until the release of the ENJOYING YOURSELF? interactive multi-disc on his own label, PSYCHOTIC DISTRACTIONS Plc. It is still not known where Vee obtained the credit rating to record, produce, market or distribute this product, but IS intelligence strongly suspects that Alexander might have been intimidated into providing at least some of the initial backing for the product. The fact that Alexander later gave Vee the rights for his original songs, although by law they were the property of PerfectPerfect and didn't have to, or that he has never attempted to claim compensation from Vee for the time and effort he had invested in Vee's career, appear to substantiate our suspicions. Other more physical evidence is also available to suggest Alexander was blackmailed and threatened, but none of it can be directly linked to Vee.'

Another bunch of hyper-nodes popped up, linked to other information concerning Milton Alexander and Vee. Johnny noticed that one was a Sat News report of a large, unauthorized 'gathering' near Alexander's country estate. He smiled, despite himself; he'd heard rumours of that before.

'Vee's album, ENJOYING YOURSELF?, sold remarkably well and provided the financial base for the subsequent expansion, both legal and illegal, of the PSYCHOTIC DISTRACTIONS Plc into the media empire it is today.' Two more hyper-nodes popped up, linked to the empire, but Johnny let Control continue.

'The first reports of terrorist activity by the so-called ONE TRIBE group begin around this period; it has been assumed that the ENJOYING YOURSELF? album not only inspired the formation of the terror group, but the money generated by its sales enabled Vee to provide them with resources and equipment.'

Along with several Vid clips of a couple of explosions and a number of bloody shootouts, another hyper-node appeared; it would access a list that would provide detailed information on the activities of the One Tribe.

'We also believe that sales of the ENJOYING YOURSELF? album provided the money for the production and distribution of this . . .' The pictures of heavily armed young girls and dead bodies were replaced by a spinning petri-dish.

Lying in the small transparent dish were a handful of yellow and black striped capsules and some round, bright orange tablets. Johnny recognized them for what they were without needing Control to tell him.

'Commonly known as OVERDRIVE, OD or SHAKE, all attempts to implicate Vee in the development, production or distribution of this drug have failed, despite overwhelming circumstantial evidence suggesting he's one of the brains behind it. Recent surveys indicate OVERDRIVE is now the most popular recreational drug in the under thirties, and there is an alarming increase in its popularity with the thirty plus range surfacing.'

Six different hyper-nodes popped up, all linked to the drug. Johnny scanned the list.

OVERDRIVE: PHYSICAL [ANALYSIS: CHEMICAL/ MEDICAL]

OVERDRIVE: EFFECTS [LAB/REAL CONDITIONS]

OVERDRIVE: EFFECTS [POLICE FOOTAGE]

OVERDRIVE: MUSIC LINK [SEE ALSO PF>VEE, EMPTI]

OVERDRIVE: HISTORY+PF>SMYTHE-JOHNSTON, REGINALD Aka GLASTONBURY [DEVELOPMENT/ DISTRIBUTION: SUSPECT]

OVERDRIVE: SOCIOPOLITICAL CONSEQUENCES [SUMMARY ONLY]

He was reaching for the 'Overdrive: effects [Police footage]' node; watching rioting was always a laugh, when a window enclosing Max and the coffee shop opened up before him. The words TEAM LEADER OVERRIDE dismantled his virtual world and Johnny found himself back at the table staring at a cold cup of coffee.

'Nice to have you back, Johnny. Get us some more coffee, willya?' Max asked.

RESIDENTIAL / PENT-HOUSE AREA ENTERVATORS – ACCESS BY PRIOR ARRANGEMENT ONLY. The door of the entervator remained shut as the girl walked up to it, only opening when she held the gold invitation card up. All persons attempting to access the residential block were first scanned by the entervators for their 'right' to enter. If the girl hadn't had the invitation the entervator would not have let her get in it. She climbed in and once more ascended, this time out of the public sections of the Plaza and into the heavily guarded residential area above.

For a second time, she received the usual scans for undeclared weapons (both plastic and metal) and any antisocial viruses she may be carrying. Biological Scan inspections were not too accurate, but if anything did show the carrier would be prevented from leaving the lift and diverted to the medical wing for a further, less discrete examination. Any undeclared weapons to show up on the scan would be alright, so long as their owner had the necessary permits and permission from their host.

The software could also scan for certain types of drugs, but that had been turned off tonight, at the request of a large amount of money.

All the information the scans obtained was displayed on the guards' screen at the entervators destination. The guards in question sat behind their neoclassical recycled iron and glass reception desk in the plush lobby above, at the start of the top section of the Plaza. The screen built into the designer furnishing in front of them remained green on all the weapons scans, indicating the girl was completely unarmed. The biological scan went amber briefly, but returned to green almost immediately. One of the guards peered at the monitor, then grunted.

'A slightly high Rad count, probably.' Not uncommon, these days. He sent confirmation to the entervator, allowing it to finish its journey.

'Could you please tell me how to get to the penthouse, please? My name is Mary; I've been invited.' The girl spoke as if she had been rehearsing the sentence on the way up. Then giggled. She took her big green glasses off and put them in one of her jacket pockets.

The two guards looked at the young grinning girl with the red hair and big brown eyes, standing in front of them. She offered one of them the invitation card.

Because the information contained on the card had already been sent to the guard, he didn't bother taking it from her, just glanced back at his screen to double-check. A corner of it had been tuned to one of the FreeNet news channels and the girl could see that the man on it was the Cam Reporter she'd passed in the lower lobby earlier, the one who had been arguing with the security guards over the blood stain. He was now standing outside the Plaza, with the building framed behind him.

'. . . the official Plaza line is that the security guard killed, a Ms. Jane Dice, was shot dead by a drug-crazed gunman as she challenged him entering the building. This version of events is almost certainly a lie. Eyewitnesses, while refusing to be interviewed on camera, maintain that the IS, the Government's so-called defenders of liberty, were really behind the killing. Security cameras near the shooting had, apparently, been turned off for routine maintenance so what exactly happened to Ms. Dice will probably always remain a mystery. The Pyramid Plaza Security Company have assured us that, despite whatever happened here not more than one hour ago, there are no more gun-toting loonies wandering around the building. This is . . .'

'Glad to see they've kicked him outta the building. Least someone's doing their job, huh Murray?' the guard commented to his colleague, before handing the card back to the girl and waving his finger at the far end of the lobby where a single entervator stood on its own.

'There you go, miss, just use that entervator there. It'll take you to the penthouse reception. It's direct.' He watched the departing figure for a moment then turned to his colleague, 'For Christsake, Murray,' he chuckled, 'How fuckin' old do you think she is?'

'I really wouldn't like to guess. Hey, can we turn this shit over? The news is starting to depress me. Besides, WarSat1 is showing a special called "American Genocide in the Twentieth Century" about now . . .'

The entervator wasn't there yet; its panel said it would be two minutes before it returned. Looking around she saw a kiosk selling sweets and mags. It wasn't an automatic, totally unmanned booth, common to most of the City; this one had a real person in it. She walked up to the counter. The kiosk assistant was standing with her back to her, boredly watching a mini Vid perched on top of a stack of DigiMags.

The Sat channel she was tuned to was showing highlights of one. of the day's Olympic competitions; the massively disproportionate athletes were warming up beside a running track, flexing and stretching their biologically/chemically-altered physiques. Several of them were even receiving last minute injections from doctors or trainers, under the watchful eye of representatives from the Olympic Drug Committee.

The various steroids and enhancers each country were using was being displayed at the bottom of the screen and the commentator seemed to be extolling the virtues of the Japanese teams endorphine compounds over that of the Ukrainians' hormone-soaked prosthetics.

'Can I have a packet of H's please?' the redhead asked.

'Certainly miss, which colour?' The assistant spun around, snapping to attention. She smiled in a much practiced manner, oozing efficiency. Then her expression changed; she eyed the girl suspiciously, 'Do you have your ID?' she added to the obviously too young customer.

The girl smiled and placed the invitation on the counter. The assistant looked at the counter's screen. It said that the girl was twenty two. She snorted. Then she saw the name on the card, and practically curtsied.

'And which colour would miss like?' she asked crisply. The choice was blue, white or red. Red were strongest.

'Red, thanks.' The invitation flashed the credit transfer to the kiosk's ice; everything, it would seem, was on her host tonight. The assistant handed the packet over to her.

'I'd like to take this opportunity on behalf of the Government to remind you that heroin is an addictive substance and that it is illegal to smoke in any public place thank you for your custom have a nice day.' The assistant chanted automatically, then smiled, without a hint of sarcasm.

While she'd been buying the cigarettes, a couple had turned up and were waiting for the same entervator as herself. They were very well dressed; he was wearing a Retro-style Hawaiian tuxedo, she was wearing a floral mink body tube. They were arguing.

'Well, I don't see why you wanted to come anyway, if all you're going to do is moan . . .' The man sounded exasperated. He was cut off in mid-sentence.

'Don't you speak to me like that! I won't put up with it. You never understand a thing I say, do you? Look, just shut up, you're just too stupid to speak.'

She looked up at the girl who had walked up to the lift.

'And what do you want?' she challenged.

Killing

'I've been invited to Mr. Alexander's party.' The girl held out her invite, giggling, 'See?'

'Oh, that's nice . . .' the woman said, imitating the girl's giggling voice. She eyed her scornfully, then turned back to the man, as if dismissing her. The girl smiled and began unwrapping the red packet in her hand.

'Do you see what I mean, now? My father gets more blatant every day. It's a wonder mummy puts up with him.' She turned towards the young girl again, not seeming to care that her comments were being overheard. 'Don't you think they're getting a bit on the young side?'

The man laughed, putting his arm around the woman's shoulder. She shrugged it off and glared at him. The girl blew a plume of sweet smoke at the couple. She didn't look in the slightest bit perturbed by the other woman's animosity.

A ping announced the arrival of the entervator.

'Welcome to the Penthouse of the Pyramid Plaza!' The voice didn't belong to the lift's ice; it belonged to a short man in a dinner jacket and sunglasses. An old dinner jacket with lapels and real buttons. He saw the couple first.

'Ah, Miss Paula, nice to see you, your mother will be ever so pleased you decided to come.'

'Yeah, hi George.' Miss Paula sounded bored with the conversation already. She strode into the lift, hardly glancing at the welcoming figure.

'Hi, I'm Lance Stu–' Paula's partner held his hand out and tried to introduce himself to the shorter man.

'Shut up Lance, he knows who you are. I had to call to clear you, stupid . . .' Paula began to castigate the man again, as he walked sheepishly over to her.

George looked at the red-headed girl. They were the same height. She giggled and looked at the floor between them.

'Hi, Mr. Alexander sent me an invitation.' She held it up and offered it to the man. 'He said that I should just hand it to everyone and I could come to his party.' She looked a bit nervous.

George held up his hand, 'That's perfectly okay miss. Mr. Alexander informed me of your invitation yesterday. He asked me to welcome you to his humble party and to make yourself at home.' He smiled at her. She smiled back at him, but didn't move. He had to beckon her into the entervator to join the arguing couple.

'Do you want some?' she asked, offering him the cigarette as she passed. He declined politely and deactivated the entervator's pause button.

The lift shot up quickly, covering the many floors between the residential lobby and the penthouse in the shortest time the City regulations would allow, if not as fast as technology could manage. It used a totally enclosed vacuum shaft, so there were no windows overlooking dramatic architecture to amuse its users. The designers of the Plaza didn't like this, but couldn't agree on how the interior of the penthouse entervator should be treated, especially after spending hundreds of man hours on different concepts. So they just installed a wrap around Vid system with 3D capacity, and all chose a piece of footage each; the future owners of the penthouse could make the difficult decision instead. Alexander had decided to run the "thunderstorm over a middle American prairie" clip, on the Dusk setting. It was very spectacular.

George, the short man in the tuxedo, leant over to the girl, the blue flare behind his glasses fading. He saw that she had her mouth open in awe at the scene, and smiled.

'I've just informed Mr. Alexander that you're here.' He leant on the sky next to her as he spoke. A small section around his knuckles became screen again, spoiling the effect. 'He's delighted that you could make it.' He leered at her as he spoke.

The lift chimed and the door opened up onto another lobby area, perhaps a hundred feet long by sixty feet wide. It was full of sofas and potted plants and large, heavily armed men and women. Most were sitting around, either talking to each other, or using decks.

Some were eating. Others stood around, tense, as if ready to react to anything, any second. They were all obviously someone's bodyguards.

'The Goon Room!' sniggered Paula, striding out of the entervator, pulling Lance by his elbow. She headed straight for the door at the far end of the room. As she walked, the chatter died down and the personal bodyguards began scanning the new couple with various devices; lights and beams strobed intrusively over them.

'This is where all daddy's paranoid friends leave the hired help. One of daddy's rules at parties; stops it getting too crowded. Obviously some of the guests get to keep one or two, but that depends how important you are.' Paula seemed to be enjoying herself, having a bad time.

The girl followed the couple and glanced back to see if George was following her.

'The party's through the door on the end,' he called out to her, remaining in the lift.

The door at the end of the room was flanked by two men sitting on stools. They both wore sunglasses, white tuxedos and held large hand-cannons. As Paula approached, one of the men spoke into his neck 'phone and depressed the door switch. The door swung open, revealing a long, beautifully marbled, totally bare and completely white hallway beyond. She breezed through the doorway without checking her stride, dragging her companion behind her. The girl walked past the guards slowly. They had identical features, as if twins. Neither seemed to notice her close scrutiny of them.

The door shut automatically behind her and she looked down the hallway. There was another man in a white tuxedo at the far end, standing to attention. He was identical to the two men outside. The couple were with him and Paula seemed to be annoyed about something.

'. . . is in now, so open the fucking door or you'll be hearing more about this later!' She was nearly yelling.

The impassive man turned and opened the only other door in the hallway. It opened out onto a large, internal balcony. Music filled the corridor around them; the penthouse was totally soundproofed with the door shut.

Directly opposite the doorway, about one hundred feet away, were two massive, slanting glass windows. They joined each other at an angle, to point out across the vast expanse of Edge Central. As she walked through the door, onto the balcony, she looked up to see the windows continue up and over her head to meet in a peak above her. There were stairs on either side of the balcony, leading downwards. She was at the very top of the Pyramid, at its very centre.

'You must be Mary. Pleased to meet you.' A woman, perhaps forty years old, stepped forward. 'Would you like a drink?' She offered the girl a tall, thin goblet. Mary took it, smiling appreciatively.

'I'm Gloria, Milton's P.A.' The girl looked confused. 'Mr. Alexander. Milton Alexander,' Gloria patiently explained.

The girl giggled. 'Where is Mr. Alexander?' she asked enthusiastically, looking around her. 'This is a cool place!' she added breathlessly.

'Milton is busy with some people right now. He asked me to say he'll be with you as soon as he can, but until then you're to enjoy yourself.'

'Uh, okay,' the girl sipped her drink and screwed her nose up, 'Yeuch, what's this?'

'Champagne. Real champagne. It's expensive, they don't make much of it any more.' Gloria said this without a trace of emotion. The girl just shrugged and began to walk to the stairs nearest her.

'Would you like to put your coat somewhere?' the P.A. called out after her. The girl turned and shook her head, smirking.

Gloria watched the retreating figure lean enthusiastically out over the balcony rail, to see what was in the room below, then continue down the stairs. The look on the P.A.'s face might have suggested to any onlooker that she had just swallowed something unpalatable.

The balcony overlooked a vast, triangular room and the windows turned out to be the two external walls of the room. They were entirely transparent at the present time. The room looked out onto an exquisitely kept Japanese-style garden on the external balcony that ran the length of each wall and then, past that, over Edge Central far below. The room was made up of several different levels, interlinked by stairs and gently sloping ramps; it had been designed purely for comfort. Some of the levels were quite small, big enough for only two or three people; these were covered with cushions. Then there were recesses set into the floor, almost like sunken beds. Other areas were much larger and appeared to be designed for walking or dancing on. There were lounge chairs and sofas of all shapes and sizes scattered everywhere and a large number of exotic plants and trees. It was impossible to tell how many people were in the room because of all the clutter, but it held them all comfortably. Both stairways swept down into the room, joining one of the higher levels of the floor about halfway along each of the external walls. The girl walked down the left hand staircase and could see that some of the guests had gone out onto the neat garden balcony; they were watching the sun set beneath the rain clouds and the crowds building up below.

Once at the bottom of the stairs the girl turned to her right and looked back up at the internal balcony. Beneath it was a cascade of vegetation, more brightly coloured tropical fauna. It fell from just below the reception balcony onto the floor far below. Almost hidden behind the plants were other balconies that would lead into the interior rooms of the rest of the penthouse. Beneath the balconies, on the real floor of the huge room, just below the vertical carpet of flowers, a large buffet had been laid out. White-coated men served the guests that mingled around the white-clothed tables. The girl started down in the general direction of the food, but slowly, looking around her at her fellow guests.

'. . . think we'll see much from here?' A fat man lounged in a hammock, on a level just below the passing girl.

'More than the poor bastards standing in the mud underneath him, dearest,' answered his skinny companion, who sat astride him, rubbing her crotch over his ample girth, 'There's going to be a big holoshow anyway, and rumours are that they're going to have real fireworks! So we shou–'

The girl trotted down a small flight of stairs, away from the couple, towards the largest dance floor in the room. She still hadn't seen her host yet.

'. . . So I told the cheap bastard that it was impossible to look like that on under 10K and that if he wanted to be seen around with a tramp then I'd buy him one for Christmas!' The small group of women on her right broke out in polite, slightly forced, laughter. The woman at the centre of the group pursed her lips, waiting for the admiration to die down so she could continue her story. Behind her, sitting on a couch, were three, to all intents and purpose naked, well built, young men. Each wore a collar with a lead and appeared to be the talking woman's property.

The girl walked past the group and clambered over the back of a settee that was barring her path.

'But it doesn't make sense! What's he got to be afraid of?' The shouting man was leaning on his companion, more for support than to emphasise his point, 'It's not as if anyone could get to him, here, is it? You've seen outside. Totally fuckin' impregnable.' Both men wore suits and were holding cans of Soopa.

'Nah, you're totally wrong, as well as pissed. Nothing's impregnable. But it isn't that anyway. He's pissed him off, and that's a dangerous thing to do to any wacko cult leader. Not his fault though, I mean, who'd have thought all this shit would happen?' His companion pushed the other man away and took a pull on his own can, before continuing.

'PerfectPerfect made him what he is today, so he's got no right to be pissed off. But the spoilt little shit ain't grateful, and seems to think he was used, and holds Milt totally responsible, despite all the compensation Milt gave him. If you ask me, the whole thing was handled badly from the start!' The man looked quickly around, realizing he'd been talking slightly louder than he should. He staggered slightly, then leaned closer to the other man to continue with less volume, 'What I don't understand is why Milt backed down and had PerfectPerfect hand over the rights to his early products; after all, they really created them, not him. And they could have prevented him from doing anything else after his release, unless they had their cut of it!'

The girl stopped just past the two men and began adjusting her hat.

'Well, this is what I heard,' the other man spoke quietly, leaning closely to the drunken man, 'Milton Alexander's at home one night, in his country residence, watching the Vid or somethin', and he sees this news flash about a mass influx of crusties into his neighbourhood. Apparently, they'd been turning up in their thousands over the last few hours and no one knew why. Anyway, he's watching this on the Vid and the picture shows an aerial shot of a huge crowd of people, gathering in a clearing in one of the woods, near a large house. He's watching it and notices the house at the centre of the group is his house. There are a good few thousand crusties, standing quietly around his house and he's watching it on the Vid. Can you imagine how that feels? Anyway, rumour has it that the doorbell rings and there's Vee on the doorstep and he wants to have a chat with Alexander about a few things,' he shrugged. 'What they had a chat about is anyone's guess, but I suggest you don't ask Milton. He moved back to the City after that and built this fortress, and I don't think he's left since.'

'Why's he having this little get together, anyway? It's not as if he likes Vee's music or anything!' the man sniggered.

An Idol

'I think it's because everyone else is having one tonight and Milt doesn't like being left out . . .'

The girl walked away from the two men, smiling. As she passed around a raised curved section of floor, she saw a large group of people to her right, standing around a very large man. The man appeared to be in his late thirties, or early forties. He was about six and a half feet tall and very well dressed, but the exquisite tailoring of his suit was attempting to disguise the fact that he was also very fat as well. The man saw her and began disengaging himself from the conversation around him. He walked over to her, trailing some of the group behind him.

'My dear girl, how delightful to see you again.' Alexander extended his large hand to her. The remains of his entourage had stopped a respectful distance away.

'Thank you for inviting me, Mr. Alexander,' the girl giggled shyly. 'It means a lot to me to be here, y'know, being able to see him in person, I'm not sure how I can thank y–'

'That's perfectly alright, I enjoy helping lovely young ladies. Oh, and please, call me Alex, most of my friends do,' the man oozed magnanimously. 'And, if I may say so, you picked the right place to watch tonight's show. I've got the best view in the whole of the City,' he boasted.

'I . . . I couldn't believe it when the dispatcher brought me the invitation, it was so . . . so unexpected. Mr. Sims said that I shouldn't look a gift horse in the mouth and go and have a good time; he knew I wanted to see the gig more than anything, but I was kinda nervous . . . I knew there'd be all these lovely looking people here, I'm just not sure I fit in, y'know . . .' the girl looked a little embarrassed and her voice trailed off. She looked down at her green trainers.

'Nonsense!' boomed her host, 'I told Sims that I liked your style and was going to invite you. Do you like being his trainee P.A.? I'm thinking of asking someone to come and assist Gloria for a while; she's getting on a bit these days. It'd be valuable experience for a girl your age.'

The girl's mouth twitched with indecision, as if she were taken back by the sudden, unexpected offer. Her eyes, however, smiled.

'Don't need a decision immediately, so don't fret over an answer just yet. We've got the whole evening ahead of us to discuss our future relationship.' He slipped his right arm over the girl's shoulder as he spoke to her and was gently massaging her neck with his hand. She looked up at him and smiled.

'Now, you just go and enjoy the party, I'll catch up with you later; got a couple of party games to arrange, to kinda get everyone in the mood for the show later. Help yourself to anything you want, it's all free . . .' He started turning away from her, satisfied with the conversation, then paused and held out a small silver tube to her, 'Nearly forgot, everyone here has to have one of these tonight.' He thumbed the dispenser catch and a small opaque square sliver fell into her outstretched palm.

He then lent down and kissed her lightly on either cheek, surreptitiously rubbing her buttocks with his free hand, then laughed and returned to his waiting entourage; they had been keeping a respectable distance the whole time he'd been talking to her. She looked at the drug a second, then, smiling, held her palm up to her mouth and touched the sliver with the tip of her tongue. It fizzed quietly then dissolved into her blood stream.

The girl skirted a couple dancing in the middle of a huge flower bed and walked up to the buffet. She picked up a plate from the nearest table and handed it to the white-frocked man on the other side. He absently started portioning out the food. Standing around the bar area, at the centre of the buffet tables, was Paula Alexander. She had her own entourage of peers around her and was talking at them in an animated fashion. The girl took her plate back and moved to the next table, closer to the group. The chef began to flash fry some strips of something.

An Idol

'. . . had the cheek to imply that this party was for those who couldn't get invites to the backstage party!' Paula looked at the faces around her for moral support. 'I ask you, who would want to be stuck two hundred floors up in that building, waiting for the crowds to disappear, with a load of journos and groupies for company?' The group around her laughed, nodding wisely as if it was a prospect they faced each day.

Paula continued, 'I, personally, can't think of anything worse than spending time with anyone associated with the One Tribe, they make me sick, to tell you the truth. I mean, it was only meant to sell product in the first place, now they actually believe it all. I really don't think it's necessary to associate with people that stupid.' Paula smiled, indicating she'd finished talking for the moment. The group around her began agreeing noisily.

'Oh, all these cult types are the same . . .'

'You're sooo right, who'd wants to go there, anyway . . .'

'She's a bloody snob, dontcha think?'

The girl turned, startled, and looked at the man who had spoken. He was perhaps thirty years old and was scruffily dressed in a very expensive, conservatively styled evening jacket. He held a steaming tumbler.

'Saw you listening to the little tart over there. She puts on all these airs and graces as though she were royalty. She's not, I can tell you, I should bloody well know, you can't have royal blood and money!' He snorted briefly at his own joke, then stiffened his back and puffed his chest out, turning to the girl beside him, 'Allow me to introduce myself, I am Prince Albert Saxdavis, third in line to the throne!' The effort of standing straight and speaking at the same time seemed too much for him, and he began coughing.

'I thought we didn't have a king or anything like that anymore?' asked the girl, nibbling some of the food on her plate.

Prince Albert slumped into a nearby chair. 'Yes, that is very informed of you,' the bluster was gone, replaced by a resigned sadness, 'but I do hope to raise sufficient support, and funding of course, to mount a media campaign for my family's reinstatement. It'd be good for the country, y'know. Good for the tourists . . .' He smiled, but didn't look as if he completely believed it would happen.

'Is that what you're doing here tonight, fund-raising?' the girl asked, sitting down next to him.

Their places at the buffet were taken by three giggling young girls, their eyes like saucers.

'You could say that, I suppose.' He didn't look at her. 'I've entered into a little wager with our host, Milton. Shouldn't be too difficult to win, I'll wager!' He laughed at his own pun. 'Well, I did, didn't I?' He took a big gulp of the steaming substance in the tumbler he was holding, then looked around. 'Damn fine place, dontcha think?' he asked, changing the subject. 'Alexander's put a lot of his own money, as well as PerfectPerfect's, into this development; seems to be quite committed to the project.' The Prince finished his drink and absently looked around again.

'What project?' the girl prompted, naively.

'Oh, you know; build a new City out there, amongst all that . . .' He waved his arm in the general direction of the Edge Central. 'You know, safe and clean for decent people; seems there's a business opportunity there, or something. Not too sure on the details myself, but I'm all for making this fine country of ours a safer place.' He pushed himself to his feet. 'I think I'll just be off to the bar, get a refill, so to speak. Can I interest you in one?'

The girl shook her head, smiling.

She placed the plate of untouched food on the chair next to her and pulled out the packet of H's. The three girls were still at the buffet table in front of her, huddled together, as if in conference. Over the sound of the music she could just pick out their conversation.

'. . . think he's brave. He is! He's going to be appearing in person. Someone is bound to try and kill him again; probably those damned

An Idol

Muslim Fundamentalists again!' The girl speaking screwed her face up at the very thought. She was about the same age as the red head, but very well endowed. The clothes she wore emphasized this.

'Nah, Carrie, it wasn't the fundamentalists,' one of the other girls objected. 'It was those IS fascists that tried it last time, and you know it's the Government who's really behind them! You shouldn't believe all that stuff on the Sat; it's all lies.' This girl was older, but similarly built and dressed.

The third girl looked puzzled. 'I thought it was the Pope . . .' she started, but stopped herself quickly as two suited men walked up to them. The three girls smiled in unison, automatically smoothing their dresses and adopting alluring postures.

'Couldn't help but overhear what you were saying, girls,' one of the men interjected, smoothly. He had a broad smile fixed onto his tanned face, 'But I'm in Promotion, and would have to say that you're being a bit naive if you believe any of it's anything more than just publicity!'

'What, you mean that it's all made up?' the older girl asked with a look of vacant surprise on her face; all traces of previous understanding of the subject suppressed. The second man put his arms around her and the girl next to her.

'Sure, it's mostly all faked. The stuff you can do with technology today, phew, you wouldn't believe it, and it's all being used to sell him. All that man's rhetoric and bogus ecological/political stance is designed to sell his product. It's not really real; he doesn't believe any of it, any more than we do; he's a capitalist, just like the rest of us. So why shouldn't he stage a few assassination attempts to help shift his units as well?' His comments were greeted with a chorus of scepticism.

'Oh, come on, I suppose he arranged to have his own band squashed then, for the publicity?' one of them asked.

'No. I'll concede that was probably just luck . . .' The group began moving away from the buffet and back towards the dance floor.

Killing

The redhead got up and walked after them, but the noise of the sound system drowned out the rest of the conversation. She walked down the length of the room, past the dance floors and party people, and out onto the external balcony. There were no plants and trees in front of the large doors and she had an unobstructed view of the lights of Edge Central before her. The sun had now dipped below the buildings opposite, leaving a dramatic blood red halo of smog in its wake. Moving to the very edge of the balcony, where the two sides met to form a tip, she leaned out and looked back and down to the Ring far below. From this height it was just possible to see over the advertising wall and watch the traffic below. It had thinned out considerably and was perhaps the lightest it had ever been. Small figures scuttled across its lanes, dodging the few vehicles on the Ring, in full view of everyone.

A couple walked into view, out from behind some bushes on the girl's left. They hadn't seen her standing there and the woman was talking quite loudly. She seemed distressed about something. Her companion looked to be trying to placate her.

'I tell you, Eddie, I'm not doing another scene with that director! This is your fault; you should have realised what Milton was up to. He fucking well knows I don't do snuff Vids anymore; it's against my image now! You should have made sure he wasn't going to pull a stunt like that.'

'Hey, sugar, calm yourself.' The man put his arm around her shoulders. 'You're taking this too personally. I've talked to Milton; he says you weren't told because they were after an authentic reaction. You know- naturalistic.'

The woman didn't appear to hear him, 'I tell you, Eddie, I should have known something was up when that girl looked surprised when the director asked her to take her knickers off.'

'Okay, sugar, okay, I appreciate your opinion, but you gotta look at it from my point of view; you shouldn't have quit until they'd filmed at least one cum shot. You know that that's your speciality and what you're being paid for. Look at the position you've put me . . .'

Pushing his arm off of her shoulder, she started shouting again, 'For fucksake Eddie, what about the position you put me in, then? What did you expect me to do? One minute I'm just getting into my stride, y'know, warming up a bit, the next minute I'm covered in that chick's blood as the prop man's axe splits her sodding head in two! I mean, it was a complete change to the script! The least someone could have done was warn me, for all I knew, he was going to start on me next . . .'

The man took the woman by the arm and led her away from the party, back towards the bushes. He was making calming gestures with his free hand.

A figure stumbled out of the party, hunched over something pressed to his face. The girl watched as it flared blue and the figure straightened to suck in the Crack3 fumes. In the pale blue flare of the inhaler she could see he was a young man, in his early twenties. He saw her and tossed the spent canister away then approached, smiling in a happy, spaced-out sort of way.

'Hey, how's it goin'? Who're you and why haven't I met you before?' He bumped into the balcony wall next to her and looked at it, surprised. He then leant on it, smiling, and looked up, about to recommence his chat up. His expression quickly changed and he straightened.

'Ah, Mary, there you are, talking to one of my programmers. I hope that he's being a gentleman.' Alexander walked up behind the girl, but was glaring at the young man who had been talking to her.

'Er, yes Mr. Alexander . . .' the young man spoke very soberly. He looked apprehensive.

'Say goodbye to Mary now, and then go and sort out the Game. Tell the Hacker I want everything made ready for our friends in five minutes. That's if they're not too drunk by now.' Alexander dismissed the man with a wave of his hand, who scurried away after mumbling something about "another time" to the girl.

'What's the Game?' asked the girl, turning to the man standing behind her. She stood very close to him, smiling up to his face. He draped his free arm over her shoulders, pulling her closer to him still. 'Ah, the Game . . . the Game was written by the Hacker. And the Hacker is very special . . .'

Johnny placed the two cups of coffee onto the table, in front of Max and Dwain. Dwain didn't notice, the blue flashes from around his glasses said he was somewhere else. So did his grin. Max grunted his thanks, but he seemed preoccupied.

'Er . . . Max?' Johnny shuffled nervously, not sitting back down, 'Is it alright to . . . er . . .'

Max's turned his head slightly. 'What?'

'I need to . . . er . . . um . . . go to . . . er . . .'

'Yeah, go on. But don't be too long,' Max waved him away absently.

Johnny walked briskly from the table, past the service counter and the nervous waitresses, and out of the coffee shop. Once outside he looked around, until he saw the sign he wanted, then ran.

Once sitting in the toilet cubicle, Johnny shrugged off his large overcoat and dropped it onto the floor. He then took the glasses off and placed them gingerly on top of it. Resting his elbows on his knees, he buried his face in his hands and began to sob.

One weekend, nearly a year ago now, he'd managed to screw up a RadWax sponsorship deal that would have led to fame and fortune, and got dumped by his girlfriend in the process. He thought that his life had got as bad as it could possibly get, then.

No chance. It had nose-dived from that moment on. Nothing worked right, it all started to fall apart; he even daydreamed about ways of topping himself.

Then, six months later, it got really bad and the nightmare really got started. With his face buried deep into his own hands, his mind's own, totally biological, built in replay facility pulled that one day back into his consciousness again; and as he had done, a thousand times before, he somehow hoped that the things that had happened would somehow miraculously change and it would end differently. Was it really six months ago? The memory was so fresh it felt like only yesterday to Johnny.

He's on the Ring, heading North. It's a hot one today; the therms are peaking nicely but there's a lot of competition for the deep reds. He's hanging back and up, taking it gracefully, checking out the competition. There's been a lot of new faces around, some nice moves have been on the Net in the past weeks. Johnny was beginning to feel old; at seventeen he'd been surfing the Ring for four years. Last year he was the best, ask anyone! But not this year; the spirit wasn't there any more. There were some kids up ahead, under-twelves, pulling Varukas and nose-divin' the freighters. Some of them were really good. Johnny resented them; it was getting that you couldn't pull the simplest aerials without some juve dropping in on your therm, or freezing your skags for a laugh. Johnny and his peers were being pushed out, it was no longer their air any more; you had to watch yourself now. Johnny shrugged. Still, you couldn't beat experience, so they said . . .

Coming past the Schwartz Multi Complex he turned his thermal imager off, banked his board slightly, then cut back, digging the skags into the thermal wave he could feel beneath him. His movement checked the board's speed slightly, allowing him to see the faces of the watching crowd on top of the low building.

He'd first met her there, on that roof, two years earlier. He'd been hanging around, just chatting, before catching the last ride of the day; then he saw her. And it just kinda happened. For the next eighteen months she came to watch him nearly every time he surfed. They had their ups and downs like most couples, but she was always there.

An Idol

Johnny scanned the faces on the roof. Kids just watching, some surfers, a few journos. She's wasn't there! Never was these days. The six months without her felt like a crushing weight on his heart.

'Get used to it,' his angry voice was muffled by the OzFilter he wore; but there was no one around to hear anyway.

He'd lost momentum and couldn't keep the altitude, so moved his weight forward and dived for the road, switching his thermal imager back on.

The scene before him shifted from Real Light. The sky remained unchanged but the ConGrip beneath him turned from its normal scorched grey colouring to an unearthly yellow, as did the buildings rising above the Ring. The now-yellow buildings lost much of their detail in the transition but were still recognizable; not just blocks. The terrestrially-bound, multicoloured, moving vehicles beneath him didn't lose any of their detail but all turned grey, as did their occupants.

And the thermal waves that he and the other surfers dreamt about became visible. They were red. A myriad of different reds, indicating density and heat and speed. The waves appeared to emanate from the very Ring itself, rising up and backwards from beneath the grey vehicles moving rapidly over the yellow surface. The waves were buffeted by the passing traffic and cross winds as they rose, forming peaks, troughs and tubes, providing the surfer with the energy and the surface with which to play on.

The other surfers remained unchanged by the ThermSoft running on Johnny's imager; it rendered himself and the others in Real Light.

As he dropped he could see a multicoloured pack of surfers ahead, writhing above the digitally generated cityscape.

AirBoards were first manufactured as toys for the super-rich and were designed to fly using thermal heat, generated by their surroundings, as their power source. NASACorp had initially commissioned their development for use in the reinstated space programme but were forced by some of their corporate backers to allow a "domestic version" to be released. They were slow and would only skim along several inches above the ground. And they were really expensive, so didn't do well in the marketplace. They were soon dropped by most major stores. Two years later, with the introduction of new synthetic fuel for cars, the boards were rediscovered by a small group of teenagers living near the Ring. Due to the higher emissions caused by the fuel, the surrounding concrete was getting hotter. The boards were going much faster and the kids found that you could get them to go higher, as well; you just had to follow a car. A small news feature on a local Sat channel snowballed into a media blitz and the boards became hot property again. Within weeks, cheaper Mexican and Bolivian boards had flooded the market. Private individuals of dubious means and suicidal intent began modifying their boards to go faster and higher and a programmer who had seen what actual thermal footage of the "waves" they were riding on looked like got the idea for the thermal goggles for surfers.

Within months, all the boards had increased in size and power and the programmer's working prototype of ThermSoft, and the ThermSpec Imagers, had just made him a millionaire. A new craze had been born.

Johnny leant back on the board, pulling at the toe straps, to lift its thin nose into the red grid passing under him. It fell down onto the roadway in a gentle slope until it mixed with other waves at car level. That was where it was hottest and the board would go fastest. You just had to dodge the cars. He was losing the pack so needed to build up some speed to catch up. At about fifteen feet Johnny watched a van pass underneath, then rolled his body sideways, twisting the board with him. The wave parted and he dropped through into the swirling red mass, just above the yellow road. He was amongst the grey boxes, his board bucking slightly. Johnny moved forward a touch, keeping the nose firmly down. His speed was increasing rapidly. He passed the van in front, flying inches above where the white line should have been. He could see the look of surprise on the grey-faced people inside the grey van. The board was changing colour now, from its normal orange to a fluorescent red hue. He passed between a grey taxi and grey mobile home and, pulling the board up with his feet clips, managed to tag the taxi's offside rear camera with the hero blobs on the board's left-most skag. Johnny began screaming, adrenaline and testosterone coursing through his body; this was more like it.

Surfers feel that they can do whatever they want and get away with it. There are cams all over the City, and the Ring is by no means any exception. But the surfers don't care; how could they ever be recognized to be prosecuted? Their boards change colour the hotter they get so cannot be used to identify the surfer, and possession of a board is not illegal (yet). You can't see their faces because of the goggles and OzFilters they wear and so many non-surfers wear goggles and Filters anyway, you can't prove that the wearer is a surfer. Some surfers will concede that they might be recognized by their clothes, or from sound bites; but their view was 'you gotta get caught to get charged,' haven't you?

The traffic around him was building up, so Johnny pulled his board's nose up and caught a wave up to five feet. He rolled his body, twisting the board into a second brake and straight across three lanes of traffic, banking gracefully back down to the yellow road. The disc he was listening to changed tracks and he could hear the blaring horns behind him. Johnny's grin was hidden behind his Ozone mask, he was briefly lost to the pleasure of being alive. A grey shape flashed past his left, veering sharply in front of him, then braked hard. Johnny nearly lost it. Momentary panic. The grey object loomed closer, filling Johnny's vision. He stared at a large grey biker, sitting backwards on the pillion of a large 'Uki, pointing an extinguisher at him. The nose of his board tipped down, nearly into the road. He overcompensated and shot upwards, losing speed, just missing some overhead signs. He watched the laughing biker stick two fingers up at him, before the bike downshifted and burned away; they hadn't even needed to use the extinguisher to screw him up.

Behind his mask, Johnny's face was flushed with a mixture of anger and embarrassment; he'd just hoped no one he knew had seen the biker do that. Fat chance of that. So long as no one had filmed it, that was all.

There was a rivalry between the surfers and the bikers on the Ring. Each thought that the other, for some reason, shouldn't be there. It had now become common practice for bikers to cut up low flying surfers and for surfers to drop things onto bikers. The surfers and the bikers normally left it up to the roadway to do the damage but some shootings had occurred as well. The bikers usually used small foam fire extinguishers; it clogged the boards intakes and made them get heavy, usually resulting in a wipeout or grounding, depending on how fast you were going.

Johnny levelled off at fifteen feet and looked ahead. There was something wrong with what he was seeing. About half a mile ahead, just before the Thames Estuary bridge, the grey boxes were all slowing down and moving into the outside lanes. Traffic jams didn't bother surfers, they even caused some of the best rides; it was the reasons behind this one Johnny didn't like. There were no roadworks scheduled on this section at the moment, so what was causing them to bunch up like that? He could see the pack of surfers ahead approaching the jam. As the first of them flew over the cars, the air around them turned blue and they disappeared.

Johnny turned back to Real Light quickly. Shit! Surf trap! The police had cordoned off ten lanes of the Ring, on the bridge itself. This had created a traffic jam in front of a clear piece of road, with six lanes of slow-moving traffic to the left. The surfers had to rise above the stationary and slow-moving vehicles to maintain speed. The police were waiting for them to do this and were pumping

Lite Ice into the air around them. Lite Ice shows up as dense blue on thermal imagers because of its immense cold. Johnny watched the surfers ahead; they were just falling out of the sky, mainly onto the cleared section of roadway, where they were being picked up by police and medics, although a couple of them had fallen into the stationary or slow-moving traffic and one disappeared over the side of the bridge, to almost certain death in the septic water below.

Johnny was committed to his present course. He was going too fast to stop and changing onto the anticlockwise lanes and going the other way was out of the question for the same reason. He just had to go for it. Flipping his imager on again, he dropped down to just a few inches above the yellow and began lining the board up. He was going beneath the surf trap, at ground level, between the stationary cars. He was gambling on no one changing lanes.

He was amongst the cars, crouched low on the board. The air above him dark blue: dangerous, cold gas. The grey boxes flashed past on either side. Then one was in front of him; he jumped the board upwards, over the turning car, then back down, missing it by a hair.

The gap narrowed and he thought he was going to touch. Then there were no more grey cars; just a clear road, and a few bodies. There was nothing else there; just wiped-out surfers all over the road. He was still at ground level, so pulled up and began turning left, towards the slow moving lane of traffic. He couldn't see the police! He looked frantically around him, then flipped to Real Light. They were everywhere! The edge of the board glanced off a cloaked figure briefly standing in front of him. The board bucked slightly, Johnny held it, veered past the next set of outstretched arms and tried to gain some height.

The chameleon cloaks the police and medics wore shimmered as they ran around the prone bodies on the road. There were perhaps thirty or forty of them; reading the few still conscious but totally mashed and broken surfers their rights, before dragging them off to the waiting Police ambulances. Johnny had obviously surprised the Police by making it through the Lite Ice in one piece. He could see that some of them were now reaching for their guns. The thermals in the cleared piece of road were cooling rapidly and his speed was dropping fast. Thing was, he couldn't see them without switching out of Real Light, which meant he then wouldn't be able to see the Police in what they were wearing; so he'd just have to guess where the thermals were. About two lanes away from the slow-moving traffic he flipped the board to the right, flying parallel to the now stationary lanes on the left; there should be an updraft along here . . .

The police opened up at about the same time as Johnny felt the thermal he wanted tug on his board's left most skag. The board and surfer rose sharply out of the path of bullets. Something exploded behind him but he didn't look back. He was trying to get amongst the cars, out of view. He swerved around a coach and into the gap between lanes.

Johnny's heart was pounding. He was flying, at high speed, through stationary traffic; all the drivers had stopped to watch the police catch the surfers. What to do? He was still on the bridge, so he couldn't get off the Ring yet . . . He allowed the board to rise slightly and looked around. Police pursuit bikes were racing down the empty lanes on his right. Shit! Johnny looked back to see where he was going. There was now a bike in front of him, speeding between the stationary vehicles, down the same gap he was flying down. Not a Police bike; it was the same one from earlier. He could almost see the expression on the face of the rearward facing pillion. The bike was going fast, only Johnny was going faster, and gaining on them. He pulled his board up slightly higher, preparing to bunny them; he didn't want to go any higher just yet or he'd be shot at by the Police. As the board rose he saw something that turned the pit of his stomach to ice. He saw a car door in front of the biker start to

An Idol

open. There was a man getting out of the door. He was holding a VidCam. He was going to film the Police and hadn't seen the approaching biker!

The biker had no chance; him, his pillion and the bike they rode slammed straight into the cam-holding obstruction and car door without reducing speed.

Johnny really tried to get his board over the subsequent explosion. His muscles were already making the moves before he'd even thought about doing them. He dug the skags into the air around him and pulled his leading foot upwards, crouching and twisting the board up at the same time.

He nearly made it.

Nearly.

The rear centre skag on his board, the big sensitive one used for stability, touched something ever so slightly.

The disc Johnny was listening to finished at the exact second the bikes fuel tank erupted. Flames engulfed him and he felt a slight tug on the board beneath his feet, then he was through the inferno. Johnny remembered how his heart had leapt, just then; he was going to make it . . .

The nose of the board began to drop. He leaned back. The board didn't respond. He realised he was about to crash and suddenly became very aware of how quiet and slow everything had become. Spinning pieces of car door, bike and biker spun around him, propelled by the blast. He watched them absently as he felt his board dip forward, leaving his stomach somewhere behind him . . .. The grey cars on either side became a canyon to sink between . . . Faces inside, mouths open, surprised . . . He watched the nose of his beautiful board inching nearer the yellow road; the resolution at this distance is incredible, look at the detail . . .

The nose touched the ConGrip.

He didn't remember much after that, not until he woke up in hospital, and a lot of trouble.

Killing

'Johnny!'

As if to answer, a toilet flushed and the boy walked out of the end cubicle. He was holding his dark glasses.

'Um, hi Dillon. I was just . . . er . . . thinking about . . . uh . . . things . . .' Johnny looked sheepishly around him.

'You okay, kid?' Dillon peered at the boy, his perpetual grin still on his face. He walked over to Johnny and took the glasses from him.

'Now, you gotta keep these on at all times, hear me? You'll be in trouble if you don't.' He slipped the glasses onto him but didn't sound angry, 'Me an' Max might need you for something.'

'Yeah.' Johnny didn't sound too enthusiastic at the thought of Dillon or Max needing him for anything. Johnny walked over to the hand basin and took his gloves off. He began washing his hands.

'Look, Dillon, I shouldn't even be here; I was sectioned, for fucksake!' Johnny was violently wringing his hands under the water as he turned to Dillon, 'and that was a fuckin' mistake. They had me down for a load of stuff I never had anything to do with! I should have got a caution, it's not fair!'

'Yeah, I see your file; you's a surfer dude, ain't ya. Caused the death of fifteen law-abidin' taxpayers and two lowlife biker types when you got caught. Yeah, I see your file.' Dillon was smirking at the boy.

'I didn't kill no one,' Johnny looked shocked at the thought 'The Police opened up at me and blew up a cab! It weren't anything to do with me. An' some biker . . .'

'Yeah, I suppose you jus' happen to be flying around, mindin' your own business at the time.' The black man chuckled, flapping his arms like a bird's wings.

'They damn near killed me!' Johnny's voice rose in pitch. He was about to say more when Dillon clamped his hand over the boy's mouth.

'I said I see your file. It tells me all I need to know so don' you be goin' on about it.' He leaned close to the boy so their noses were almost touching, 'Now you listen to me, boy, I got some news for you: you ain't the only draftee aroun' here, so don't go thinkin' you in for some special treatment or nothin', cause you ain't. You're gonna put up with it.' He released Johnny's mouth, then stepped back. Johnny looked at him, shaking.

'I suggest you apply yourself to the business of the evening, understand?'

Johnny nodded.

'Okay, Johnny Boy,' Dillon was smiling again, 'shall we go and sample some more of the wonderful coffee?' He elaborately motioned towards the door.

'Who else was sectioned? Dwain?' Johnny asked, as they made their way back to the coffee shop. The terrace was getting very busy now, especially on the side overlooking Edge Central.

'No, Dwain's a redneck army man. When his last tour of duty ended he was volunteered for IS.' Dillon held open the door of the coffee shop, allowing Johnny to enter first. 'I'm the other draftee.'

Johnny looked at the man.

'What you lookin' so surprised at, boy?' Dillon asked indignantly. He walked over to the counter. The shop, unlike the others on either side, was still virtually empty. Apart from Max and Dwain, there were only a couple of other customers inside and they were at the other end of the room. The rest had decided to leave for some reason.

'Uh, I didn't mean to . . . it's just, um . . .' Johnny couldn't find the words to express himself out of trouble fast enough.

' 'S okay, I know what you mean. I was one of the first "social deviants" to be sectioned, so I been doin' it a while now.' Dillon was still smiling but he looked as if he were miles away, 'Yeah, I been aroun' a while. Been aroun' a while longer than our Mr. Vee, anyway.'

Killing

Dillon and his family, his mother, three brothers and two sisters, had lived in Edge Central before it became Edge Central. Back then it was just known as the Inner City. Dillon couldn't really remember what it was like; his first real memories were of Relocation Camp Six, and they weren't anything to smile about. That was where he grew up. As a virtual prisoner, stuck in a no-man's land between the contaminated heart of the City and the soaring towers beyond the new, ever expanding, roadway.

New housing for the disposed families from the old city centre was provided on their ability to pay for it, although this was never stated in so many words; if the homeless in the camps didn't have anyone in the City or surrounding suburbs with whom they could stay with, or the credit to find and pay for rented accommodation (including the deposit and mandatory Non-Payment Insurance Tax), they weren't allowed to leave until charity housing was available. So Dillon lived in Relocation Camp Six for nearly ten years. He watched his mother die through malnutrition caused by an old cliché: she gave too much of her own food to her starving children for too long. He also watched two of his brothers grow up and get murdered in the violence that surrounded their everyday existence and eventually resorted to pimping for his sisters just to survive.

When Dillon left the camp it wasn't to take his place, eventually, amongst the society that had so neatly abandoned him; he travelled the other way, back into the contaminated heartland of the old city, to the place that eventually became known as Edge Central. There he met others like himself, who'd given up on the false promises and escaped the brutal captivity of the camps for an equally harsh freedom, and finished his very modern education.

Dillon took his place amongst those who preyed on the City to survive; one of a new breed of dealer hustler pimp spawned in the barbaric autonomy of Edge Central. Using the skills he had honed during his formative years, he slipped back into the City that had shunned him to compete for the only business he knew. He was very good at it.

An Idol

He looked up at Johnny, 'Want some more coffee?' Johnny shook his head.

Dillon turned back to the counter and spoke briefly with the waitress. He then looked back at Johnny.

'Judging by your reaction earlier, you don't really like our Mr. Vee, do you? Know anyone who got caught up in that One Tribe bullshit?'

'Uh, yeah, I knew someone once . . .' Johnny started answering but Dillon didn't really seem interested in the answer; he carried on speaking.

'I known hundreds, fuckin' hundreds! Watched 'em turn up day after day; like a plague or somethin'. Fuckin' incredible. Nearly got myself hooked, 'n all. Scary. Drugs talkin' that. "Unite with the One Tribe for the sake of the world" was what everyone was sayin'. Shit, you'd have to be on drugs to believe that.' Dillon was shaking his head at his own folly, still grinning though, 'Problem is that I'm not sure what to believe no more. I know the government don't tell the truth but they never have, so no change there . . .' His monologue tailed off as some fireworks exploded in the near distance. Johnny was watching him closely.

'It's easy to believe in drugs, man. Makes you think it's all okay, especially if you're with a lot of other fucked people doin' the similar. I 'mem the Ravers Return when that was prime. Ooooeee, did we have some fun there.' Dillon turned to Johnny again, the big grin back on his face at this happier, less complex memory, 'I used to do business there, and that's where I took my first Shake. That was jus' after your man Vee was released. Never forget it! It went on for twenty-four straight, no bull. Fuckin' miracle, I thought. Did a lot after that, and made some good business for a while, seein' as it was totally illegal, like.' Dillon's expression almost became serious.

'See, at the time, I never realised why they wouldn't let us just get on with it. I never realised why that drug was any different from Daze4s or SuperCools. Or why, if everyone wanted to get totally fucked and all loved up, dancin' an' gigglin' an' shakin' into the dawn, why the man wanted to stop us? All it ever did was start a riot, property would get trashed, y'know.' He picked his coffee up and began walking towards the others.

'Why do they try to stop the parties then? And the surfing, and everything else?' Johnny asked quickly, before they were within earshot of Max and Dwain. Dillon stopped and looked at him.

'Didn't they teach you anything in the academy?' He sipped his coffee, looking at Johnny, who performed what appeared to be a cross between a shrug and a head shake.

'They try to stop the parties and the surfin' and the draggin' an' everythin' else, not because they're antisocial and against the policies required to maintain this society but because it's a control thing; symbol of their authority to tell us what to do. An' it also gives people something else to think about; keeps their minds off the things that are really important.

'OD, Shake – whatever you want to call the drug – is the fly in the soup though, 'cause it's a totally social drug with really antisocial side effects; that's why it's illegal where most of the others aren't. Instead of keeping the population indoors and isolated, stoned in front of the screen, OD gets people outside and together. They're less controllable when in large groups. Add to that the side effects of upsettin' anyone who's on Shake . . .' Dillon shrugged 'Obvious isn't it?'

'Well, well, well . . .' Max had been mumbling to himself for the last half hour; things were strangely wrong with the penthouse's ice but he couldn't figure out exactly what, because he didn't know what he was looking for.

'What's happening, Max?' asked Dillon.

'Seems that Milton Alexander is the owner of the penthouse. That's about all I can find out from the Plaza's ice 'cause the penthouse has its own. I suppose I'll just go an' have a look-see myself.'

'Is that the only area to secure?' Dillon was watching a group of suits stagger drunkenly through the door of the coffee shop as he spoke to Max. Max grunted an affirmative.

Johnny was only half listening to the conversation. He was staring out over the expanse of Edge Central, towards the tall, skinny building in the distance.

Dillon watched the group of suits freeze when they saw the four men; they had obviously not noticed the IS men sitting in the shop before they had entered. They had probably thought it was their lucky night because they had found a spare table somewhere.

'What did you tell Control about the security guard and the red neck here?' Dillon asked, nodding at Dwain.

'The truth.' Max scratched his nose. 'That Dwain's a trigger happy psycho who shouldn't be allowed out. Control knows that. Told me there's a shortage on functioning operatives 'cause of the scale of tonight's little exercise, and to put up with him.' He shrugged and the sides of his glasses sprang back down, signalling that the conversation was over. Dwain didn't appear to have heard what was said about him; he just sat there, grinning in another virtual world behind his glasses; he was also rubbing his crotch, oblivious to those around him.

The suits were standing uncertainly at the counter. They were arguing, very quietly, not about whether they should stay or not, but how soon they could leave without attracting unwanted attention.

'Do you think it'll be a long shot, Dillon? I mean, from here, or one of the other buildings?' Johnny turned around from the view and looked expectantly at the man.

'Nah, we'll be sitting here all night, bored stupid.' It wasn't Dillon who answered; it was Dwain, back from wherever he had been.

'You sound pretty sure, Dwain. You workin' on inside information or somethin'?' Dillon chided, then added, 'Or are you worried about the distance? Distance shouldn't bother no pro, y'know what I'm sayin?' he grinned.

Killing

'I know what you're sayin' Dwain rose to the bait, 'Shit, I've been a pro all my adult life, not swannin' around some crack ridden' 'hood, so outta my fuckin' head I didn't know what day it was . . .' He began to rise out of his seat, squaring up to Dillon.

Max's gun appeared at Dwain's temple, a small red light flashing just above the trigger guard; the safety was off. 'You're not getting out of your seat without prior instructions, are you Dwain?' he croaked.

Dwain froze, remaining halfway out of his seat for several seconds, as if trying to decide whether Max was serious or not. The gun remained firmly levelled at his temple, the safety light blinking.

Dwain sat back down, opposite the ever grinning Dillon. Max casually put the gun away without saying any more. Johnny watched as the group of suits began to nervously make for the door. They seemed in a hurry.

'I'll tell you what this pro thinks, Johnny Boy.' Dwain was smiling again, he didn't seem too concerned that he kept incurring Max's wrath, 'It's gonna be a bomb!' He pointed at Johnny, 'You mark my words, they'll use a SmartScan bomb or somethin'. They'll fly it right up that faggot singer's arsehole and it'll be goodbye babe security, goodbye faggot! We're jus' up here for the view.'

'Easy to scramble, that sort of shit.' Dillon was lounging back in his chair. 'It wouldn't get near him, jus' fly off an' blow some other mother apart.'

'Would he have access to that sort of Tech?' asked Johnny.

'Course, he buys his shit from the same places as everyone else,' Dillon replied.

'Why not a static bomb, y'know, planted earlier?'

'Nah, too much security around the tower before tonight. If you weren't a face, you was history. 'Sides, they're easily detected.' Dillon seemed to know what he was talking about. 'Anyway, blowing him to pieces ain't gonna teach anyone anythin', y'know, there wouldn't be enough left to prove it was ever him.'

An Idol

'So what do you reckon, Mr. Professional? Close hit? Get someone to jus' walk up to him an' pull the trigger?' Dwain was warming to their conversation now.

'How would you find anyone that stupid?' Johnny looked at Dwain, incredulously, 'Whoever did that would be ripped apart.' Dillon and Dwain both turned to look at Johnny. Dwain started laughing.

'There are ways, shall we say . . .' said Dillon, mysteriously. Johnny didn't get to question the smiling man any further. Max started swearing.

'Well, that's just fuckin' great!'

The blue light around Max's glasses faded. The other three watched him closely as he took his glasses off and rubbed his eyes.

'Want the bad fuckin' news, or the really bad fuckin' news?' he asked them, sliding the glasses back onto his nose. 'There's a fuckin' party going on up there! Y'know, dancing and all that. Rich types, couple of hundred of them, I'd say. Some of them look political.'

'You mean radicals?' Dwain asked.

'No, I mean fuckin' politicians; real ones. They've got their own bodyguards an' everything, some of them appear to be vat-bred and all are tooled up to the back teeth. That's the bad news.' Max reached into his coat pocket and pulled out a crumpled packet of cigarettes. 'Now, the really bad news is that Control says that doesn't change shit. Control's just told me that nearly all the other "building teams" are reporting large party gatherings at their locations as well. Seems that the population isn't satisfied with watching tonight's gig on the Sat; there's some retro craze about seeing things in real-life, so everyone is outside, watching Edge Central!' He lit his cigarette.

'What the fuck does anyone expect to see from this distance?'

'No idea, Dillon, no idea. I've given up trying to understand how the worms think. What it means for us, though, is we're stuck here. We aren't going to get relieved and we're not going to get backup unless we're in the target zone.' Max took a long pull on his cigarette, 'We better hope nothin' happens, hadn't we, Dillon?' Dillon nodded, still grinning.

'So what're we doin' now? Jus' sittin'?' Dwain looked bored, and a room full of bodyguards sounded like fun.

'No, Dwain, you're coming with me to help me find out who's in the party.' Max looked at him, 'Won't be as interesting as the thirty-sixth floor women's shower room though . . .' Blue light flared around his glasses as their sides dropped, and he didn't finish the sentence. Dwain snorted but followed, leaving Johnny and Dillon on their own.

———————————————— His royal highness, Prince Albert Saxdavis, pumped another round into the shotgun and casually aimed at the last, heavily bleeding guard before him. The big bore weapon splattered most of the man's upper body over a large section of the wall, leaving the rest of his remains twitching and kicking on the floor. The Prince moved forward along the corridor towards the door at the far end.

'Well done . . . well done, that's nearly 2 Mil of credit so far.' The dapper looking gentleman walking beside the Prince sounded as if he was talking to a small child.

'Bit easy, dontcha think?' asked the Prince, swaggering a bit, 'Where's the sport in this, Milton?' The question wasn't addressed to the man next to him; so, for some reason, he spoke upwards towards the ceiling.

Alexander put his arm around the girl, 'Watch! This is where the fun begins. Up to now the Hacker's been keeping it dead easy for the fat slob. Now you might see what's so special about the Game.'

The young redhead watched the two figures in front of her, the Prince and the Hacker, walking along without moving; they were suspended in the air in front of her, inside a large portion of a virtual gaming area. Part of the game area surrounding them had been rendered for the audience alone to see where the danger was to come from next, and that moved as the two figures moved.

The secret trap door in the section of ceiling the Prince had just walked under slid open and an armed figure dropped out.

'Behind yooooou!' the smartly dressed Hacker, evaporating, warned.

His royal highness turned and fired at the armed figure; and missed. He pumped the gun again and fired a second time, as his new adversary fired back. The guard crumpled but winged his foe. The Prince staggered, dropping the shotgun to grasp his injured arm; a look of utter disbelief on his face.

'Ahhh, ahhh . . . fuck!' was all he could manage.

The dapper figure reappeared, laughing. 'Does that hurt, my Prince? Maybe you should find a Medipack now,' he suggested.

'What the fuck's going on?' the Prince asked, plaintively, clutching his bleeding wound.

'This is the sport, Al. The game's wired to your nervous system; the software's written just for pain. If you get shot, you get hurt. You didn't think I was just ripping off some kid's arcade game for the sake of it, did you?'

Appreciative Ohh's and Ahh's from the audience around Alexander and the girl signalled their delight and renewed interest at this unexpected turn of events; many of them had started to get bored with the game and begun drifting off.

Alexander beamed broadly at the obvious success of his little show.

'We caught the Hacker trying to access some very personal stuff from my private ice, about two years ago,' he told the girl next to him. 'It wasn't the first time someone had tried, and he fell into a little maze I'd had installed. He couldn't get back to his body before some of my men found it; and now it's too late. I keep him in that over there.' He indicated a small black box on a black slab table, just visible through the holo projection. 'He's very useful, if slightly mad, and writes some very clever software just for me.'

'Why's he mad? Because he's angry at being caught and can't get back to his body?' the girl asked.

'Yeah, probably; he hasn't got a body to go back to any more.'

Alexander chuckled, then added in a more serious tone, 'But we also think it's something to do with accelerated time when you're digitised; most people we've attempted to capture like this have ended up unusable and have to be deleted.'

The Prince had picked up his gun again and was staggering, bleeding, down the corridor. His health score was dropping point by point as he lost more blood; his left side was drenched bright red. He was making for a Medipack in the middle of a junction in front of him when he saw the next guard step away from the wall towards it. He raised the gun and depressed the trigger. Nothing happened.

'You have to pump it for it to work . . .' the dapper Hacker offered helpfully, if slightly sarcastically.

The guard shot Albert in the chest, sending him spinning back the way he'd come. His royal highness looked down at the ribs protruding from his shattered torso, then up at the guard, raising his gun a second time. The guard slowed down.

'Pump the gun, Al, then shoot him. This will get really boring for everyone watching unless you try harder. To make it easier for you I've put this one into slo-mo; but it'll be the last time I help.'

The Prince, through a haze of pain and tears, somehow managed to lift the gun and slide the fore grip back to pump another shell into the chamber. He levelled it at the slowly moving generated guard and fired.

The gun's discharge kept real time until it made contact with the guard, then it slowed down and sprayed the virtual man, ever so casually, over the wall.

'Now get the Medipack . . .'

The audience watched as Albert Saxdavis, with a health score of ten percent, dragged himself along the floor, towards the piece of software that would reconstruct his shattered body, leaving a bloody trail of his own intestines in his wake. There was much laughter and approval at the scene from the audience but they were all sporting enough to clap and cheer when the Prince finally made it to the software.

Albert looked beyond hearing; his flushed cheeks were streaked with tears at the intense anguish his body felt.

The Medipack dissolved into the shattered body and the Prince's bones and skin began to knit rapidly back together again. It looked like it hurt almost as much as getting shot in the first place. Eventually he stood up, whole again, except his clothes remained ragged and stained; the only indication of what had happened to him.

'Give him the machine gun, will ya?' Alexander asked the Hacker, 'This could get very predictable, otherwise.'

The Prince, clutching another, much larger gun, stood by a closed door, obviously debating whether to go in or not. He was no longer as confident about playing this game as he had once been.

The door opened and he started firing immediately. Bodies dropped in front of him and he stepped into the room beyond, still firing. There were several large explosions and an impressive amount of beautifully rendered carnage before the Prince eventually ran out of foes. Afterwards, he waved both of his arms in the air, still firing his gun, until the ammunition ran out.

'Ha, getting the hang of it now, dontcha think?' he swaggered.

'No, not really. You've got no ammo left, stupid.'

In the middle of the large room, on top of a small flight of steps and underneath a transparent bubble, was a flashing credit sign and a big box of ammunition. The Prince shrugged and walked carefully over to it. He looked around it briefly, to see how he could get the bubble off the treasure inside. Nothing. He turned around and saw an impressive looking switch on one of the walls of the room.

'Ha!' he exclaimed, running over to it.

The Hacker suppressed a snigger as Alexander grasped it. The switch exploded, disintegrating his hand. Alexander staggered back, dropped the large machine gun and fell through a trap door that had opened up behind him and down into a razor-lined tube. The virtual drop sucked the screaming man along a roller coaster ride of slicing torment (the guests at the party watched a transparent tube unfold rapidly beneath them and disappear, smeared with blood, above them; the Prince stayed tumbling where he was, in full view in front of them) and into the inevitable green chemical lake below. The Prince's health score began to plummet as his skin was stripped from his thrashing body.

'Does anyone else want to come and play? This bloke's crap!' cackled the Hacker, hysterically.

Alexander and the girl walked outside, leaving the whooping crowd, and onto the balcony. They passed the real body of Prince Albert Saxdavis, wired to the Hacker's black box sitting on the slab table next to an expensive looking entertainment system and an ice terminal. His body was unscathed but the expression of sheer agony on the twisted face suggested that the pain, if not the game, was very real.

The sun had disappeared totally now and the City was fully illuminated. Lights had started appearing in Edge Central as well, although most of these had a different sort of luminance from the lights in the City; they were softer, less defined. Directly in front of the couple, rising from the low lights around it, was the Ministry of Truth tower. It was lit from top to bottom and had a single blue laser mounted on the roof, fanning upwards.

'He's so far away!' The girl sounded disappointed. 'How will we be able to see anything from here?'

'I've got a load of these in.' Alexander pointed to a stack of cartons by the balcony door. 'They're Army issue BiNoks. They've got auto trackers and vibration dampers on them; apparently you can dance wearing them.' The girl looked suitably impressed. Alexander walked over to the cartons and, tearing open the upper-most packet, pulled out a pair of the BiNoks. She took off her hat to allow him to put it on her. He stood behind her, pressing himself up against her as he adjusted the head strap.

'Of course, they're only a gimmick really. When the novelty wears off, there's always the 3D Sat system inside for anyone who wants to see the show properly. How do you feel?' He began stroking her hair.

Through the glasses she could see the tower clearly. It was about the same height as the Plaza but much, much thinner; just a round column reaching towards the stars. It had been constructed within the last two months, rising rapidly to its present height, although the foundations must have been laid earlier without anyone noticing. There had been a great deal of interest in the structure from nearly everyone in the City. Where the materials had come from and what it was to be used for had been the most commonly asked (and unanswered) questions. Everyone knew who was behind it, though. Then, just under a week ago, the rumour about Vee's free concert began to spread and the tower was given a purpose and a name: the Ministry of Truth.

There were roadies swarming over the roof of the building, making final adjustments to the sound and Cam equipment that had already been set up. There was no sign of Vee or anyone remotely famous yet. She began panning down the tower. Nearly two thirds of its overall height was covered by a wraparound VidWall, now playing Trance patterns to the crowd below. Later, when Vee came on, live Cam footage, filmed from the roof, would be played on the wall. Vee would be over two hundred stories high when singing, his image towering over Edge Central and the horde below.

Below the VidWall were the speakers. The lowest twenty floors of the tower were completely hidden from view, obscured by the biggest sound system the world had ever seen. The girl zoomed in onto the throng. People were packed solid around the tower. It was difficult to estimate how many people there were but everywhere she scanned was crowded, shoulder to shoulder.

An Idol

'Wow!' she said, breathlessly. She tracked back across Edge Central, towards the Ring. As the light levels fell, the BiNoks auto enhancer cut in; she could see that there were still huge crowds making for the illuminated tower from every direction, a moving wave of humanity converging on the technological totem that was the Ministry of Truth tower. On the City side of the Ring were more people still. Those who were too nervous to go into Edge Central, but didn't want to miss out on the party, were struggling to find the best vantage points they could. They were massing on the tops of buildings and car parks, on plush gardened balconies or hanging from street signs and lighting; anywhere that provided a view of Edge Central and the Ministry of Truth tower. They were even perched precariously on top of the Ring's vast advertising wall.

Alexander pushed his nose into the girl's hair, closing his eyes as he breathed in. He was smiling, as if in anticipation of delights to come, 'I'm glad you're impressed by them. Things from the Army don't come cheap.' He flipped the catch on the back of the BiNoks and gently took them off the girl's head. He dropped them onto the floor behind him, not bothering to see how they landed.

'Have you thought about my proposition, yet?' he asked, as she turned around to face him. He stroked the side of her face with his index finger. She smiled at him and looked down at her feet, shyly.

'I think perhaps we should go somewhere, er, slightly more private, to discuss our future relationship, don't you?' Alexander took her by the elbow and, without waiting for her to reply, smugly led her back into the large room. She smiled, struggling to put her hat back on with one hand as they walked.

The game had already finished; the Holo projection had reduced down to a few square metres, just large enough to show the Prince was being slowly eaten by a large purple creature, his health score a constant 1%. He was still conscious but unable to do anything about it.

Killing

The Hacker stood next to him.

'Well?' the Hacker asked when he saw Alexander.

'Yeah, go on then; enjoy yourself.'

A grin spread across the Hacker's face and he and the half-eaten Prince faded away. Alexander pointed to Albert Saxdavis' body, as it stood up and stretched, then ran its hands over itself, but didn't unplug the cable from the black box.

'I can convince the Hacker to write and play these games by giving him something he hasn't got. For a short time, anyway.'

The Prince's body turned around and smiled at them. 'That's better. How long have I got?'

'Until the end of the party. Don't damage his body too much, will you?' Alexander chuckled, not really caring what the Hacker did to his borrowed flesh. He winked at the girl next to him, 'He's a bit careless sometimes. He gets carried away, y'see; we don't let him have physical feeling simulations in the capture block very often, it only makes him morose later. Sometimes, if he's been a good boy, we let him borrow a real body to do some feeling with.'

One of the waiters passed them, so Alexander took another glass of champagne and used it to wash down a small pink capsule.

'Want one?' He offered her a small dispenser, 'It's an OverDrive enhancer, you must've tried them before, haven't you?' he added.

'What does this one enhance?' she asked coyly. He leered at her and handed the drained glass back to the waiter. She pumped one of the capsules out of the dispenser and swallowed it. As the waiter walked away, a woman, of approximately thirty years old, walked up. She was trailing three near naked young men behind her. Ignoring the girl, she spoke directly to Alexander.

'So, Milt, are you taking your little friend to play with your activity centre before the show, or are you going to wait until later, like a real host?' There was ill-concealed venom in her comment.

'Fuck off, Liz!' Alexander leant towards the woman, baring his teeth at her, 'before I get security to shoot your toys!' he spat, nodding towards the young men behind her. The woman strode off, smiling. She appeared pleased to have upset him.

'Who was that?' asked the girl, quietly.

'My fucking wife. I'd have divorced her, or worse, years ago, if Paula, my daughter, would have let me.' Her host shook his head, then once again took the young girl by the arm, 'Her problem, Mary, is that she has never forgiven me for being born after her!' He looked as if he was serious.

Alexander led the girl through the large room, towards the almost hidden balconies behind the vegetation on the far wall. Passing behind the buffet and beneath a rose-covered arch, he led her into a small lobby. There was a spiral staircase on one side, leading up, but there was also a lift. Alexander pressed the pad next to it and its door opened.

'So, you're looking forward to tonight's show, then?' he asked, stroking the girl's neck. They stepped into the lift and it shot quickly upwards.

'Oh yeah,' she sounded excited, 'he's been my idol ever since I was young.' The door of the lift opened and they stepped out onto one of the higher balconies, then turned left and walked down a corridor, into the heart of the penthouse.

'Well, you've got me to thank for that.' Her host swaggered; but he wasn't trying to impress her any more, just himself.

They were heading to a black door at the very end of the corridor.

'We go back a long way, me and Vee, but I'm sure you know that. I helped make him what he is today, not that he gives me any credit for it,' he added tersely, stopping by the black door. The door didn't have a handle on it, or any visible type of control pad, to indicate how it opened. Alexander pulled a small card out of his pocket and tapped it on the door frame. The door clicked open and he walked in, holding it open for her.

'Oh, I wouldn't say that,' said the girl wistfully, walking into the room after the man.

He looked at her, confused. 'Wouldn't say what?' The door

clicked shut behind him.

'What you just said. Vee knows you've been a great help. He's always saying how he feels he hasn't thanked you properly,' she answered, smiling.

'How would you know . . ?' Alexander's voice trailed off, a look of horror forming slowly on his face.

The girl didn't answer immediately, just grinned at him broadly, then stepped forward and sidekicked him in the right temple.

She stepped over the body and checked that the door had shut properly, then turned and looked at the room. It was predominantly black and about forty feet wide by fifty feet long. At the far end of the room was a huge bed, held off the floor on industrial style legs. It was covered in shiny material and cushions; all black. Between the girl and the bed was what looked like an executive climbing frame made out of chrome tubes. Hanging between the tubes was a web of foam-covered straps. The rest of the room was decorated with various pieces of antique weaponry, some art and a lot of pornography. Next to the bed was a small touchdeck; linking the room to the penthouse's ice. The girl walked over to it, dropping her coat onto the bed as she passed, and turned it on. The screen unfurled and she surfed the initial menus into the Penthouse's SecCam system, and displayed all the views simultaneously on the screen. She then turned and looked at the unconscious figure of her host, lying by the door.

Mary had first met her idol, the rock god and eco-activist, Empti Vee, a year earlier at a party. It wasn't an exclusive rock stars and groupies only type party that you needed to know the bouncers or have a special invite for; it was just a normal Saturday night Edge Central Shaker, being held in one of the many decomposing office blocks on the restricted side of the Ring. The day before the shaker, her boyfriend told her that he wanted to go on his own; he'd said he had some "business" to attend to. They argued about it; Mary couldn't understand why he needed to be on his own to do that, and besides, he was always doing that to her, disappearing, trying to find reasons to go out without her, to get away from her, wasn't he?

He'd argued that it was hardly professional, bringing your girl along and, more to the point, didn't she trust him or something?

Mary was adamant: she wanted to go to the party and didn't see why she shouldn't. What was so professional about a business meeting in a shaker, for Christsake? She then suggested that she went on her own and, if she saw him, would pretend she didn't know him; that way his professionalism would remain un-challenged.

He went mad. They continued arguing until she told him to fuck off again and he stormed off.

Mary felt guilty about it afterwards and decided not to go. Her decision was partly due to her (ex)boyfriend's arguments; she didn't want to screw up the deal he had miraculously landed (shite jobs were scarce, well paid ones almost impossible to find) but also because Edge Central was dangerous, especially if you were a fourteen year old girl on your own. So she decided to let him stew in his own juice for a while and would call him in a day or two to accept his apology.

She spent the next day watching the Net and avoiding her stepfather. She'd tried to call Speed anyway and patch it up but couldn't get in touch with him.

She changed her mind about going to the party when Terri, her best friend, turned up with a dubious individual called Skutz and a large bag of OD. Skutz was from Edge Central and had "borrowed some credit from somewhere" and wanted to take Terri and the bag of drugs to, coincidentally, the same party that Mary had wanted to go to. Terri confided to Mary that she didn't trust the man as far as she could throw him and that she, Mary, was going to be coming with her to make sure Skutz behaved himself. It took

Killing

Terri under a minute to convince Mary to get changed.

'So, how's Speed doin'? I heard he's about to hit the big time.' Terri sounded impressed, which pleased Mary. Terri had never liked Speed; she thought he was an asshole. Mary looked at her friend; she was pacing around the room like a caged animal, the pupils of her eyes massive. She decided not to tell her they'd split up . . . again.

'Yeah, really wild, isn't it. Seems it's not all sorted yet but should be soon. It'll mean changes, an' I'll be seein' less of him when he's doin' the circuit.' Mary beamed, struggling to pull her boots on without undoing the straps.

'Well, when the credit starts a rollin' in, don't you be forgettin' your friends now . . .' Terri watched Mary finish getting ready and urged her to go faster, 'Hurry up, willya, it's getting late. We've gotta go.' She seemed anxious to be on the move, although they had plenty of time to get there. Skutz was already standing by the door of Mary's small bedroom, pulling on his coat. His eyes were hidden behind some old fashioned sunnies but, as Mary knew, they would be the same as Terri's; they'd both dropped some OD earlier in the day and were moving up to the fourth level by now, judging by their inability to stay still and their anxiousness to get out of the cramped apartment and into the open.

'What about me?' Mary asked, nodding at Skutz's bag.

'Huh? Oh, yeah . . .' Skutz fished around for a second, then held out his palm to her. She took the capsule and put it in her mouth, holding it between her teeth. Terri and Skutz watched absently as Mary bit down on the membrane, releasing its content onto her tongue. She paused a second, then inhaled sharply, sucking the rapidly dissolving capsule and its contents into her brain.

'I ain't got any Skips on me; we'll get you one on the way.' Skutz smiled, opening the door of her bedroom.

Once ingested, the drug OverDrive works in six stages, over a twelve to eighteen hour period, depending on the strength and quality of the batch. The first two are ambient levels that make the user mellow, listless, almost totally inactive. The Sat or Net becomes interesting and just thinking becomes fun. Sex is totally incredible. The third level is mainly hallucinogenic and begins to mesh the user's nerve endings and brain stems onto the template introduced by the drug. Things, previously unconnectable, connect; life and reality start to fall into place and make sense, and a subtle feeling of satisfaction and well being infuses the user. The fourth and fifth levels are very visual and the user feels incredibly euphoric and speedy; the full impact of the drug on the nervous system begins to take effect. The user is unable to stay still and is highly susceptible to outside stimulation, like music. At this stage most users feel compelled to "go out" and be with other people experiencing the same effects. It is nearly impossible for any user on these levels to remain inside, unless in a very large space. These feelings are normally accompanied by insane, uncontrollable laughter. The sixth level is the fully blown part of the OD trip. The user is in a high state of euphoria, their body uncontrollably active. Dancing becomes a necessity; the body's natural stress reaction is used to stimulate and fuel the user. This is coupled with a linking of the senses at a cerebral level: sound is felt, light is tasted, touch is heard. At this stage a user, in the presence of another user, will feel a psychological bonding take place between them. Everyone loves everyone else, at least for the duration of the trip.

Mary's mother was sitting in the living room, crying, as the trio trooped past. She was watching another blubbering woman pacing around the coffee table. Mary was careful not to walk through the hologram of Mrs. Brakenbury but Skutz and Terri just stumbled through it, smirking, making the soap star wobble and distort. Mary's mum didn't seem to notice.

'Still grieving over Donna, huh?' Terri asked Mary's mother, trying hard not to laugh.

'It shouldn't have happened; it's so unfair! She had her whole

Killing

life ahead of her . . .' Mary's mum blubbed, reaching for the box of tissues next to the packet of blue H's.

Mr. Brakenbury walked into the living room from the kitchen and asked his wife if she'd like a nice cup of tea. Both figures froze and the Chunda Valley theme tune started its familiar refrain.

'I can't stand Holo-Soaps, all these strangers walking around your own home, you don't get any privacy . . .' Skutz opinionated, as Terri pushed him towards the front door.

'Don't be so stupid, they can't see you . . .' she countered, clipping the grinning boy around the head with her hand.

'I'm going out with Terri and Skutz . . .' Mary began, but her mother was sobbing loudly again and didn't seem to notice her daughter was speaking to her. Mary whirled around and followed the others out, grabbing the door with one hand and pivoting her body weight on the door step, she leaned back and slammed the door behind her as hard as she could.

After the trio had crossed into Edge Central, Skutz stopped by the first dealer he recognized and swapped some of his OD for a Skip for Mary and a couple of enhancers. The Skip would do what it said, speeding up the first three stages of the OverDrive, taking her quickly through the ambient levels, ready for the party. It didn't do this by shortening the trip though, she'd be spending the majority of the next twelve hours on the higher levels only. He pushed it into the mouth of the giggling girl, as she stared vacantly upwards at the sky.

'Can we sit down here for a while? It's really nice here, I think I saw a star . . .'

The enhancers were slightly different from skips; they didn't speed up stages but prolonged whichever one you were on when you took it. There were also other secondary OD-linked drugs that could produce a variety of other effects on top of the OD effects, but skips and enhancers were the most common and, by default, the easiest to get.

An Idol

Mary saw her (ex)boyfriend about two hours later, when the effects of the OD had really taken hold. She really loved him. Soooo much. She started pushing her way through the pumping dancers around her, making for the gantry he was standing on; she'd forgotten about their argument and his business meeting already. She'd lost Terri and Skutz ages ago but it didn't matter, she'd just been dancing. She reached the gantry and walked up the iron stairs.

He'd gone.

She looked around, trying to focus past the visuals projected around her by the lighting system, and then past the visuals her brain was producing to the rhythm of the music. In front of her was a group of tech-heads hanging over the rail, staring at the dancers below. Some bouncers stood nearby. There was a couple snogging at the end, near the bar. A woman was pushing her amour's head into her ample cleavage, and enjoying it. The couple split apart and the man turned around.

Speed! The visuals around Mary, the ones that only existed in her brain, darkened and closed in on her. He saw her then, and his expression froze. The girl next to him noticed his distraction and looked at Mary. She said something to him and he walked over to her.

'What the fuck are you doing here? You're gonna ruin everything. Who're you here with anyway . . .'

Mary couldn't speak, the blood rushing in her veins seemed so loud she could hardly hear him.

'I thought I told you I needed to come on my own? What are you doing, checking up on me or something? Shit, you don't realise . . .' He was angry but looked anxious at the same time.

Mary looked past him, to the woman waiting by the bar. She was very beautiful and well dressed. Expensively successful. 'Who's she?' Mary managed to stammer, cutting him off.

'This isn't what you're thinking; she's an agent. She's going to . . .'

'And is that how she normally discusses business?' Her voice was louder now, a red haze beginning to cloud her vision. Her boyfriend's face was beginning to distort, the shadows more pronounced, becoming evil.

'Hey, what is this? What's your problem? You don't own me! Shit, You told me to fuck off, yesterday. I thought . . ' he raised his voice and looked anxiously over his shoulder, towards the woman at the bar.

'You sly fucker! You're a lying bastard . . .' As she began shouting, each word she uttered pushed a drug induced spike of hate and pain into her own head.

'Hey, keep your fucking voice down . . .' He grabbed her by the upper arms, wanting to shake some sense into her. His touch tasted like sulphur in her mouth.

'How can you do this to me? I thought we were in love . . .' The words fell out of her, a last plea to help her maintain her grip on herself and the drug inside her.

'Yeah, well . . .' he looked sheepishly at his feet, 'I'm not so sure I am . . .'

The full impact of his words slammed into Mary's mind in a nano second. Her screaming red vision began flattening out, exposing the demons in shadows. The strobing lights around her clawed at her sanity. She screamed and lashed out at the object of loathing that held her.

The boy tried to avoid her kicking feet and pushed her away but someone behind him bumped into him at the same time, so he stumbled forward as he pushed. Too hard. Mary tumbled backwards, totally unbalanced, and down the iron staircase behind her, into the dancers below.

She lay on the floor for a second, unaware of her surroundings or herself, dazed by the fall. Hands reached down to help her stand. The OD cut in. She was on her feet in an instant, knocking away the outstretched arms of the small crowd that surrounded her.

'Watch it, she's havin' a bad one . . .' someone laughed. Mary didn't hear, the urge to escape the red haze and the oppressive crowd that hung around her was unbearable. All the faces surrounding her were those of the laughing, well dressed woman and Speed; festering in their infidelity, rejoicing in her pain and hurt. His words echoed around her to the tempo of the music, assaulting her over and over again. She started to run. Nothing could stop her. Her limbic system was lit up like an Xmas tree, the music flaring red and violent in her mind, scratching her eyeballs through the tears. The dancing figures in her path, if they saw her, quickly moved out of her way, subconsciously aware of what was happening to her. Those that didn't see her she knocked out of the way, effortlessly.

Door. Stairs. Up. Run. Run. The red haze, their faces and his words still surrounded her. Run. Up. She pushed past people as she went, the smell of sweat and alcohol swam before her. They were loathsome. The touch of her own clothes on her body tasted sour in her mouth. She was loathsome. She continued running upwards, trying to escape herself as much as those around her. She had to be on her own; it was all that was important now. She reached the top of the stairs. A large form moved in front of her, blocking her path. She cannoned into him, knocking both of them through the door he had sought to prevent her reaching. She landed on top of him, on the floor. He grabbed her tightly, wrapping his huge arms around her, pinning her arms by her sides.

'Hang on, Joe, we'll turn her off in a second . . . there's a deactivator around here somewhere . . . Glastonbury, where are you?'

Mary heard voices but was unable to identify the meanings of the words any more. She started to hyperventilate and her vision had reduced down to a purple slot; the pressure of the man holding her had become too much for her to bear, she thought she was about to die. She thrashed around, trying to break free, her head fit to explode.

She felt a slight pressure on the neck, then a sharp shooting pain enter her brain. Almost instantly a tide of overwhelming normalness swept through her body, her vision cleared and the voices of the people around her lost their visual quality and became only sound again. She looked at the man beneath her; she was lying on top of a large tattooed skinhead, wearing a white T-shirt and red braces. The skinhead winked at her.

'You can let her go now, Joe; Glastonbury's juice'll work almost immediately,' a strangely familiar voice said behind her.

Joe the skinhead released her and she turned around to see who had spoken. There was a grinning hippy standing over her, holding a large syringe gun. And behind him . . . she nearly blacked out again.

'Have a nice trip?' Vee asked, holding out his hand to help her up.

Milton Alexander was beginning to regain consciousness as the girl tightened the last of the catches on the foam-covered web. Backing away from the chrome frame and the hanging figure, she stepped over the heap of his discarded clothes on the floor and sat down on the bed, facing the naked man. Alexander was suspended in an upright position, moaning. His head lolled on his chest, saliva dribbling from his chin. She waited patiently until his eyes opened.

'How's it going, Milt?' she asked, as if they were friends, meeting for a friendly drink in a bar.

His head groggily moved as awareness returned. It then snapped upwards and he glared at her. He began to struggle violently in the frame.

'What the fuck is going on? Get me out of this fucking thing now!' he exploded. The frame flexed slightly but otherwise held steady, Alexander's exertions only succeeded in oscillating himself from side to side.

An Idol

The girl sat on the bed, a look of glee on her face. She obviously found the sight of the naked man struggling like this highly amusing. Alexander saw her expression and stopped straining. He looked at her with ill-concealed anger, his eyes bulging. He was breathing very rapidly. The girl pulled the green PuffaMac jacket across the bed and onto her lap, and started to fiddle with the lining.

'This is a nice room, Milt. D'you do much entertaining here?' she asked, looking around. Alexander's choice of decor made her giggle. Mixed amongst the paintings of nineteenth century plump nudes were more recent "action" shots of the rape and torture of young girls and, in a few cases, boys. Bondage equipment hung from wooden plaques like ancient hunting weapons and if she looked at them closely, she would have seen that they were stained from recent use.

The jacket she held came apart in her hands and she opened it out into a full length coat. Inside, clipped into the lining, were some plastic tubes.

Alexander didn't bother to answer her question, 'Who are you, and what do you want?' he croaked.

She ignored him and just smiled, then unclipped a couple of the tubes from her coat and emptied their contents onto the floor in front of her.

'You'll never get away with this, you know that? Security will cut you in half as soon as you step outside that door!' Alexander began shaking the frame again, 'Who's put you up for this? At least tell me that . . .' His expression changed, remembering what she'd said just prior to knocking him unconscious. He stared at her in disbelief, then began battling against his bonds as violently as he could.

'I know who fucking sent you; you're one of his sodding bodyguards! Oh my god . . .' He looked very, very worried now. The girl sat on the bed, giggling and kicking her feet with pleasure.

'You know screaming isn't going to work, Milt. You were the one who had this room secured so that your special guests wouldn't disturb your family with their screaming, remember?'

'Why's he doing this? Why? I thought we'd come to an arrangement.' Alexander had stopped struggling again, and swung there, shaking.

'You didn't keep your side of it, did you, Milt? You had your chance once before and made a load of promises which you had no real intention of keeping. It's too late now, anyway.'

'Look, I'll do anything, just tell him I'm sorry and . . .' he started begging. She just looked at him, contempt on her face.

'Please, talk to me, will ya? Look, I'm sure that this is just a mis-understanding that can be easily sorted out, I mean, look, I can understand he's a bit pissed off, right, but this is a bit much . . .'

'Shut up whining, Milt.' She stood up and approached him. 'If it'll stop your bleating, I'll tell you why I'm here, you're in that and what's going to happen next.' She ran one of her gloved fingers down the nearest chrome support, 'I'm here because someone – and I don't think I really need to say who – thinks that there is a good chance that he could be assassinated by someone from here, tonight.' She smiled and pushed Alexander with her finger, so that the naked, swinging man started to swing a little faster.

'What would you do, if it was up to you?'

Johnny paused for a moment, as if considering his options, 'I'm not sure, but it would have to be in public, or who's gonna believe it happened? Anything can be faked. And thinking about it, I agree an explosion wouldn't be right, for the same reasons; there might not be enough left to prove it had happened. I'd go for a shot in public.'

Dillon chuckled, 'Well, Mr. Apprentice, seems like you're learnin'. That's good.'

'Do you think anyone really believes he's serious?' Johnny asked, after a pause.

'Who?'

'Vee.'

'Yeah, they must do, or we wouldn't be here. I wouldn't put anythin' past that crazy mother or anyone who's with the Tribe on a full time basis; they believe all sorts of shit . . .' Dillon seemed about to add more, but Frank folded into their reality, interrupting him.

'Just been talking to Control,' Frank appeared to sit down at the table but Johnny couldn't help noticing he wasn't sitting on anything, 'Max's started sending footage through; you boys have got an interesting party on your hands. The host of tonight's penthouse bash is none other than Milton Alexander himself.' Dillon whistled.

'He fucked Vee over in the past, didn't he?' Johnny decided to act knowledgeable, as if he was on top of the situation.

'Yeah, he tried to, anyway. Nasty piece of work, if you believe the gossip,' Dillon corrected, staring intently at Frank; he didn't seem particularly impressed with Johnny knowing who Alexander was. 'What's Control say about it?' he asked Frank.

'Not much, really. It's not relevant, apparently. Control has told Max that tonight's operation, if necessary, is to go ahead exactly as planned. Max isn't happy, but then, he never is,' Frank answered and winked at Johnny. Johnny really didn't like the way Frank kept looking at him; it was giving him the creeps really badly.

'Neither am I. Shit, this is gettin' worse by the minute.' Dillon didn't sound happy, but Johnny noticed he was still smiling slightly. 'What about backup?' he asked.

'Not a hope in hell,' Frank grinned. 'It's chaos, tonight. I've been monitoring the cross talk while you lot have been sitting around drinking coffee. There's parties at nearly all the other area locations this high; everything's stretched to breaking point already. On top of that, every other cult, loony fringe or political party are holding some sort of rally or demonstration tonight as well, and things have hardly got going yet. Guess we just gotta cope.' He seemed to be genuinely enjoying himself.

OVERDRIVE: PHYSICAL [ANALYSIS: CHEMICAL/MEDICAL]

OVERDRIVE: EFFECTS [LAB/REAL CONDITIONS]

OVERDRIVE: EFFECTS [POLICE FOOTAGE]

OVERDRIVE: MUSIC LINK [SEE ALSO PF>VEE, EMPTI]

OVERDRIVE: HISTORY+PF>SMYTHE-JOHNSTON, REGINALD AKA GLASTONBURY [DEVELOPMENT/DISTRIBUTION: SUSPECT]

OVERDRIVE: SOCIOPOLITICAL CONSEQUENCES [SUMMARY ONLY]

Johnny touched the fifth virtual hyper-node and the window, floating in front of him above the coffee cups, fragmented into the face of a young, long-haired man. He had decided he should know more about the drug OD, seeing as it was scaring the living daylights out of everyone at IS and in the Government, so he jacked back into his ice, but kept the window scaled down to a floating frame so that he could see what was happening in reality at the same time.

Johnny had always mistrusted OD and a lot of other, mainly hallucinogenic, drugs. If it stopped him from surfing he didn't want to know about it. Of course, Zippys and Amph inhalers were totally different; he didn't see anything wrong with putting a little bounce into your step once in a while.

Control appeared in a postage stamp next to the small frame and began the narrative. The first section was about someone called Reginald Smythe-Johnston's childhood; the image of the hippy was replaced by that of a small boy.

Johnny skipped to the next section.

Control began again as the figure turned back into the young hippy, this time with slightly shorter hair.

'Smythe-Johnston's early promise at science resulted in a biochemistry scholarship at BP University, then into a doctorate at Keynes University. His highly successful academic record at both colleges was balanced by a series of social offences towards staff and peers which eventually led to his subsequent expulsion and brief imprisonment in the final year of his PhD.'

Hyper-nodes began popping up, next to a hyper-group of student and national news sheet articles. They all concerned a series of mild poisonings that had resulted in hallucinogenic experiences and/or very strange psychosexual behaviour.

'Smythe-Johnston is first believed to have met Vee at the New Scrubs penal reform institute several months later. He was being held there, awaiting the results of his appeal. They were detained in the same wing for three weeks.' An animated fly-through of the institute began playing in the frame in front of Johnny. The commentary continued.

Killing

'Smythe-Johnston's appeal succeeded and he was released from prison. He left the country shortly afterwards, to begin working as a chemist for the Lo Fung natural biotics company in Indonesia.' Deserted Indonesian beaches filled the frame, overlaid by the company's logo and stock-market statistics. 'He worked there for the next three years, as part of their recreational drug design team. He left, apparently without warning, on the 13th December. That's two days after Vee was released from his detention. It is not known whether Vee contacted Smythe-Johnston, or vice versa, but our undercover operatives' reports suggested they began working together almost immediately.

'Six months later, Vee released the ENJOYING YOURSELF? album. The first reports of the drug known as OVERDRIVE preceded it by two months . . . ' The window split into two images, one of Vee promoting the album; the other, the drug.

'So initially the link between the album and the drug was not noticed; several large pharmaceutical consortiums had applied to the Government for licenses to produce and market OVERDRIVE type drugs already, so we at IS assumed the drug had been developed by one of them and the reports of its usage in and around the Restricted Zone were just unofficial user trials. The license would have been granted if the Neo-Kensington riot hadn't taken place.'

A hyper-node appeared, linked to the riot, and Cam footage was played; it showed a large pack of male and female suits rampaging through a shopping mall, seemingly intent on wrecking as much of it as was possible. All of them were totally out of their heads and looked almost rabid. Some of them were obviously injured, they were covered in blood, but they didn't appear to notice and it certainly hadn't affected their ability to defile their surroundings.

Control continued, 'IS were immediately notified because of the type of people rioting; they weren't the usual mixture of juves and dossers from Edge Central or one of the suburban slum districts; they were yuppie types from the Neo-Ken area and the surrounding offices.

'After they were arrested we ran some of them through the IS labs. Medical reports on these subjects indicated that large amounts of an unknown substance found in their spinal cortex and brain had triggered their extreme behaviour reaction. A further compound analysis of the substance was performed and it turned out to be a mutation of the drug OVERDRIVE.

'All licenses were immediately refused and IS began an investigation into the drug, its effects and who was behind it.

'Subsequent research identified the cause of the drug's mutation as the live broadcasting of the '41 election results: The Conservative Party lost and the dissatisfaction the result caused amongst those supporters who had ingested the drug triggered it into mutating inside them.

'It turned out that the pharmaceutical consortiums who had applied for the license hadn't developed it; they'd just been sent a small test sample with a brief description of its normal effects and a price for sole production and distribution rights. They'd been impressed by their own happy subjects' reactions to it and wanted in on the action. The strange thing was that neither company could successfully synthesise it; so they weren't responsible for its illegal distribution. Both companies were unable to say who was behind the drug's development, claiming that they had a contact addresses on the Net only, no names.'

A hyper-node labelled OVERDRIVE: PHYSICAL [analysis: chemical/medical] appeared with a spinning DNA strand. Johnny ignored it; he'd never understand chemistry if he lived to be a thousand years old, although he had heard that OD came from only one source.

'The IS investigation quickly indicated that the source of the drug was somewhere within the Restricted Zone; no other security force around the world had reports of its usage yet. The link between Vee and the drug was suspected from this moment onwards, and has been justified judging by his exploitation of the drug's effects.'

Killing

OVERDRIVE: MUSIC LINK [see also PF>VEE, EMPTI] appeared but Control continued unchecked, 'Smythe-Johnston was not associated with its development for some time, it was only when IS undercover operatives began infiltrating the ONE TRIBE that the extent of his involvement with Vee and the drug became known to us. It seems that Smythe-Johnston alone was behind OD's initial development; he had been playing with it in his spare time for a number of years, perfecting it before trying to sell it to a big corp. But when the licences were refused and it was awarded illegal status, Vee stepped in and provided him with the backing to develop and expand the drug's illegal production and, using the ONE TRIBE, with the means to distribute it.'

A hyper-node marked THE ONE TRIBE appeared. Johnny was tempted to use it but decided to finish what he was watching first.

News clips began to play in the window above the table, charting the rise in popularity and increasing public concern about the drug.

'In the last five years, OD and the various Amplifier and Accelerator derivative drugs associated with it have become one of the most popular recreational drugs in our society. All attempts by various Government and religious agencies to limit its expansion and use have failed.'

The footage being played was now a mixture of news clips and Police/SecCams of raids on ConApts, large housing blocks and a variety of warehouses. In each instance the footage showed a great deal of resistance to the raids; the people being arrested seemed intent on destroying anything and anyone in their path, with no thought to their own safety.

'One of the major problems with enforcing the law against OD is catching anyone in possession of it. Because it has been designed to be taken privately, several hours before the user goes out, and its main effects don't establish themselves for several hours afterwards, it is nearly impossible to identify a user in the early stages of an OD experience without a time-consuming, and relatively expensive, brain scan.

An Idol

'And when a user is apprehended, the drug mutates and resistance to the arrest is almost inevitable.'

When the raid clips had finished, a very low quality piece of footage began running in the window. It had no sound associated with it and appeared to have been shot through a gauze, even though it was enhanced. It showed a very grainy Smythe-Johnston arguing with a short man in a hooded jacket and OzFilter, and a larger man with no hair. They were standing in the middle of a large white room surrounded by tables manned by naked men and women. The naked men and women were filling capsules and vein guns with a fluorescent powder substance.

'The smaller man with Smythe-Johnston is alleged to be Vee himself, the other man is known to be Vee's chief gopher-come-bodyguard. They are standing in the middle of an OD factory. Our informants suggest that there are perhaps several hundred of these factories across the Restricted Zone, maybe thousands worldwide, by now. And, because of the peculiar chemical make-up of the drug, all of them must be under the control of Smythe-Johnston and Vee, and are being run by members of the ONE TRIBE.

'In recent months we have been receiving reports that there is a power struggle going on between Smythe-Johnston and Vee for control of the OD production and distribution network, although this cannot be confirmed by independent sources.

'They seem to have had a disagreement over the street price of OD. Our sources suggest that Smythe-Johnston wants to raise the price of the drug and limit its availability, increasing the profit margin, while Vee wants to maintain the drug's artificially low price and keep the supply as high as possible.'

The window changed again, this time into a multicoloured bar graph of OD prices throughout the world; it showed massive price differences in the cost of the drug, depending on where it was purchased. Another graph was overlaid over the first, showing the minimum and average wages of the respective countries. Johnny could see they were the same shape.

'As you can see, there is a high correlation between the information the two graphs represent. OD is being sold at a fixed percentage of each countries' minimum wage; anyone, anywhere, can afford large quantities of the drug.

'This has made it an extremely popular choice amongst the young, and poor, around the world. And since the introduction of the relatively expensive Amplifier and Enhancer sub-drugs, OD's appeal to the richer, more affluent, classes has risen considerably in the past year.

'Arrest warrants have been issued for Smythe-Johnston throughout the world community but he has successfully evaded arrest up to the present time. His whereabouts are currently unknown.'

Johnny paused the ice's information and checked his surroundings. Frank had disappeared again and the others were still sitting around the table. He didn't seem to be missing anything, so he went back into the virtual briefing. Control seemed to have finished talking about the man who had developed OD and flashed some of the previously available hyper-nodes back onto the Window. Johnny went to press the One Tribe node but touched the one marked OVERDRIVE: MUSIC LINK [see also PF>VEE, EMPTI] by mistake: he'd associated the wrong node with the One Tribe label. He shrugged to himself and settled back to watch what he'd selected, anyway.

Extremely old Vid footage began running in the frame; a group of black men with long, matted dreads were sitting in a sunny field smoking large hand rolled cigarettes, the soundtrack boomed slowly.

'Certain types of drugs and certain styles of popular music have, in the past, psychologically reinforced the use of one another, at least for certain types of users.' The Vid changed to another old clip; a group of white men and women running around another field, naked, with flowers painted over their faces and genitalia. The sound track accompanying it jangled and phased away in the background.

'In other words; some users' experience of one type of drug will heighten the pleasure of a certain style of music, and vice versa.' The footage changed again and Johnny watched as a seething mass of people writhed in time to pulsing lights and strobes and rapid techno. It changed once more and a room full of motionless bodies appeared with an extremely ambient, almost nonexistent, Slo-Bop track.

The image froze and a list of substances and dates scrolled over the frame.

'Cannabis, LSD, Ecstasy, NoBrainers, Groovy Juice, the list is endless. All these drugs can be associated with certain types of music and/or semi-public event. The "linking" phenomenon seems to have some sort of cultural or racial basis at first but eventually the drug and the music, together or separately, seem to cross from one cultural subgroup to another over a period of time.'

Statistical graphs began flowing across the frame, 'The new drug and new music aren't adopted by the new subgroup en masse, the adoption only normally taking place with certain members of the younger generation, spreading slightly to other areas of the society after it has become established, or is changed to mimic another form that has already gained wider acceptance.'

The album cover of ENJOYING YOURSELF? unfolded, over the statistics, 'Initially, OVERDRIVE and SHAKE music, pioneered by Empti Vee, were not linked. The success of the album ENJOYING YOURSELF? was attributed to his past exploitation by the PerfectPerfect recording company. The six different mixes of each track on the album were not associated with the six levels of OVERDRIVE because the drug wasn't widely available; its effects on users were not known.'

Striped OD capsules appeared in the frame, 'After the Neo-

Kensington riot, sufficient data was collected by the IS to link OVERDRIVE with Vee's album,' the OVERDRIVE: PHYSICAL [analysis: chemical/medical] hyper-node appeared again, 'During the evening at the Neo-Kensington night club, many of the tracks played were from the ENJOYING YOURSELF? recording and OVERDRIVE was given out free to the customers.'

A SecCam clip from the club ran as Control talked. A fat man in a straw hat seemed to be doing good, if not entirely subtle, business with the suited customers.

'None of the rioters, later, said they were really aware of what music they'd listened to that night, but under hypnotism responded positively to certain tracks from Vee's album, indicating that they were familiar with certain sections of these tracks.

'When analysed in detail, IS scientists discovered Vee had coded psycho-triggers into parts of these tracks, designed to activate part of the DNA strand of the OD drug. Listening to certain tracks from ENJOYING YOURSELF? will cause the OD within a user to mutate, but no reaction will occur; it lies dormant for the duration of the trip unless the user gets upset in any way.

'As soon as that happens the drug changes in nature and warps the users' frontal lobes; he or she will then develop extremely antisocial behaviour that will last for several hours.'

Control didn't need to add any more about the riot. Instead, the window ran the classic PoliceVid clip of the now famous riot again. Johnny couldn't help chuckling to himself at the people in suits throwing bottles and furniture at the police and generally dismantling the plush mall around them.

'Associating a drug with a type of music to enhance the appeal of that music is nothing new; many performers and companies have done that before. However, Vee is using his media influence to promote the drug, not vice versa. The IS tech report on the nature of the drug and its construction concludes that the mutating side effect has been developed intentionally, expressly for the antisocial impact it has on society. The Government subsequently had the drug banned and awarded an illegal status; its rise in popularity since has been phenomenal.'

News clips, artwork, Vids and stills flashed over the frame, charting the rise of the Shake/OD craze, as Control tirelessly continued.

'Other popular musicians around the world began releasing 6Mix Discs soon after the success of ENJOYING YOURSELF?, using the properties and increasing availability of the drug to enhance their own respective sales. This was predicted. What wasn't expected was the similarity in the content of message in their music. Vee had used the lyrics of his album to promote dissatisfaction and discontent with our contemporary capitalist society and current ecological system, and laid the blueprint for the rest to follow.'

Johnny snorted. Anyone could have told you that; everyone into the Shake scene was 'ecologically aware' and politically motivated. Or at least said they were.

'It was obvious to us at IS that Vee was getting into the power game but the Government's analysts erroneously expected the craze to "die back" after a year or two and be replaced by another, newer, fad. Against the recommendations of IS, they chose not to act directly and let events run their natural course. Subtle pressure was put on the Sat and Net channels to reduce any "positive" Shake-related airtime and increase their editorial opposition to Vee, Edge Central and the users of the drug OVERDRIVE.'

News clips condemning OD and Vee, blaming both of them for a wide variety of problems, ran through the window, accompanying Control as she talked, and were eventually replaced by a C-generated spinning skull and cross bones.

'Our Government-enforced inactivity allowed Vee the time to set up the foundations for his present day media empire. Unknown to us at the time, he had been reinvesting the credit made from album and drug sales into Net and Sat channels around the globe; some legal, others illegal. Within two years Vee had broken the established Government/Corporate stranglehold on public communications. Not only was it now impossible to keep his activities quiet and reduce the amount of positive media exposure he received; it was no longer possible for our government, or any other around the world, to control what was "news" and how it was presented to the population. His channels began challenging the information supplied by the existing news sources and exposing other issues that the population would not have been aware of before.

'Vee's channels brought a new meaning to the term 'public access entertainment'. He encouraged and financed "Little Brother TV", flooding the screen with anti-corporate and anti-government propaganda made by individuals or organizations that had, up to now, no real way of reaching a wide audience. He was also responsible for the introduction of Anti-Ads to give alternative information about the so-called "real" effects of products on us and our environment.

'As fast as his legal channels were sued and had their licenses revoked, and the illegal ones were scrambled, others sprang up in their place. Keeping track of his ever expanding media empire has proved nearly impossible.'

The virtual window dissected itself into smaller windows, each contained a news channel from a different country. All the anchor men and women were very young, the graphics used around them were of the highest quality, the Anti-Ads were similarly well produced; very different from the more conservative broadcasts shown before.

'Vee's channels, when not used to promote himself, have concentrated on so-called political, corporate and ecological exploitation mixed amongst specially commissioned, highly thought-provoking, popular art/entertainment programming.

'He is attempting to use his media empire the way he is using the drug OVERDRIVE: to undermine the very institutions that support our modern day society, and promote civil unrest and dissatisfaction within as large a subgroup of the total global population as possible.'

Various statistics and a breakdown of time and content studies finished the section on OD and the media; then the floating window faded out and Johnny was left with a single hyper-node, marked simply THE ONE TRIBE. He thumbed it.

The ice responded to the request for more information; the window solidified again and Control began another part of the virtual briefing.

'The name THE ONE TRIBE began to appear in reports from the Restricted Zone while Vee was still in prison. At first, IS assumed it was just another criminal sub-community; non-political, and certainly nothing to do with Vee. After his release, the reports started to indicate that THE ONE TRIBE's influence was much larger than had been previously believed and they had started to act more like an unofficial Police force within the Restricted Zone than the criminals they are, reducing much of the violence within the camps and unofficially occupied areas, and also acting as a welcoming committee to the juves that have been entering the Restricted Zone from the City. They also started running the parties.

'Vee included references to THE ONE TRIBE, in the album ENJOYING YOURSELF?, within his lyrics, referring to them as "the last generation": those who realised they had "no future, except to protest and die". He appeared to be appealing to individuals who agreed with his Eco/Political stance and was inviting them to join THE ONE TRIBE and him in his destructive ambitions.'

The lyrics appeared in the window, the relevant sections highlighted.

'Although his lyrics have been used as a rallying cry by perpetrators of antisocial behaviour since, and there is a great deal of evidence to suggest that THE ONE TRIBE run the distribution of the drug OVERDRIVE, Vee has consistently, and successfully, denied or simply ignored any attempts to link him directly to THE ONE TRIBE's terrorist activities.'

Killing

A Vid clip of a news conference ran in the window and Johnny watched an openly laughing Vee deny any involvement in the hostage shootout at one of the City's Primary Educational complexes. The incident in question involved a class of seven year olds who had held their teacher and headmaster hostage with, amongst other things, a thermal detonator. They had been demanding, in the name of the One Tribe, a world ban on nuclear energy production and all forms of the internal combustion engine.

'Indeed, there has been widespread speculation about whether THE ONE TRIBE really exists as a terrorist organization, with any form of leadership, or whether it is just a concept or class of individual, like a surfer or biker; just a collection of individuals with an underdeveloped set of morals, no unifying cause, and no real structure to their activities.'

More news clips were run by the programme about a variety of different offences, ranging from vandalism and graffiti, to a spate of suicide bombings on fertility clinics and the hijacking of a nuclear power station. All were attributed to the One Tribe.

'In actuality, both views are correct. Many individuals, detained for criminal offences, will say that they are members of THE ONE TRIBE and have committed their crimes in its name. Subsequent investigations into their offences and their lives often show that they have had no direct contact with Vee or any of his organizations, and that their crimes aren't even associated with any of Vee's recognized political, ecological or social goals. Our psychologists believe that part of Vee's popularity stems from giving these people a cause to blame for their actions.

'Many of the more serious offences, however, are planned and executed meticulously. Equipment recovered from injured or killed perps has been of a very high quality, some of it military issue.'

An IS-labelled clip unfolded in front of Johnny, showing a heap of hi-tech looking weapons lying next to a larger heap of corpses, amongst a few dishevelled looking trees. He recognized some of the weapons from his brief training in the academy; amongst the

An Idol

handguns and subs were several anti-aircraft disposables and what looked like a Hotload rail-cannon (banned in most of the civilized countries across the globe).

'This footage was shot after the failed assault on the Redwood Chemical Institute on the outskirts of the North Eco-park. Several of the perps killed during the offensive, believed to have been carried out by THE ONE TRIBE, have been identified as members of Vee's personal bodyguard.'

The heap of bodies and guns was replaced by a grainy, much enhanced satellite shot of a beach. A naked man was walking along it towards a large cacti-covered rock jutting from the white sand, surrounded by a small group of equally naked women. Even with the quality of the picture it was possible to see that the women were all heavily armed.

'Popular opinion about Vee's bodyguard would suggest that the heavily armed young girls he employs is really only a publicity gimmick; there for show and to massage his ego. This is a quite inaccurate misconception. His bodyguard is more like a private army in numbers and has thousands of members worldwide, both male and female.'

The group on the beach sat down in the shade of the large rock, the man still at the centre of the group of girls. The camera panned out, the rock was covered with straw-roofed cabanas and hammocks. There were perhaps thirty or so people lounging around amongst them, watching the setting sun. The camera panned back further, exposing the far side of the rock. The beach continued into a small bay but was covered in heavily sweating, exercising people, encouraged by violently gesturing men. There were row after row of them; some practising a type of unarmed martial art, others using heavily weighted practice weapons.

'This is Zipolita, Mexico. Vee uses this private beach as a training ground for his bodyguard and to vet and brainwash his new recruits. We believe he is using army deserters, from several different countries, to train both men and women in different

Killing

aspects of terrorism and warfare. Infiltrating this area has been virtually impossible, so more detailed information on their training and any other activities that might be taking place here is not available. IS believe that he uses the bodyguards brainwashed here to exert his influence on the various parts of his organization, and to run his drug activities.

'They are, in fact, the real ONE TRIBE, and are deadly.'

The beach scene disappeared and three different Vid clips began to play simultaneously in Johnny's floating window. Each showed the same scene but shot from a different angle.

Control maintained the commentary, 'Vee began appearing in public with heavily armed young girls shortly after the second known assassination attempt on his life. This SecCam footage is of the fourth known attempt and illustrates extremely well the problem caused by THE ONE TRIBE. It isn't just the skills and level of weapons technology they have access to that make them such an impressive force; it is the level of commitment they have to Vee and their cause that is the problem.'

The window's title block told Johnny that the Cam footage came from Verona airport's security system, two years earlier. He watched as Vee, and an entourage of mainly young girls, stepped onto a powered walkway, surrounded by perhaps ten running journalists and Cam operators. They were watched by a segregated crowd of fans screaming wildly from the other side of the concourse. Control highlighted the Airport security presence in the background. 'If you watch their actions it is obvious that they are preparing for something to happen; we are almost certain that they knew of the attempt in advance.

'Please note that none of Vee's bodyguard were armed at the time because they'd all just stepped off a transcontinental flight; the airport security had refused to give them their licensed, but still confiscated, weapons back until they'd left the complex.'

The footage slowed down in each of the clips as a muzzle flashed from above the onlooking crowd and one of the girls around Vee suddenly pushed him forward. The shot hit her squarely in the chest, causing a large red crater to appear there before sending her over the top of the walkway's glass sides.

The muzzle flashed again as Vee started to run. This time one of the stunned journalists was hit; his head changed into a haze of blood and brain as his body jerked into the Cam op next to him.

One of the images zoomed in onto the gunman as he switched his weapon to automatic and opened up properly; he was lying on top of a flight of stairs beneath the arrivals/departures holo. The airport security still hadn't responded to the attack yet.

At the sound of the automatic fire Vee was thrown to the moving floor by the two girls nearest him, just before the bullets ripped into them all.

The powered walkway continued its ponderous journey across the concourse, taking them directly past the assassin. All the young women, instead of trying to avoid the bullets and find cover, dived onto the bloody pile on top of Vee, catching the hail of soft-nosed shells with their own bodies; intent on protecting their idol at all costs.

Johnny watched the carnage unfold, feeling slightly queasy, as the twitching pile of bodies moved slowly along the glass sided walkway, smearing and pumping blood across the transparent walls as the shots continued to rip systematically into them.

When the bloody mess ran out of walkway, and slid sickly onto the polished floor at the end, the airport security eventually reacted and one of them shot the assassin dead.

'Vee escaped without so much as a scratch. He was lucky; if the assassin had used a laser, or armour piercing rounds instead of dumdums, he'd be dead. Every other person with him was seriously injured, or died; that's including the journos. The unsuccessful attempt is believed to have been Vatican-financed, with the blessing of the Mafia and Italian coalition government. All it succeeded in doing was start a riot that caused so much damage the airport closed for two months, and persuade Vee never to appear, announced, in public again.'

──────────────────────────────── 'He's going to be what?'

The girl grinned widely at the look of surprise on Alexander's face, and walked back to the bed. He was still swinging in the harness because the frame had a complex set of gears linked to the webbing which would maintain the oscillation of his body, at the same rate and speed, until it was stopped or sped up. She flopped onto the bed and began sorting the contents of the opened plastic tubes into piles. There were several thinner metal tubes, some heavily engineered blocks with slots and grooves cut into them, a couple of foam-covered handles with buttons over them, half a dozen flat discs about four inches in diameter, and one six inch high cone.

'How does he know he'll be hit from here? Is he certain?'

She continued to ignore him, and started fixing the engineered blocks onto one another.

'Why didn't anyone tell me about this? I could help! Look, I've got excellent security here; they're vat-bred, the best!'

'Transgenic life forms are disgusting; you should be ashamed of yourself for using them, Milt. In a massively overpopulated world as well. Tut tut! Besides, they're not as good as me.' The girl sounded offended by his suggestion at first but smiled at him to show she was only teasing. She returned to the task at hand, slotting the tubes through their engineered blocks.

Alexander began thrashing around in the harness, causing the oscillations to increase. He was looking very anxious again.

'Oh shit! He thinks . . . He doesn't think I've got anything to do with this, does he? C'mon! Look, you've got to tell him, please. I know things have been said in the past, but this . . .' Alexander began to cry, tears welling in his bulging eyes, then streaming down his flushed cheeks. He was shaking uncontrollably now, and sweating profusely.

'If you continue like that, you'll give yourself a really bad trip!' she said, sweetly, picking up one of the foam-covered handles. The handle fixed, with a satisfying click, onto one of the tubes protruding from the group of engineered blocks, then folded back, along its length. The girl attached the second handle directly to the blocks themselves.

'What's that?' Alexander asked eventually, although he had a pretty good idea.

'A flachette sub-cannon. It was in the cloaking tubes hidden inside my coat. They don't show up on normal scans! Neat, huh?' She beamed brightly, leapt up and turned around, then aimed the short, stubby weapon at the bed and depressed the trigger stud on the rear handle. The gun spat briefly, making a wet, almost silent noise, and the mattress on the bed was ripped apart by the force of the weapon's discharge, sending chunks of compressed foam packing and other pieces of material into the air. The girl started laughing.

'My god, you can't be more than sixteen! Jesus!' Alexander looked totally terrified, his eyes were bulging unnaturally from his head, 'Where the fuck does he find you people? What in god's name does he do to you?' He began to scream.

Mary had stayed with Vee for the rest of that first night. Holding her gently in his arms he had told her she'd start to feel a bit sleepy because the drug Glastonbury, the hippy, had given her to suppress the OD would knock her out for a bit. She'd said she didn't mind so long as he didn't leave her because she felt really safe with him. In fact, she told him dreamily, she felt more relaxed than she had ever felt before, which was surprising really because she'd always dreamed about meeting him and had thought that if she ever did, she'd be really nervous and on edge, but she wasn't, which was really strange . . . She fell asleep wondering why.

The next morning, to her surprise, she found that she hadn't been dreaming the night before, and, even more surprisingly, that Vee was still with her. She woke up with one of his arms draped, protectively, around her shoulders. She hadn't wanted to open her eyes at first, but carefully opened one, then the other, and peered up. His gaze met hers, and he smiled at her.

She decided to hang around with him, and his entourage, for the rest of the next day, in the large room at the top of the crumbling warehouse. Everyone was really friendly towards her, accepting her presence there as if it were totally natural. Vee was very protective and gentle towards her, constantly making sure she was all right, and had everything she wanted.

He introduced her to his bodyguards, his band, the roadies, several producers, another couple of bands that were hanging out with him at the time, the hippy Glastonbury and a skinhead called Joe. They were all really nice, even Joe, who'd been knocked through the door by her the night before, and he looked really scary; covered in tattoos, piercings and scars that all looked self-inflicted. Vee said Joe was used to girls behaving like that with him, and everyone laughed, except Joe. He just smiled sheepishly, and mumbled something about "always playing hard to get" and "personal taste".

What surprised her most about all the people she met was their willingness to listen to her, and that they didn't take the piss out of everything she said, like Speed and his mates always did. These people seemed genuinely interested in her. And they had something to say for themselves. They talked about music and art, pollution, the Government and the corporations; important things, not just about wipeouts, the latest teen fashion and who's shagging who.

Vee didn't speak much; he watched and listened. And took drugs. An impressive amount, by anyone's standards. When he did talk, she noticed a slight lull in the conversations around them, and

Killing

everyone listened. He was never interrupted, and hardly anyone ever disagreed with him. When they did, he would just shrug, as if it didn't really matter, anyway. Then find something else to distort his own senses with.

Later, maybe even the next evening, it was impossible to tell because of the massive shutters on the windows of the warehouse, Mary watched Joe stride into the room and up to Vee. She was sitting on the opposite side of the room, being, rather unsuccessfully, chatted up by a sound engineer. She watched Joe lean down to Vee and shout briefly into his ear. Vee burst out laughing and looked away from the speaker he was fiddling with, and over to where she was sitting. He said something to the bodyguard next to him, handed the girl his screwdriver, then walked over towards Mary.

'What's your real name?' Vee asked.

'Mary, why?' she answered defensively.

He looked at her, a smile playing on the corners of his mouth, 'Are you sure? Joe seems to think it's something else.'

'How did he . . ?' her voice trailed off, and she squared up to the man in front of her, her face hardening, 'Okay, if you must know, my real name is Virginia. Mary is my middle name. Nice combination, huh?' She stood there, arms folded across her chest, legs apart, defiantly, as if daring him to laugh; she'd had too much abuse about her name when she was younger to take any more from anyone, ever again. Even from Vee.

'It's a wonderful name!' he beamed. 'Most apt, I think,' he added, almost to himself. 'We're leaving. Have you got anything you have to stay behind for, or are you going to come with us now?' he asked. Mary felt her jaw drop open.

Four hours later she was on a beach on the west coast of Mexico, laying in a large hammock next to Vee, sharing a bottle of Mescal. They were both extremely drunk, although she'd hardly touched a drop of the potent liquid. Vee had managed to drink most of the bottle on his own. Around them in a loose circle, the nearest person perhaps twenty feet away, were the remains of the entourage from the warehouse. They all lounged lifelessly in hammocks or on the sand, out of the heat of the afternoon under straw-covered cabanas dotted along the beach. Everyone, including Vee and Mary, were transfixed by the scene before them.

On the beach in front of the wall-less huts, stretching as far down the beach as they could see, were beached dolphins and whales. Most were motionless, and quite dead, but some were still writhing in the burning sun. The skin on each was a discoloured white yellow instead of grey, and they had traces of red around the open and suppurating sores they all seemed to be covered with. Their eyes were swollen shut, and the few living creatures that remained were crying loudly. The eerie sound reverberated around the bay, bouncing off the surrounding hills and back down to the onlookers; an echo of death that seeped deeply into the soul.

Every few minutes another, equally sick mammal, would hurl itself through the Pacific Ocean's white fringe of crashing breakers, and up onto the sand, ready to die in full view of the crowd that had gathered along the white, shimmering, palm lined beach.

'We had to stop swimming here three years ago because the dolphins started attacking us. They're not stupid, y'know,' Vee was trying not to slur his words. 'They know that we,' he pointed to everyone around him, and lastly to himself, 'We're killing them. Killing them and every other fuckin' thing on the planet larger than a fuckin' rat . . . Now look at 'em; they know they're dead, so they've come to show us what we fuckin' well done to them.'

Mary was having a hard time following him but didn't want to interrupt him.

'We're the nastiest animals this sad planet has given life to. I wonder whether they realise we've done to it to ourselves as well?' he added wistfully, swigging from the bottle.

'Who?' Mary asked.

'The dolphins. I wonder whether they realise we've killed

ourselves as well as them and the rest of the fish? I guess they don't,' he sniggered. 'After all, most of us are too fucking stupid to realise it, so how can they . . ?' Vee's drunken smile faltered, and he threw the just-empty bottle at the nearest dying creature. It landed short. He was becoming increasingly agitated and angry at the genocide before him, and had been sporadically ranting in the same vein since the Mescal had been uncorked.

'This is why it has to be done, why I've got to do it . . .' Vee was struggling against the hammock, attempting to get out, 'It's gotta be done soon, or there'll be nothing . . . nothing . . . 'cept roaches . . .' He tipped the hammock too far, and both he and Mary fell onto the cool sand. He lurched to his feet and staggered off towards the nearest carcass.

Mary picked herself up, and followed. As soon as she stepped out into the sun she had to start hopping, to stop her feet from burning. A couple of other girls, members of his bodyguard, followed them. Mary slowed down, allowing them to catch up; she had met them on the flight and thought they were really sweet people.

'It's ingrained in our fuckin' nature, we were only trying to survive . . . all going fine as well, 'cept we got too good at it . . .' Mary couldn't tell whether Vee was talking to her and the other girls, himself, or the dying dolphins he was walking through.

'We started living too long . . . that's where it went wrong. Nothing to cut us back, reduce our numbers . . . killed or tamed everything that could harm us, the only thing left was ourselves, and we got too scared to do that properly . . . now it's caught up with us, just like it has with you . . . 'cept you admit it, we don't . . . we just carry on . . .'

Mary could see Vee was crying openly, but looked more angry than sad. She was a bit concerned about him; things had been fun until they left the warehouse, then Vee had started to act strangely. At first he had just seemed paranoid, which was understandable under the circumstances; he was still officially a wanted criminal, and had, to date, survived at least five assassination attempts that she knew about. His mood had worsened on the secret flight from Edge Central to Mexico, when an aide had told him about the dolphins. Since arriving, he had just got drunk and angry.

'What's he going on about?' Mary turned to one of the bodyguards, she thought her name was Shade or Jade, or something.

'You should listen to him, he's speaking the truth. It's important.' Rayed was staring at Vee as she answered Mary, a determined expression on her face.

'Most people choose not to listen, they bury their heads up their own arses and pretend it's not happening,' Mary turned to look at the second bodyguard. She couldn't remember her name at all.

'Vee's sayin' we've fucked ourselves and everything else 'cause it's in our nature, and we won't even admit it, even though we've all known about it since the turn of the millennium.'

'I, um . . . not sure I understand. You mean someone knew this was going to happen?' Mary pointed her bare toe at the nearest dolphin. The once majestic creature's skin was rotting away in places, and a mixture of pus and blood had discoloured the burning white sand around it.

'Yes, we did!' She absently waved her gun at the hammocks and huts back up the beach.

'I mean humans in general. Fuckin' humans! We're the ones that did this, on purpose, without a second thought about the consequences for us and the rest of the planet, and we've been doing things like it for years.'

The guard knelt down and peered closely at the dying creature, 'Not just things that have caused this; it's everything else as well. You've been hearing about it every day of your life, a little bit here, a little bit there.

'Everyone knows what's happening now 'cause it's staring them in the face every day and they can't escape it, but most people still choose to ignore it, and everyone just carries on regardless, without

any attempt to come to terms with what's going to happen next.'
She looked up at Mary's baffled expression, 'It's over, too late,
finished,' she added emotionlessly.

'What is?' Mary asked, moving down the beach to the cool sand
near the breakers.

'Everything. The whole thing. All poisoned, cancerous or used
up. Everything!'

Mary looked confused; she still didn't watch the news much,
only by accident, really, but she was sure someone would have
said something about it if it was true. She'd seen greenies on the
Vid going on about this road widening or that nuclear test, but . . .

'What do you mean, it's too late? There's nothing that can be
done?' Mary looked at Rayed, wanting her to have a different
opinion.

'How come no one's noticed yet?' Mary added haughtily.

'The rich countries are pulling all the resources from what they
call "the Third World" and the rest of the poorer countries in Europe
to sustain their own levels of consumption; and it ain't going to
last long.'

Rayed shrugged at Mary's expression, 'You did ask what he was
going on about.'

'But surely someone will think of something . . . I dunno, maybe
some scientist will . . .' Mary never finished the sentence; she
stopped when the two girls started laughing. Rayed put her arm
around Mary.

'It was those stupid bastards that have got us into this situation
in the first place, and they're not going to be able to get us out of
it.'

'Scientists? Did you say something about Scientists?' Vee had
heard her comment. He stood, quite still, glaring at the young girl.

'Let me tell you about Scientists,' he seemed quite sober, all of a
sudden, 'Scientists are human, like everyone else. They are just as
short-sighted, just as self-centred, just as sure of themselves as
everyone else. Trusting our collective soul to the holy grail of

An Idol

Science, without question or doubt, has proved to be the single, most destructive, insane, unpardonable act we have ever done to ourselves and everything else on this fucking planet!

'Every time there was a problem to be solved, or a goal to be achieved, or just a desire expressed by a large enough carrot or a big enough stick, Science has gone to work and managed to give the engineers and designers of this world just enough to get the ball rolling. It's immaterial that they then spend the rest of their time trying to keep up!' Vee's shout trailed off, and he looked at Mary steadily before adding in a quieter tone, 'And once the work's been done, it can't be undone.

'You see, Scientists are resourceful, just like all other humans, and as if by magic the problem seems solved, the goal achieved. But by wielding this magic they create a false security in their own abilities, so when their actions create an unwanted side effect or two, everyone is encouraged to just ignore them, not worry about them: Science'll sort them out if they become a problem.

'Everything Science has done has been driven by individual or corporate interest and greed. It has shaped how Science has progressed; so everything Science has become or achieved has been driven by the need to keep our technological society on the path it has been following for the last two hundred years.

'Science has just compounded the initial problems caused by unrestrained capitalism and made it a whole lot worse. Hey, you want to live longer as well? No problem. You want to go faster? No problem. Unfortunately, there was a problem. Now, if you want to live longer than you did in the nineteenth century, but you live in any urban area in the Western hemisphere, you've got to wear 'Zone masks and RadBlock when you're outside 'cause there's more ozone at ground level than anywhere else . . . and the RadBlock is a joke in itself, 'cause it turns out to be toxic anyway, and it all started 'cause you wanted to go faster, and Science said you could.'

Vee was ranting freely now, addressing everyone within earshot.

'D'you remember when the fossil fuels virtually ran out? What

Killing

happened? Science teamed up with the corporations and developed Synthetic Fuels! Fuckin' great! Everyone's happy 'cause it would work in old-style engines, with a bit of modification, and there wouldn't be any drop in the car's overall performance; you can still go much faster than you can cope with! Of course, there wasn't any drop in the emissions the engines produced, either. The new fuels are worse, they burn much hotter causing the ozone problem to get worse and on and on and on . . . And no one really gives a shit. Who cares? We can carry on like we always have, pretend nothing's changed, safe in the knowledge that Science'll come to our rescue and sort it out.

'Shit! All that fuckin' happened was people started surfin' on the fuckin' discharge and discovered a new craze . . . I fuckin' hate the lot of 'em: Designers an' Engineers an' Scientists! All complete cunts, every last one of them! They all know that designing photocopiers, or some other useless piece of mass-produced disposable shite like that, is as bad as designing a fuckin' bomb: it's just that they'll kill us all later rather than sooner . . . An all the fuckers'll say in their defence is, "If I don't do it, someone else will"! Fuck! I hate . . .'

Eventually, Vee passed out and was taken to bed by Joe. Mary paddled in the warm water and watched as the skinhead carried him away from the beach, towards the cacti-covered rocks and the weird huts above. She spent the rest of the day hanging around the two bodyguards, eventually drinking and smoking herself into a stupor. Later, someone gave her a light blanket and told her she could crash wherever she liked. A little later still, she did.

The next day she woke just before dawn, pinching herself to make sure she wasn't dreaming again. She wasn't, so got gingerly out of the hammock. Wrapping the blanket around herself to stave off the pre-dawn chill, she decided to explore. The first thing she found was Vee on the beach. He was sitting with his back to the surf, facing the inland dawn, with an ancient looking laptop on his knees.

An Idol

When he saw her, he waved at her to come over. Mary was surprised to see him without any bodyguards.

'I've got something to show you, you might find it interesting,' he called as she got nearer.

'What is it?' shouted Mary, grinning wildly as she ran across the sand.

'I was wondering what caused you to freak, back at the warehouse, so I've been looking at the security Vid,' he answered, a mischievous grin on his face.

'Oh!' Mary couldn't disguise the hurt tone in her voice. Saturday night had been the last thing on her mind, and she didn't really want to have to think about it right now. She sat down heavily, next to him, and grudgingly looked over his shoulder at the screen.

'I thought it was going to be something nice.'

'Ah, give us a kiss, and cheer up!' Vee smiled at her, baring his lips. Held between his teeth was a small striped capsule of OD. She kissed him, taking the capsule as she did.

'Can you remember what happened?' he asked.

She shook her head, 'No, not really, just pieces. Speed, my boy . . . my *ex*-boyfriend, was there. He was with someone else, I think the bitch was blonde. I can remember talking to him, then not much else. Everything went a bit red. I . . . I'm not sure. Just running. And stairs . . . then you.' She smiled at the last bit, and put her arms around his shoulders. 'Thanks!'

She kissed him. He put his arm around her, but instead of kissing her back, pulled his face away.

'I'll show you what happened; watch . . .' He turned towards the screen, 'What did you take, and where did you get it?' he added, resetting the options for the Vid playback.

'A Shake, I think it was orange. Skutz gave it to me. He's a friend of a friend. And a Skip. We got that from just inside Edge Central, just past Checkpoint Chaz.'

'Yeah, that figures . . . Watch this.'

The ancient screen opened into a window labelled .\CAM6edt2.osp and contained an image of a packed warehouse.

Vee punched a few keys, and it panned in on to a couple on a raised walkway, near some steps. The couple were gesturing at each other violently, and appeared to be arguing. They were standing on their own, the nearest person to them a bouncer about three metres away.

The clip zoomed in closer, Mary's face, on the ancient screen, was a mixture of anger and hurt, the boy had his back to the Cam and was jabbing his finger at her accusingly.

Suddenly the boy lurched forwards, towards Mary, and she disappeared from sight. The angle changed to another Cam, and Mary watched herself fall backwards, four metres or so, and on to the dancers below.

'Now, that wasn't very nice, was it? I'm not surprised you had a little, er . . . "reaction". Keep watching.'

Mary watched as she sprang to her feet almost immediately, surprised she hadn't broken anything. She had some bruises but couldn't remember exactly how she had got them; she reckoned the fall accounted for most of them.

She watched as someone put their hand on her shoulder, perhaps to ask if she was alright. She saw herself turn around, and slap the hand away from her, then begin to run. The Cam tracked her across the dance floor as she reeled blindly towards a large door on the other side of the warehouse. Any dancers that got in her way were just brushed aside.

The Cam view changed as she reached the stairs and began to climb. Then again and again as she ran up flight after flight. Mary's jaw dropped as she watched herself go; she hadn't realised she was that fit.

Joe the skinhead was standing outside the door on the uppermost floor and stepped in front of her, to prevent her from going any farther. Mary watched as she careened into him, without even checking her pace. His feet left the ground as he was knocked backwards. Although completely winded, he somehow managed to hold onto her as they both crashed through the door behind him.

'Wild stuff, isn't it! I mean, look at that,' Vee replayed the moment of impact again, in slo-mo, 'Joe must weigh at least two hundred and fifty pounds; look what you did to him!'

'What did Speed do, after he pushed me down the steps?' Mary asked the question quietly, her expression was one of curiosity, but her eyes burned with anger. Vee was watching her closely, and smiled slightly at the question.

'He had an argument with the blond girl. Do you want to see that?'

'No!' Mary answered quickly. She felt quite upset now, the elation she had felt earlier had now gone. She felt used and abused. And pretty angry.

'Don't let it cut you up. He's still in that shit hole of a city; you're on a beach thousands of miles away, jus' lazin' in the sun. If you're still pissed off with him, get vindictive and make him suffer, but don't moan to me about it. If you can't live with it, do something about it. You'll feel better if you do, it always works.' Mary looked at the man next to her. He was quite serious.

'How? He's too far away to hit.'

'Use your imagination, maybe ask some of your new friends to help . . .' he answered cryptically.

Mary decided she wanted to change the subject, she was uncomfortable with this conversation, so she asked him about what he had been saying the day earlier.

'What do you want to know?'

'How it's all got as bad as you said it has. I mean, why wasn't anything done sooner, and what's going to be done now?' she asked, almost dreamily; the OD was beginning to take hold.

'Well, it's kinda difficult to lay it all on any one doorstep, if you catch my drift. It's a bit complicated but really boils down to our nature as humans. The rich, throughout history, have always tried to cut themselves off from the poor and the social consequences of

Killing

their own standard of living. In the past they used a social class system to perform the segregation. Today, they live in heavily guarded enclaves, like this one we're in at the moment. Nothing more than a beautiful prison, really. An environment that is designed to filter out anything unpleasant and allow them to ignore the shit outside.

'That's why the world has been suffering under a particularly virulent brand of uncontrollable, unrestrained, and very uneven brand of capitalism for the last hundred or so years. Those who have benefited from it have chosen to ignore the cost. It's part of human nature to just overlook anything that doesn't conform to a peach-flavoured version of reality, in the hope that it might go away. The problems have been swept under the carpet for "future generations" to sort out.

'And because it's in our nature to behave like this, to ignore instead of solve, the problems around us have just got worse. Now we've run out of time.'

'Don't scientists solve problems, though?' Mary asked.

'Yeah, but not the problems that really matter. The problems Science solves are selected by those with capital and resources, so Science is generally used to make new toys for the rich, or increase corporate profit margins. Any benefit it has had to the rest of the world population is purely coincidental.

'But it's not scientists on their own that are to blame, you mustn't make that mistake, it's humans in general; all of us. Scientists just provide the information without any regard to how or why it's going to be used, or without any real understanding of its implications, and they know it! They fucking well upset me more than the really ignorant because of that.' He snarled.

She looked at him, and tried to frown, except the drug inside her would only allow a brief furrowing of her brow. He recognized her expression, though, and tried to explain again.

'Well, it's like this. We, I mean humans generally, treat technological progress as a pathological necessity, because that's how we've always survived in the past. Because it's new, it's good. We no longer consider properly whether the advance actually improves our lives when we adopt it; we just adopt it out of habit. This problem has been compounded by scientific advances, Science's wonderful ability to solve problems by creating new ones; the technology being used has become so complex that it is no longer possible to accurately predict the outcome of the processes we devise. But we still adopt them, digging ourselves an ever deeper grave without ever acknowledging it.' He looked at the nodding girl, and smiled. She smiled back, wondering what in hell he was on about.

Days began merging together, easily stretching into weeks. Mary was no longer sure whether it was Saturday or Sunday . . . or Thursday. Everything was free, including the best grass she'd ever smoked in her life. Some days she would be up at dawn; other days, not before the evening. It didn't seem to matter, no one minded whether she did anything, or not. Someone told her that the place was called Zipolita, and that it had been a "happy, hippy, druggy, sort of hangout" since the late twentieth century. Later, it had been bought, lock, stock and hash pipe, by a Japanese software company, as a corporate retreat for stressed-out programmers and executives. They'd kept it looking the same, all straw huts and hammocks, but added the luxuries subtly. It gave the programmers and executives the impression that they were slumming it, out on the edge, getting their act together back in nature.

The software company also installed a massive security system to keep any unlicensed dealers, prostitutes or holiday makers out, and to keep their own employees under full recorded surveillance while they unwound. Apparently, Vee had somehow conned the software company into leasing him the entire bay for a week, four years earlier. He decided he liked it there and just stayed, over-running the place with the One Tribe, and the software company decided not to even bother asking him to leave.

Killing

Mary didn't see Vee much after her first month there. He was always coming or going and no one ever knew where he was, until he turned up, which could be any hour of the day or night. She got to know a lot of the people at Zipolita in the periods without him. Some were a lot like her; normal teenagers from the City, or the other large conurbations around the world. Others were Survivalists or gun freaks from backwater farm areas in East America or the Ukraineland (a few of whom had surprisingly right-wing attitudes). There were also a few religious types; mainly Druist, Buddhist or Hindu, who Mary avoided.

Some of the others were at Zipolita to train for Vee's bodyguard, or for other roles in the One Tribe, but most were just hanging out, enjoying the continual party. All of them seemed totally committed to Vee or his causes, in one way or another, but would make a big thing out of not actually worshipping him if goaded on the subject; "Hey, he's just a human, like everyone else".

She also found a few ecologists, botanists, chemists and other types of researchers around the bay. Vee seemed to fund quite a lot of scientific research, despite his alleged hatred of scientists, and much of it was based in, or near to, Zipolita. The scientists were quite approachable but were too busy to spend much time hanging out. On some days Mary helped out, measuring dead dolphins and taking soil or water samples from the surrounding bay, but it got quite depressing sometimes, so she didn't do it very often.

And then there were the deserters. They kept themselves pretty much to themselves. They were here to maintain the security of the retreat, and to train the One Tribe. Mary tried to talk to them but they would only answer in grunts or monosyllables and seemed unsure how to treat her; she wasn't "in training", so they couldn't shout at her, and they didn't seem to know how to talk to normal people. Vee told her that many of them were really sick, mainly due to the African thing. They couldn't deal with real people any more and weren't able to stop hating; they'd seen and done too much that had nothing to do with normal people's lives. He said

An Idol

that a lot of the deserters understood him much better than anyone else, because they found it easier to accept a lot of what he said was actually real and happening, right now.

She also met some hackers that were staying there. She enjoyed listening to their stories about "Dangerous Ice" and "Military Code Breakers", even though she could only understand a fraction of their technical jargon. Subconsciously it reminded her of "skag-angle" conversations from home. They told her that they were employed by Vee to "cause a bit of bother" in the Net; he had them rearranging and borrowing information from corporate and government ice stacks across the globe. They seemed to think it was all a bit of a laugh, really. Mary liked the hackers because they didn't seem quite as fanatical as everyone else; they were into enjoying themselves, and spent most of their time out of their heads. It was through talking to them that she got the idea how to get her revenge on Speed.

She got one of the hackers to get her into The City's Police ID Data Bank, and accessed Speed's file. She grabbed it and flipped through the files listing from the MINOR OFFENDER/<5 OFFENCE category, to the PERSISTENT OFFENDER/POSSIBLE SECTION REQUIRED category. She dropped Speed's file into the new category, and the hacker helped her introduce an X-Ref Virus, linked to the alteration. The virus would add detailed information to Speed's file, taken from other offenders records; the next time the Police accessed his file they would find a whole history of previous offences.

She then set up a Scan Bomb, linked to the virus and Speed's ID Card's code. The next time his ID card was scanned by the Police's card reader system the Scan Bomb would wipe the card clean, and then rewrite it with new information from the X-Ref Virus. The Police scan would then yield a whole load of false, and highly damning, information and Speed would be up to his neck in it.

Later, when she thought about what she'd done, Mary wasn't sure whether she did feel better now that she'd got her own back.

She didn't tell Vee about it either, although she was sure he'd be pleased with her.

The weeks turned into months; Mary was getting used to where she was, although the hammock still gave her neck ache, some mornings, and she still kept over doing it with the drugs by accident and lost a few days here and there. She started training with the deserters, not because she was going to join Vee's bodyguard or anything, but because it was something to do. She'd also started reading, something she had never done for pleasure before. Not DigiMags either, but books. Old books. They were lying around everywhere, scattered about under seats and tables, no one person's property, so that anyone could read them if they wanted to. Some were just stories, and most of these were old-fashioned Sci-fi or fantasy novels, but nearly all the rest were about ecology and pollution.

Mary preferred the Sci-fi stories. She loved the technological daydreams about faster than light engines and the space ships they powered, and the mysterious alien worlds the engines took the adventurers to, the capsules or booths that crossed time and spanned astral dimensions, parallel universes, black holes, cyborgs, big guns; they were great. The ecology stuff was just depressing, and she soon learned to avoid anything with a picture of the planet earth on it.

When Vee saw she'd started getting into the books he told her to read the others as well.

'Nah, they're boring. These are great, though. I never realised, they're much better than the Vids.'

'Yeah, aren't they!' Vee replied. 'I've been dreaming about stuff like that for as long as I can remember. One of the first memories I have is a dream I had about flying irons or something. I remember waking up and running to the window to see if it was really happening. I saw War Of The Worlds years later, an' it was just like my dream.' While he spoke, Mary watched his eyes re-focus on nothing but his memory; she thought he looked happier than she'd ever seen him before. They then re-focused on her, and his smile changed. He pulled out a spliff and began to light it.

'I'd love to see it, y'know, space travel. I mean real space travel. Maybe someone'll invent a deep freeze or something so I can,' she giggled.

'It's never going to happen, I'm afraid,' he answered dourly. He put his finger over her mouth to stop the inevitable questions, and added, 'We're going to die out on this planet; there'll be no glorious colonization of space in our future because we don't have one. If you want to know why, read the other books. They spell it out plainly enough: It's survival of the fittest, and we no longer fit. The cockroaches and scorpions will probably survive, but not much else will.'

So she read them, and his outbursts about scientists and humanity started to make a sort of sense to her. At school she'd been told about pseudo-religious sects that were based around prophecies of world doom and the apocalypse. Many of these, laughably, she thought at the time, had stated that the world would end at the turn of the millennium, the year 2000 AD.

According to the books she was reading, these sects had actually been right and the apocalypse had happened. It was just taking a few years for the disaster to become truly noticed. It was all to do with something called "exponential growth of the world population, industrialization, pollution and food production", and "the exponential decline in natural resource and usable land" on top of the outlandish energy requirements of the modern, affluent, corporate driven capitalist societies that were dominating the globe.

Vee had to help her understand the term, exponential.

'Exponential growth is achieved when something increases by a constant percentage of its whole in a constant time period.'

Mary looked at Vee blankly. He tried again.

'Okay, think of it as "doubling time" and answer this riddle.

Killing

Imagine a pond, with a water lily on it. It'll double in size every day, and unless you do something about it, it will cover your pond and kill everything else in it in thirty days.'

Mary nodded.

'It seems small for ages, so you decide not to do anything about it until it covers half of your pond. What day will that be on?'

Mary shook her head.

'The twenty-ninth day. That's what exponential growth is. Humans have allowed their shit to get too big for too long, and now it's going to smother us!' He laughed at the look of indignation on her face.

He then told her that it wasn't any big secret, really; the hyper-rich had known for years that there was no real hope of saving the human race. The Earth would survive of course; it just wouldn't be able to support humans, or any other largish mammal. Vee explained that most of the rich, which included everyone in the City and the other conurbations, had adopted the attitude that they might as well make the most of it while it lasts and not think about it, although some of the really rich hadn't given up just yet, which is why the space race had started again in earnest.

Mary couldn't believe it. She asked Vee why nothing had been done, or even attempted, by anyone, to relieve the problem. He told her that the information had been freely available to everyone else for years, before the World Governments had started, very quietly, repressing or distorting it, but that no one had taken any notice of what the books and some "troublemaking" scientists and ecologists said. It would have meant too much of a change in everyone's cosy life styles; no one wanted to do without their cars and disposable luxuries, they thought they were theirs by right.

Mary knew that Vee had broken the government stranglehold on communications, and the facts were being broadcast again, but most people still weren't interested. She couldn't understand the apathy.

An Idol

Vee's explanation was, 'Humans are only interested in themselves and other humans at the end of the day. Everything we do is centred around ourselves. We are continually looking at ourselves and comparing what we see to those around us. Everything else is just a backdrop for our own egos. We've turned this self-obsession into an art, created everything from religions to soap operas around it. How do we live? How do we die? How do we fuck? And how do you live? How do you die? How do you fuck? are the only things we're interested in.' He waved at the world around him, 'This is just a backdrop for humans to perform on. It's not as important as us.

'Our whole society is based around showing us images of ourselves: that's what we're really into, to the exclusion of nearly everything else. And when we're told that the bad stuff we see every day is going to happen to us and our loved ones, we just refuse to believe it. Our egos tell us we're too important to be part of the statistics, "it won't happen here" so don't worry about it.

'And nothing is ever done about any of the bad shit that happens to other people because the people with the power are making money out of it, and the rest of us haven't personally felt threatened enough to change anything.'

'Are you having a nice time? You're shaking a bit.' The girl sounded concerned, but the big smile gave a different impression. Alexander was visibly trembling in the harness, sweat pouring off his naked body.

'You really shouldn't take drugs if you're not going to enjoy them.'

'Get me out of this fucking harness!' Alexander bellowed, 'You're going to regret this . . .'

The girl just smiled at the ranting man, and dropped the gun on the wrecked bed. There were a few unopened tubes on the floor. She knelt and opened the nearest one. It contained two hydro-syringe guns; one filled with an orange liquid, the other blue. She placed the blue syringe's nozzle against her forearm, and depressed the trigger. The initial jolt of the hit caused her eyes to roll backwards under their lids. When they came back down, her pupils were like pin pricks and she glared malevolently at Alexander. He stopped ranting, and stared at the expression on the girl's face.

'It's your turn now, Milt. Stop your whining and take your medicine like a good boy.'

He watched as she walked over to him, the orange hydro-syringe held up where he could see it.

'What's . . . what's in the syringe?' he stammered.

'I thought you wanted to come and party with me?' she chided, stroking his cheek with the tip of the syringe, 'Isn't that why you brought me in here?' She stepped back, and twisted one of the frame's controls. The harness swung Alexander's body into a horizontal position, with his feet slightly above the level of his head.

'Oh, wow, what a great toy!' the girl exclaimed. 'This is fun! I'm glad you asked me come and play with it,' she added, twisting another of the frames controls which pulled Alexander's legs apart, from the knees, exposing his genitalia fully. She began stroking the syringe tip along the inside of his thigh.

'Oh, come on, Mary, a joke's a joke . . .' her host began pleading again.

'What's wrong, Milt? You don't look happy. Have I done anything wrong?' Pretend realization dawned on her face. 'Oh, I see, I'm supposed to be in that, and not you!' Her expression hardened. 'Well, tough shit, Milt. It doesn't always work out as planned.' She pushed the end of the syringe against his taught scrotum, and depressed the trigger, injecting him directly in his left bollock.

Her action was immediately rewarded by a scream of pain, then Alexander's flaccid penis expanded into an uncontrollable erection.

'That's very sweet of you, I'm glad to see you still like me, but I don't think you're my type . . . ' she giggled.

'What have you done to me? What . . . wha . . . wha . . .'

Alexander's body became rigid almost immediately, his teeth were bared but he couldn't open his mouth to speak.

'That was some OD. You've always boasted about how you could take more drugs than anyone else, so I guess we're going to find out just how much more.' She walked slowly around the frame, so that she was standing beside his head, and bent down so that her mouth was next to his ear.

'So wadda you want to do, now? Huh? Do you want to listen to a little story?' She gently pulled his ear lobe with thumb and forefinger, smiling. 'I think you should. Once upon a time, about eight, short, confused years ago was a little girl; a member of one of your potential customer profile groups. You sold her someone . . .'

Johnny walked over to the window; he was curious to see what Dillon was looking at. Max and Dwain didn't notice him get up, they were still jacked into the Penthouse's ice, taking a virtual walk through the party upstairs. He couldn't see Frank any more, but that didn't mean he wasn't around.

'I see they still haven't managed to cut their power supply. Don't see why they bother tryin',' said Dillon conversationally, as Johnny got nearer. Dillon was looking out towards Edge Central and the beacon of pulsing lights at the centre. He didn't look as if he was in the slightest bit concerned about anything, and was just enjoying the view.

'Where do they get the juice from?'

'A little bit here, a little bit there. Loads of power cables runnin' under or near to Edge Central. They just dig one out and do a spot of rewirin'. Tha's how Edge Central runs. Tha's how they built the fuckin' tower: most of it was stolen from this place when it was bein' built.'

After a pause, Dillon asked, 'What you been doin'?'

'I was going through the data again, I . . . um, thought it might be useful later, if I did . . . um, y'know, knew more . . .'

'An' do you?'

'Yeah, kinda. I guess I didn't really know how big Vee had got. I mean, sure, I know he's probably the most successful celeb in the last fifty years, and that he's really the leader of the One Tribe, an' they deal for him an' all that; but I didn't realise he'd become as powerful as Control said he has. Y'know, with all that influence; I knew he ran his own Sat and Net channels but I didn't know he owned all the Eco ones as well. And, like the training camps an' that, I thought they were jus' communes, y'know, for blown away Shakeheads and other dropouts, not fucking military training grounds! An' I didn't realise the One Tribe virtually ran Edge Central these days!' Johnny felt indignant at the amount of power Vee seemed able to wield.

'Yeah, lotta people was surprised at how fast he done all that!' Dillon agreed. 'And how do you think all this new found knowledge is goin' to be useful to you later?' he added, still watching the gathering people below. He was smiling.

'Er, I . . . um . . .' Johnny still wasn't sure why he was there, dressed as an IS assassin with three real IS assassins, and he had absolutely no idea what he was going to do if things started getting dodgy later. It also dawned on him that it didn't matter whether he knew what was going on, or not; it was totally irrelevant and beyond his control anyway.

'I wouldn't worry about it, Johnny Boy, we're given all that shit info 'cause the IS middle management are into some sort of "self-empowerment" bull at the moment, but no one's goin' to ask you your opinion about anythin', so it don't matter what any of us really think or know.

'If anything does happen here tonight, Frank'll be tellin' you what to do. Frank's got all the information, you're jus' along to make up the numbers.' Dillon's grin had widened as he spoke, but he still looked directly out of the window and not at Johnny. Johnny thought he still wasn't being told the whole story, but decided not to push it.

'There's a lot of people out there, tonight,' Johnny said, after a short while.

'Yeah, whole lotta people. Whole lotta little time bombs, waitin' to go off.' Johnny turned to look at the man, and noticed he was smiling grimly, with absolutely no trace of humour in his expression. 'Shit, look at 'em. It ain't just a few no more, it looks more like everybody. I been standin' here, watchin', an' I seen whole families down there, actin' as if they're on a day trip to a fun park. No, this isn't good.'

'I never understood what everyone sees in him, y'know, and I've met quite . . . ' Johnny started.

'That's 'cause you never listened; all you was interested in was your surfin' an' your hair cut. You weren't interested in no man who was givin' you bad news, so you never listened to what he was really sayin', even though you watched his Vid channels an' listen to his music.

'See, you probably weren't into Shake much, before you was sectioned; I hear most surfers don't do it, 'cause it kinda fucks up your balance.' Johnny nodded, but Dillon wasn't concerned whether he agreed with him or not.

'An' what Shake does, amongst other things, is to get you in the mood for listenin'; that's at the early levels, anyway. You never really listened to what ol' Vee was goin' on about, so you ain't gonna see what others see in him.

'Amongst other things, he's givin' people somethin' that they ain't used to gettin'. It's really rare an' you sure as shit can't get from anywhere else; the truth. He's tellin' them what's going on around them, not tryin' to lie or tell 'em it'll all be okay. That's why you don't understand what a lot of the people down there see in him; 'cause you've never really been interested in what's happenin' around you, anythin' that was on a bigger scale than you can actually see.

'Those people down there aren't dropouts, tryin' to escape from society like you're told; that's what the real people are doin'. Real people are the ones that spend their days watchin' the Vid, sedated outta their minds, just like the Government wants them to, mindlessly consumin' what the companies give them.' Dillon put his palms on the window and leant so close to the glass his breath became visible on its surface, 'Those people down there are taking

An Idol

an active part in society, some of them are tryin' to change it, an' they're all havin' a ball. Vee's made 'em scared and angry about what's been happenin' and they're beginnin' to question things they've always accepted. That's what makes him so dangerous; he's tellin' them the truth, and they're startin' to listen to it.'

Johnny was a bit bemused by what Dillon was saying, and stood for several minutes trying to digest, before speaking again. 'You sound like you agree with him; I thought . . .'

'Johnny Boy, you gotta learn to listen. You're not here to think, so don't try. I'll say it again, jus' for the record: What you or I think or believe don't mean shit. We're here to do a job; we have no say in what that job is or how we do it, understand?'

Johnny nodded but Dillon didn't seem satisfied, 'The sooner you realise that, the easier it'll all be on you. How long was you at the Academy, anyway?'

'Er, three weeks . . . nearly.'

Dillon finally turned and looked at Johnny, his grin widening at Johnny's answer.

'Yeah, that makes sense. You don't know your arse from your elbow and don't even know that, yet. No wonder we've got Frank along.'

Johnny didn't know what to say, so he sort of half nodded and shrugged at the same time, and wished he'd remained sitting down, playing with his ice's virtual briefing. He was desperately thinking of something to say that wouldn't further undermine Dillon's confidence in him.

'So, er . . . how long ago were you at the Academy?' was the best he could come up with. Dillon tilted his head downwards, pulling his glasses down to the tip of his nose with one finger, and stared at Johnny for a moment, with an expression approaching utter disbelief on his face.

'Do you really want to know?' Dillon asked, shaking his head. Johnny nodded, he decided he wasn't going to say anything more for the rest of the day, if he could help it.

Killing

'What you really mean is, "How come you ended up in the same shit as me?" huh? Well, seein' as we ain't got anythin' else to do at the moment, I suppose I might as well tell you. I was sectioned nearly six years ago. I tol' you I was one of the first? Yeah?' Johnny nodded, and Dillon carried on with his own personal history.

'At first, I thought I'd jus' got myself banged up again. There'd been rumours about draftin' convicted perps goin' around while I was on remand, but it didn't bother me much; seems the last government had tried introducin' the draft, and fucked up, so I thought nothin' about it. Right up until they found me guilty I thought I was headin' for Canvey Island and ten. Imagine my surprise when they declared me "mentally criminally prone" under the '35 Criminal Psychology Act, and sectioned me!' He grinned at Johnny. 'I couldn't believe it when the judge explained that meant they could psychologically adjust me without needin' my consent. I was taken into a little room, an' some suit asks me whether I want to be turned into a vegetable, or sign up for an extended tour of duty with one of the Services.

'I jus' looked at him an' said, "give me the pen, fucker, where do I sign?" The dude even gives me the choice of which "service" I "join", so I picks the IS. I didn't want to go an' die in no African wasteland an' I don't like foreign food anyway. I figured I'd hang around for a while, check it out, then scoot ASAP.' He turned around and looked directly at the boy, ' 'Cept it didn't quite work out like that.'

'I'm a sealed unit, linked indirectly to the IS main ice. It has its advantages and disadvantages.'

'You're wired up inside?' Johnny was part impressed, part horrified.

'This is old technology,' Dillon said dismissively. 'There are other ways of controllin' people these days, an' some don't require it. Everyone gets given a psychological test; some'll follow orders and are controllable after verbal readjustment, others aren't. I wasn't, but they decided they were goin' to use me anyway, so I got hardwired. They inserted a couple of processors into my spine, linked them to a chunk of ice in my stomach, an' stuck a whole batch of probes into my brain, and just turned me on.'

'Wow! What's it like?' Johnny asked reverently.

'I now do some things because I have to, not 'cause I want to. I'm compelled to do what I'm told, an' I jus' do it. Simple as that. At the time it doesn't even cross my mind to question what I'm doin'.'

'So why haven't you tried to, erm . . . y'know . . .'

'What, run? Where would I go? Besides, they can blow the ice in my guts at any time they want. Apparently the charge isn't enough to kill you immediately, just enough to turn your intestines into so much sludge; you die watchin' your guts ooze outta your arse.'

Johnny gaped at the man; he couldn't believe that Dillon was talking about it all so calmly.

'It's not all bad news, though. As a thank you, and to keep me from taking drugs any more, they've spliced part of my brain with a mood inhibitor and tuned me into a permanent buzz. I feel real good all the time now, whether I like it or not!' His widening grin looked, to Johnny, as if it was going to spread right off his face.

'Is, erm . . . is Dwain the same?'

'No, Dwain's a product of military trainin'. He's been brainwashed in the age-old lo-tech fashion of boot camp, nothin' more. He's naturally gung-ho anyway, due to his inbred white trash background. With a little bit of weapons trainin' he was prime material for Africa.'

'So, how come he's with IS now?'

'Because he didn't die there. Dwain had three tours in Africa, and somehow survived. The Army don't like it when their cannon fodder remain intact for too long; they eventually begin to notice that no one wants to want to win anythin' and realise that they're only there to test the weapons and control the excess population. So Dwain was transferred to IS before he tried to desert. I don't think he's very happy about it; bit too much like hard work for him. They've had him on buildin' clearance duty, an' that gets a bit hairy. It ain't like shootin' unarmed niggers from an assault chopper.'

Johnny was about to ask something, his mouth was open, when a large flash, very near to the base of the Ministry of Truth tower, demanded both of their attentions.

Dillon's glasses flared blue on to his face as he jacked into the Net. 'I'm hackin' into the Sat channels, find out what they say happened. Get Max.'

Johnny nervously turned around and walked back to the coffee table. Max already knew about the explosion and was talking to Control. Frank was sitting on air near the table, looking as dejected as Dwain.

'Just fucking brilliant. What a waste of time,' Dwain was moaning, as Johnny sat down.

'What's going on?' he asked.

'If he's been off'd, us sittin' here wasting our time is what's been going on.' Dwain looked really upset.

Frank shook his head in disgust, but at what, Johnny wasn't sure. Dillon walked over to the group by the table.

'The right-wing EuroSat and Stateside Sat channels are blaming either Muslim fundamentalists, surprise surprise, or saying it's purely drug-related and criminal, while the left-wing channels are blaming the right-wing Christian Militia, the Government, the Army and us, while the Asian channels are blaming everything in the West that has a power base. Strangely, Vee's own media network isn't really commenting, except to say an explosion has occurred near to the Ministry of Truth tower, and there are injuries.'

'How was it done?' Johnny's heart was beating rapidly; if Vee was dead, then tonight's operation would be cancelled. It didn't occur to him that they would probably be assigned elsewhere.

'Smart missile,' Max answered, adding, 'but nothing has been confirmed yet, so nothing has changed yet; we wait for further information.'

Dwain groaned, and shuffled impatiently in his seat. Johnny noticed he didn't stand up to relieve his cramp.

'What's the situation in the party, Max?' asked Dillon, 'Jus' in case we still have to gatecrash.'

'It's still a party, with a mixture of famous and infamous faces, there's even a few politicians and an aristo knocking around.' For some reason, Dwain started giggling.

Max ignored him, 'There's a couple of problems though. Alexander disappeared with a bimbo about half an hour ago, but I can't access the room they went into; it's a shielded grey area, so we got a potential problem there. And there's also no sound from any of the penthouse's systems either. We can't hear anything from up there, and I don't know why. Control's checking it for me. The rest is fairly standard. I suggest you go an' have a look yourself. Take the boy with you, if you want.'

Johnny thought it was like actually being there, at the party, except it was completely silent. And they were floating. First they had drifted through a lobby full of bodyguards, who were just milling around, passing time. The guards' mouths moved but the sounds they made were absent, like a very old sort of Vid. Johnny wanted to stop and count them but Dillon just punched their total up into the air in front of him.

273 assorted bodyguards.

A weapons rundown was obtainable behind a hyper-node next to the figure but Johnny decided not to look.

'This is weird. We should be able to hear what they're sayin',' Dillon shrugged. 'C'mon then, let's have a look around.'

Johnny realised that Dillon was "towing him" through the virtual representation, and tried to relax. He was never comfortable unless he felt in control of himself. He even hated buses and tubes because of that. This was so real it felt the same. The illusion was caused by the ice he wore. It was linked to Dillon's, both pieces had constructed a real-time virtual penthouse, then put them both into it. All the information needed to do this was stripped from the penthouse's surveillance Cam system by Max's earlier hack.

They passed, unnoticed, up to the door at the other side of the room between the two vat-bred guards. It opened in their simulation, but the guards didn't respond, so Johnny wondered whether it had opened in reality or not. He shook his head incredulously as he recognized the clones; they were from the Arnie Corp Laboratories and physically based on their founder.

Johnny floated down the white passage and into the main triangular room, feeling like an unseen ghost, haunting the penthouse. They had no density, so the guests and furniture appeared to pass right through them.

Dillon ignored the silent laughing and dancing people around him and sped them off, on a fly-through of the penthouse's layout, dragging Johnny behind him.

The image around Johnny froze, and he was flipped unceremoniously back into the coffee shop. Control was sitting in front of him. Max was grim-faced, and Dwain was sitting to attention. Dillon was the only one who looked relaxed.

Control began talking, 'Situation update: the bomb blast at the tower was not actually in the building. The bomb was deflected and detonated in a section of the crowd nearby.'

A holographic miniature of the base of the Ministry of Truth appeared over the coffee table, and a massively slowed clip of the attempt ran. The missile shot across the picture from right to left, towards the speakers. Just before impact the missile changed course abruptly and veered away, detonating almost immediately. It left an almost perfectly round crater next to the building, polarizing a huge area of dancers in the process.

'We do not know who is responsible for the attack yet, but it indicates that someone in or very near to the tower is equipped with a sonic net, shielding the building from smart weapons.'

'Ooooeee, willya look at all those bodies! Reminds me of Kenya . . .' Dwain was grinning at the carnage, watching the aftermath.

Johnny could see his fingers moving, as if touching keys; he was manipulating the picture somehow, probably rewinding and replaying the moment of impact again and again. Johnny let his own clip continue to run. He was amazed at how soon the bomb blast area was overrun with people again. Some seemed agitated by what had happened and were wailing or shouting, although others didn't appear to have even noticed and hadn't stopped dancing; they were seemingly oblivious to the bits and pieces of unluckier revellers scattered around them. Within minutes the whole area was covered in people again, obliterating all traces of the explosion.

Control cut through the transmission, 'Your mission is now active. I repeat, your mission is now active.

'You are to proceed to your designated area and secure it, then await further instructions. Your mission objectives are to take precedence over all other considerations.'

Control blinked out of existence, leaving Johnny staring dumbly at the air where she used to be. He couldn't believe that it was actually going to happen. He looked at Frank. Frank was grinning.

'Frank, get ready. Dillon, help the boy strap on Frank.' Max got to his feet, issuing orders as he unclipped his own weapons.

'Dwain, you may stand up now,' he added. Frank winked at Johnny before folding elegantly into nothing.

'Stand up, Johnny Boy, I gotta attach this to your ice. Oh, and take a couple of those orange capsules as well.'

Dillon was standing behind Johnny, and waved the bag Johnny had carried up from the cruiser over the boy's shoulder. Johnny reached into his pocket and pulled out the pump dispenser Max had given him earlier. He popped two of the capsules into his palm, shrugged and swallowed them, then watched as Dillon unclipped the catch on the bag and pulled out a small clam-shaped plastic and chrome disc, and another hand-cannon. He handed the new gun to Johnny.

Out of the bulges on either side of the plastic and chrome disc came two fibre-optic cables. Each cable had one large pin adapter at the end.

'What do the orange capsules do?' he asked.

'Oh, this and that. They've got a blood clottin' agent in them, amongst other things; helps if you get hit,' Dillon answered cheerfully, then added, 'Stand up.'

Johnny stood up, and apprehensively eyed the object Dillon held. 'What's that do?' he asked.

Dillon just smiled, and motioned to Johnny to turn around. Johnny turned around, and felt the man lift his coat up, behind him; his ice was attached to his belt in the small of his back.

'Aren't those pins a bit large for the ice?' he asked. He'd remembered seeing a few sockets on it, but they'd been for very small pins. The pins on the cables Dillon was holding were at least four inches long.

'Nah, it'll fit. The pins don't go in there, anyway,' Dillon said confidently, dropping the coat back down. Johnny then felt Dillon's fingers on the back of his head. He was about to turn around to see what was going on when he felt a brief stabbing pain in the back of his neck, followed by a tingling sensation run through his body.

'You're all done. Turn around.'

Johnny heard Dillon, and turned around to look at the man. At least, he tried to. Instead he felt himself turn the hand-cannon he held over, and watched as he began stripping it, very expertly, down.

'Fuck off Dillon, you know the little shit can't!' he felt, and heard, himself say.

What the fuck is going on? He actually thought he'd said it. It felt like he had said it, but he didn't hear the words come out.

An Idol

What's happening!! What the fuck is happening? FUCK FUCK FUCK FUCK FUCK . . . he began screaming as loudly as he could. *Shut up, you little shit. I can fuckin' well hear you well enough if you just talk, alright?* It was Frank. *I've taken control of you, my little friend. The jack plugs fit into your head, not your ice, stupid. Did you really think they'd let a toe rag like you loose with a gun on an important operation like this?* Johnny watched as he finished reassembling the gun, and clipped it onto his belt, beneath his leather coat. He then glanced up at the waiting trio.

'Yeah, I'm ready, let's go,' he felt himself say.

I'm only going to say this once, alright? Your body depends on me, if you distract me by shouting and screaming in my head, or trying to struggle, I can't guarantee what'll happen to it; remember, if you get shot up, it doesn't really bother me, much, 'cause I'm back at the academy. Frank started laughing, but only in Johnny's head, not with his mouth, and followed the others out of the coffee shop.

Johnny, dumbstruck by what was happening, saw the look of relief on the faces of the coffee shop staff as they left.

Walking to the entervator still felt like walking to Johnny. He could feel the floor beneath him, the boots around his feet, his trousers brushing together, his muscles making their exertions. Except he wasn't doing it. He wasn't actually doing it. It was coming from somewhere else; his body was only experiencing half the signals it normally felt and was quietly screaming at the abnormality of it. It felt a bit like pins and needles, mixed with cramp, but just in the brain.

'So what's it feel like to have legs an' shit like that again, Frank?' Dwain leered at the boy while the entervator rose.

'Fuck off, Dwain!' Frank replied tersely, through Johnny.

'Hey, Johnny, you listening?' Dwain asked, suppressing a smirk, 'Ask your pilot why he ain't here, himself.'

'Shut it, all of you. We got business to attend to!' Max gruffly interrupted, as the doors pinged and their destination was announced. He stepped out into the lobby, and strode up to the nervous looking guards at the reception desk. The guards were fully aware that the IS men were about to step out of the lift, because they'd set off nearly every sensor on their control panel. Dillon, Dwain and the boy followed.

Max didn't beat around the bush with needless conversation, 'You are, under no circumstances, to let anyone else come up to this level. Understand?' Both guards nodded.

Why aren't you here? Johnny asked Frank. He'd started thinking about what Dwain had said, and was very concerned indeed.

Shut up, I'm busy. Johnny could see that he wasn't, he was just watching Max scare the shit out of the security guards, so asked again, only loudly this time.

For fucksake, don't do that. You're really pissing me off.

Johnny continued asking; he had nothing else to do and no one else to talk to, and he didn't seriously think he was going to make it anyway. He was past caring.

Alright, I'll show you, Frank finally conceded, and a small frame appeared in front of the boy. In the frame was a real-time of Frank. Frank was just a torso, lying on a disability couch, wired to an expensively large slab of ice and a booster.

Frank smiled at the Cam taking the shot, and opened his mouth to speak.

Happy now? he said.

What happened? Johnny asked, staring at the mutilated figure.

Around Frank he could see other mutilated figures, some with even worse injuries than Frank, but all wired up to similar hardware. There were also technicians, or perhaps nurses, administering the damaged operatives.

I didn't shut up when I was supposed to! The frame abruptly disappeared, without any delicate transformation first. *So fuckin' well shut up and let me do my job, willya?*

The four men walked towards the penthouse lift; Max had got the guards to call it, but without transmitting who really wanted it. He noticed the kiosk.

'You! Hands on your head. Frank, check her!' Max pointed towards the girl inside it. For a moment she looked uncertain, then put her hands on her head.

Max turned to Dillon, 'He'll be wired, snag his shades while I remove him from the situation.'

Johnny watched Dillon nod as he moved, uncontrollably, towards the nearby kiosk. He reached confidently for the handle of the door and entered the small work area. The girl was nervously staring at the floor.

'Turn around!' Johnny felt himself say. The girl turned, and he began to frisk her for weapons, rapidly checking her arms and legs first, then torso. Johnny then felt Frank slow his movements down, and began gently rubbing his hands over the woman's breasts, eventually cupping them in each palm, and squeezing the nipples beneath the thin fabric of her uniform with his thumbs. Johnny felt his grip tighten, until it felt as if he was gripping her as hard as he could. She started to shake, and eventually cried out in pain. Frank started rubbing Johnny's crotch into her buttocks as he held her. The girl began to sob as Frank moved one of Johnny's hands down her stomach and between her legs, pulling her tightly up against the body he inhabited. Johnny could feel his erection digging into her as Frank continued grinding his crotch against the trembling girl.

'Frank, stop pissing around and get over here! Now!' Max screamed, impatiently.

Frank let Johnny let go of the girl, and stepped back. The girl didn't turn around. She stood, shaking, with her back still towards him. As he left the kiosk, Frank turned the boy to look back at the girl. Johnny could see the tears streaming down her face as she looked at him, an expression of ill-disguised hate, mixed with total fear, on her face.

He felt himself smile broadly at her, then licked his lips.

What the fuck did you do that for? Jesus, she'll think that was me . . .

Killing

Johnny began, but immediately stopped again because the entervator arrived.

The doors slid open. Dillon stepped forward and whisked the glasses off the man inside the lift, as Max shot him in the chest. The boy watched as Dillon quickly clipped an optic lead onto the glasses, downloading a pre-designed programme into them.

'Yeah, all done; whoever's on the other end is getting the late arrivals show you put into the penthouse's ice earlier.' Dillon nodded to Max, dropping the glasses onto the dead body.

As the lift rose, Johnny stared mournfully at the bits of body stuck to the wall; they were spoiling the effect of the prairie scene.

'Frank, you take point, for the obvious reasons.'

If Johnny had control over his own body, he would probably have soiled himself there and then. Max's words made horrific sense to him. He felt Frank answer, but wasn't aware of what Frank had made him say, his mind was screaming, urging his body to obey his commands and get them both out of there. Then the doors opened.

Here we go, Johnny Boy. Frank sounded as if he was enjoying himself. *Now remember, no screaming, okay? It'll put me off.*

Johnny felt himself step firmly out into a room that had two hundred and seventy three heavily armed bodyguards in it, and watched them all turn and look at him. He tried to scream.

—————————————— 'Once upon a time, about eight, short, confused years ago was a little girl; a member of one of your potential customer profile groups. You sold her someone . . .' the red-headed girl's sing song voice paused as the door buzzer sounded twice. She bounded across the room, towards the door, the gun raised in her hand. A voice from outside was piped into the soundproofed room, and a small frame on the door unfurled, showing her who was outside.

'Milton! What the fuck are you playing at? You've got a party out here that needs a host!' It was Alexander's wife, and she obviously couldn't see into the room. The girl stood motionless next to the door, the gun levelled firmly at head height, pointing towards the source of the disembodied voice.

'Can you hear me, Milton? Are you going to answer me or not? The Vid's saying that the little shit'll be on soon, so stop playing with that little tart and your activity centre and get out here, now!' The girl grinned at Alexander's wife's comments, and turned and winked at her captive host.

'Shit, you could at least have the decency to answer me! Have you got your mouth full or something?'

The girl watched Alexander's wife storm away from the room, before lowering the gun and walking back over to her host. He stared at her with bulging eyes, the veins at his temples pulsing. He was trying to say something but seemed unable to open his mouth properly; his efforts were just causing spittle to spray randomly over his sweating, inclined body.

'Finding it hard to speak, Milt?' she asked. 'It must be the drugs you take. What level are you on now?' She was giggling as she leaned over the restrained man to check the straps. The OD she'd injected into Alexander's phallus was causing him to shake spasmodically from head to foot, waves of contractions spreading out across his body like ripples in a pond. The girl leant very close to his face, and gently parted his lips with her left forefinger. Spittle sprayed over her face, but this only caused her to giggle more. She inspected his teeth. She could hear them rasping against each other, and watched as he involuntarily ground them backwards and forwards in time to the spasms wracking his body. Small pieces of enamel were already breaking off.

'I wonder whether you'll be able to wear away your teeth before your gums give out?' she cheerfully commented, then added, 'We've got enough time to find out. The "little shit" won't be on just yet.'

The girl began circling the frame, inspecting the trapped man from every angle, watching how the contractions moved from one muscle group to another. As she paced, she began talking again in her little girl voice 'What was I doing before that nasty woman interrupted me? Can you remember, Milt? Oh yeah, that's right, I was telling a story. Do you want me to carry on?' She didn't bother waiting for the answer she knew wouldn't come, and started anyway: 'Once upon a time there was a little girl. And her name was Mary, except it wasn't really Mary. And she was just like every other little girl, except she thought she was different, y'know, somehow special, like most little girls do. Anyway, she developed this crush on a certain rock star. You know the one I mean, don't you? 'Cause that was all down to you, you clever man . . .'

Alexander was trying to follow the girl with his eyes, but the muscle spasms were making this almost impossible; they kept rolling backwards into his head, exposing the bloodshot whites around his irises. He was only half listening to her; he was involuntarily remembering the only time he had ever met Vee properly, and what they'd talked about.

Alexander recalled how he'd felt when he had seen his house on the news, surrounded by the crusties. More annoyed and confused than anything else. He'd tried to call his internal security but they hadn't responded. Then he tried to call the Police but the terminal didn't respond.

Then the door bell rang. He had angrily gone to answer it, thinking it was one of his guards to apologise and tell him the crusties had been dispersed. He remembered he didn't even bother to get a gun, he'd been so annoyed.

The girl continued her story in a singsong voice, 'Several years later, as fate would have it, the girl and her idol met. He was charming; she was entranced. And then he found out she wasn't really called Mary; she was called Virginia Mary.

'The girl hated her name, mainly due to the ridicule it had caused her throughout her short life. Don't you think children are really cruel? It has always amazed me how they can cause so much pain and suffering with the most innocuous of weapons.

'Anyway, he seemed to like her name and actually got quite excited about it. Later, he told her he'd found it inspiring and that it was a coincidence that was too good to miss. Her idol it seemed, has a great belief in fate and coincidence. Anyway, she had no idea what he was talking about, but was happy anyway because he was happy, and he'd also taken her with him, away from the nasty city . . .'

Alexander was now bleeding from his wrists and ankles, and his body seemed to be swelling up as his muscles bruised themselves with their continual movement. His skin was stretched quite taught, and beginning to discolour. The involuntary movements he made were causing the padded straps to cut into his bloated flesh.

His eyes had glazed over by now but tears still streamed down

Killing

his cheeks.

He was still very conscious.

In Alexander's mind Vee had just walked into his house again, as if he owned it.

'I want to show you something, then we're going to have a little chat,' Vee had said.

Alexander remembered he hadn't answered, just followed the man into his study. He remembered he had been thinking about what he was going to have done to Vee when his security turned up, then Vee had informed him that all the security guards were unconscious, or dead, depending upon how committed to their job they had been, and that the Police were being prevented from getting to the house.

He then watched as Vee casually detuned the Sat receiver to a different type of signal.

The screen had blanked briefly then cut into a hand-Cam clip, shot inside a white room. In the clip, in a chair, next to a bald man, had been his latest mistress; a young singer he had "discovered". She had been stripped naked, and tied down with wire, judging by the way her skin was pinched and bleeding.

'I think we should have a little chat, don't you?' Vee had said.

'She thought he'd just taken her on a little holiday to the seaside, but this wasn't strictly true. You see, this rock star had met loads of people, just like her, before. He knew their desires, their fears, their confusion, because he was once one of them – before you had him locked up and turned him into a sort of a god, anyway.

'He'd watched them and listened to them and realised how they could be useful to him. So, as she sunned herself and had a good time, she was introduced to the "ecological" cause, and the One Tribe, and the machine he had constructed to make her useful. She eventually decided, as they mostly all do, she wanted to be a part of it instead of just one of the audience; "part of the solution, not the problem" was how she phrased it.

An Idol

'She didn't realise it at the time, but she was already well on her way to being one of its major cogs. You see, unknown to her, while she had been asleep, others had been awake. Virginia Mary was already changing, with a little help from Science.'

The girl smiled, and stroked Alexander's head.

He was beginning to turn purple in places, the lactic acid building up as his muscles bruised with severe overuse and no recovery periods.

The spasms were now travelling up and down his body in waves, rather like displaced water in a large bath tub. The shaking would start at his feet, move rapidly up his body, activating all the muscle groups as it went, then back down again, towards his feet. Each wave was greeted by an almost inaudible moan. But the man's mind refused to let go and deliver him into oblivion. The conversation that had changed his life continued its replay.

Vee had informed Alexander that the image he was watching, of the girl tied to the chair, was not a recording. To prove it he said, "Wave Joe" and the bald man had waved at the Cam. Vee had then wanted to talk to Alexander about the royalties and rights to the songs he hadn't had anything to do with. And about being exploited and left to rot in prison. And about why Alexander was so greedy and power mad, anyway.

And whenever Alexander had tried to argue back or threaten him, Vee had talked about what the bald man in the warehouse was going to do to Alexander's young mistress. The man in the warehouse had then done it, despite all Alexander's pleadings for him not to.

But he had still refused Vee's demands, though; it was the principal of the thing.

Eventually Alexander's mistress had died.

Vee had then told him that it would be his wife next time.

Alexander thought that he must've betrayed himself somehow, because Vee added, 'Or maybe your daughter?' and smiled a terrible sort of smile. One that said 'I know you . . .'

Killing

Alexander remembered the series of concessions and promises he had eventually made to Vee to make him leave.

The girl squatted down on her haunches, next to the man's head, still stroking his hair tenderly. With her lips next to his right ear, she continued her story in her singsong voice.

'Do you know what "pheromones" are?

'That's smell, really. Do you like the way I smell?' she asked brightly, holding her armpit nearer to his nose.

'Mary, the girl in this story, hadn't ever thought about smell, it was just something people did, especially in Edge Central.

'But smell is more than just smell; smell is individual. It's like fingerprints or DNA. Anyway, smell was one of the ways she was changed by Science. They changed her pheromones so she'd smell like someone else. Any guesses who?'

Her host's muscle spasms had increased in frequency and magnitude now, and were no longer moving over his body in waves; each separate muscle now twitched and pulled randomly, his whole body jerking in the frame as if connected to the electricity supply.

He was also bleeding quite badly from where he was held by the straps; they had dug into his bloated skin to a depth of almost an inch by now.

The girl moved back, but only slightly, to avoid getting any of the blood on her bright green clothing.

Alexander had been badly shaken by the whole experience of Vee's visit, and the way himself and his property had been violated, but he had held it in restraint.

He had done what Vee had asked; released the royalties, ate humble pie in front of the world's press and all the rest, all the time planning cold revenge on the upstart.

He had found plenty to rally to the cause, especially in the Government. Vee had very quickly upset a great many powerful people. They had decided that the re-population of the restricted zone seemed like as good a place to start: make the bastard homeless again.

He pumped billions of his own money into the promotion, then execution, of the plan.

Alexander had found a cause in life, other than the pursuit of money; he wanted to destroy Vee.

'Mary didn't know anything about what was being done to her, though, and kept asking her idol what she could do to help the cause. He kept putting her off, telling her she wasn't ready; she thought he meant that her physical and weapons training wasn't going well, which annoyed her 'cause her instructors seemed pleased.

'Eventually he asked her if she'd do a small job for him, and she jumped at the chance. She was so eager to become involved, to actually do something herself to help. She was a bit disappointed when he told her he wanted her to work as a friend's personal assistant; Mary wanted to do something a bit more glamorous, y'know, kinda dangerous, but he persisted. He told her that she wouldn't really be working for his friend, and she'd only be there for a short time anyway; just long enough for her to meet someone else.'

Alexander was now totally rigid and he seemed to be having real problems breathing. His muscles had seized completely and the lactic acid building up in them had no method of release; he appeared to be in a great deal of pain. He was turning quite blue in places, due to internal haemorrhaging.

The girl stood up, and moved around to the front of the frame, raising the tormented man into an upright position so she could stare directly into his eyes.

Alexander had thought it was all going well. He thought he had made himself untouchable in the fortress he had built, surrounded by a fortune in bodyguards, and his friends in high places had told him Vee was about to fall.

Killing

If it wasn't for the pain, he would have hardly believed what was actually happening to him.

The girl's story continued unabated, 'Mary asked him who she was to meet, and the idol described a very nasty man, who had very nasty desires and a great deal of money and power from his nasty business dealings.

'She then asked him what he wanted her to do, once she met this nasty man. He said nothing, just get really close to him. The rest would just happen naturally, and she'd be invited to a party by him.'

Her voice changed from the agreeable tone she'd been using to tell the story, to a harsh, contemptuous snarl, 'Is this story ringing any bells yet, Milt? You see, that young lady's idol knew that the nasty man would like her, and invite her to his flash pad because he would want to play with her in his nasty, nasty little way.

'Not just because she was young and pretty and reasonably innocent,' she grasped her host's mouth and pulled his head up to face her properly, oblivious to the blood and teeth that spewed over her hand, 'but also because she subconsciously reminded him of the person he wanted to fuck most in the whole wide world; Mary smelt just like his own daughter!'

The door buzzer went again.

'Shit!' The girl turned, releasing the man's face, and bounded over towards the door, gun drawn.

'Milton! For christsakewillya leave her until later!' Alexander's wife was back, and she seemed angry, and not a little drunk, 'You've still got a party out here to look after!' The woman staggered against the door, spilling her drink over herself, 'Fuck! Milton! Security have also just told me there are more guests on the way up, so get your fucking arse outta there and meet them, cause I'll be fucked if I'm going to!' The girl watched the woman storm away, before going back to her captive.

Alexander hung limply in the harness, quite still. There was blood streaked all over his discoloured body, and blood, faeces and intestine falling from his slack anus.

'Oh Milt, you're dead!' She sounded surprised, then started giggling at her own pantomime acting, 'And you didn't get to hear the rest of the story. Never mind.'

She walked past the dead body without a second glance, picked up the last of the canisters and her jacket from the floor, and went and sat on the remains of the bed, next to the touchdeck.

'I wonder who the late arrivals are?' she asked herself, sarcastically, accessing the SecCam's system. The deck's screen unfurled and lit.

As the screen adjusted, she pulled her green glasses out of her jacket and placed them next to the deck. A blue light inside the glasses began blinking, indicating it had established an information field between itself and the ice within the touchdeck.

The girl watched the four late arrivals in the lift, and grinned. Standing in the virtual prairie were two fat men in suits, smoking large cigars. With them were a couple of young, very beautiful girls, dressed in long fur coats. They seemed to be chatting amicably with the man in the dinner jacket.

Across the screen the words IS HACK: FAKE FOOTAGE. BEGINNING RECODING appeared, and the blue light inside the glasses turned red. While she waited, the girl emptied the remaining canisters onto the floor and expertly began to assemble the assorted components.

The glasses gave a brief noise to attract her attention and the message on the screen changed to IS HACK DIVERTED: RECODING COMPLETE, WATCH! The words faded out and the scene shifted. The SecCam view of the lift remained the same, except there were pieces of gore hanging over the prairie sim now. The man in the dinner jacket was a corpse in the corner and the four guests had turned into heavily armed IS assassins.

'Oh, what a surprise!' she said sardonically, tapping the touchpad lightly. The image fragmented into close-ups of the four men and her glasses began to hum.

The words DOWNLOADING NOW appeared on the screen but the girl didn't notice; she had already returned to the task of assembling the components in front of her.

In a surprisingly short time the girl constructed a jumping detonator linked to a photo-optic/vibration cell. She stood up, and walked over to door. Stopping about three metres away, she turned and knelt, and began to secure the device to the floor. She adjusted its field sensor to face the door and surrounding area, then looked back towards the screen to check on the late arrivals.

The downloading had finished and the screen had split into two images. The left-most image was a static shot showing three of the IS men still in the lift, hugging the walls. The other was a panning SecCam shot of the fourth IS man; he was striding confidently through the guards in the lobby.

The girl stood up and quickly crossed to the bed. She gathered her remaining items, the coat, her hat, glasses and gun, and turned to leave the room. She paused a moment, then turned around and reached towards the touchdeck. Her hand above the buttons, she stared at the screen.

The IS man had his back towards the cam and appeared to be chatting amiably to the two identical vat-bred guards sitting in front of him. The rest of the bodyguards in the room were giving this odd trio their undivided attention; the IS turning up seemed to be causing them no little concern. She watched as the IS man casually put both hands into his long leather coat's pockets, then raised a couple of large hand-cannons and nonchalantly started emptying their contents into the seated clones.

A slight grin touched her face, then she jabbed a couple of buttons, and the view switched to a mosaic of the rest of the party. Her eyes flicked quickly over the images. In one, Prince Albert, under the control of the Hacker, was being physically molested by a small crowd of laughing young men. He seemed to be enjoying it

An Idol

as much as they were, and was even helping with the mutilation. She forcibly depressed the off switch and stood up. The screen blanked, then folded back down into the deck. The girl turned and left the room, briefly stooping to activate the device she had left on the floor. She glanced at the gently swinging carcass, smiled, then extinguished the light as she shut the door.

Moving quickly, she retraced her steps along the corridor towards the overgrown balcony, the lift, and spiral staircase. The party below was still in full swing and the music, if anything, seemed louder. She ignored the lift and started down the stairs, taking them two at a time. As she ran, she pulled on the jacket and slipped the glasses onto her face. Reaching the second floor, she swung off the staircase and turned left, away from the balcony overlooking the rest of the party and moved purposefully down the corridor that greeted her.

Placing the hat on her head and adjusting its veil with one hand, she walked to the door at the very end.

Unlike Alexander's "study", this room had a door handle, but when she tried it, the door gave an engaged beep and refused to open.

She quickly glanced back down the corridor, then fished inside one of the jacket's pockets, eventually pulling out a small black card. The music abruptly ended. She touched the card to the door frame, next to the handle, and the door clicked open.

'Hey, why don't you just barge in . . .'

Paula Alexander was standing in a large bathroom, repainting her face in the large mirror above the sink. The girl stepped into the room, shutting the door behind her with her foot. Paula turned her head slightly and saw the girl in green reflected in the mirror.

'Oh, it's you!' she snorted, haughtily. Then added, 'I didn't expect to see you again . . .'

The girl in green, grinning, raised the small hand-cannon, and flipped a node on the side of the butt; a smaller chrome tube beneath the gun's main muzzle slid forward, releasing the safety.

Killing

Paula's voice trailed off, and a look of consternation crossed her face.

'Wha– ?'

The girl depressed the gun's trigger for a fraction of a second and the chrome tube spat a silent stream of flachettes into the surprised face.

Paula's body jerked backwards into the shell-shaped bath tub in the corner of the room, her shattered face sprayed an arc of gore over the mirror and pure white wall above her. She twitched spasmodically for a few seconds, then slumped over.

The girl stepped to one side of the bathroom door and stood, quite still, facing the inert body and matted trail of blood and hair that clung to the wall.

A couple of fingers on her left hand moved slightly, and she settled back, resting on the wall.

And waited.

A short time later, she smiled, and her left hand moved briefly in the air again, as if touching an invisible switch. Her entire outfit, from the hat on her head to the trainers on her feet, began to shimmer and pulse with a myriad of barely perceptible colours. She raised the hood of her jacket and zipped it up.

———————————— Johnny watched himself walk up to the two identical men flanking the door at the end of the room. He began moaning involuntarily as he strode past Alexander's guests' bodyguards, realizing that he had their complete attention.

Shut the fuck up. How the hell am I supposed to think with you wailing like that?

Johnny shut up wailing. *What are you doing, Frank?* he asked instead, almost hysterically.

My job, so shut it!

Frank stopped the boy in front of the two Arnie clones, and made him smile broadly at them. Johnny was too scared to be able, or even want, to think about what Frank was going to do.

'Hiya guys, how's it going?' the boy boomed.

The guards just looked at him. *Bit stupid, vat-bred goons. Still, what can you expect?* Frank chuckled, for Johnny's benefit.

Johnny didn't say anything; he could feel both his hands, unbidden, reach into his jacket's pockets, and through their fake bottoms, towards the smooth, cold plastic of his hand-cannons' butts. They adjusted slightly as he grasped them, forming comfortably beneath his fingers to achieve optimum grip traction.

Here we go, now, so don't distract me . . . Before Johnny could say anything, both guns were out and he'd began firing them simultaneously into the first guard's lap. Johnny watched helplessly as the bullets ripped it apart, and the clones red, very human-like blood sprayed back at him. He felt it spatter over his face, and wanted to scream at his inability to wipe it off immediately.

He moved slightly, and turned both of the cannons on the second one. It was rising from its stool, but hadn't had enough time to level its own gun at him. The flat-tipped shells slammed into it, sending it splattering over the wall.

He then expected Frank to dive him for cover, maybe rolling and firing at the same time.

Frank didn't.

Frank just turned the boy around to face the rest of the dumbstruck bodyguards, and started shooting at them. The closest few began to drop before the first shots came back.

At the same time, Max, Dillon and Dwain opened up from the far end of the room.

Frank stopped firing with one gun and started to reload it one-handed. The other gun jammed and Johnny started screaming again.

Oh for Pete's sake . . . Shit!

A massive invisible wall of pain slammed into his chest, spinning him off his feet. Johnny watched the ceiling turn above him, and honestly thought he'd just been killed.

He rolled twice, then was back on his feet again, once more firing into the melee with a miraculously reloaded gun. His chest felt as though it were on fire, though.

See what I fuckin' mean? If you insist on distracting me while I'm working you'll only succeed in getting yourself killed. Good body armour, isn't it?

Silently, with a feeling of complete helplessness, Johnny watched as he casually strolled around the room, firing randomly at the remaining bodyguards. Max and the others had done a remarkably efficient job at pacifying most of the them before they had realised what was happening. The bodies already outnumbered the living and they were keeping the rest pinned down in a deadly crossfire.

Most of them had their backs towards him and Frank was just

leaving him standing there, picking them off one by one.

Johnny had seen real people shot before; it was sometimes on the Sat. You could get Vids of it from Africa and the Med States, and he'd seen it happen in real life once, but this was surreally more real than he could possibly have imagined.

The weird, horrific, almost implausible impact of each shell on each body ingrained itself in his mind; the terrible feeling of power the act of killing gave him, tempered by the suppressed knowledge that it wasn't actually him, both excited and appalled him.

He couldn't have spoken if he had wanted to; it was all a bit too much for him to cope with.

He didn't even make a noise when he felt something tug at his left arm.

Oops! Sorry Johnny.

'C'mon, we're wasting time. Dillon, get that door open. I'll hit the SecCams in the party to see if we've been noticed yet.' Max had stopped firing and began touching invisible buttons around his left hand, leaving Dwain and Frank to finish off the stragglers. He walked past the boy, ignoring the dead and dying bodies around him, and up to the door.

'Hey, Johnny Boy, ain't this great!' Dwain yelled, with a huge grin, almost as big as one of Dillon's, across his face.

Frank stopped the boy, and made him reload both weapons. Dwain joined him.

'Best fun I had since the transit camp clearances last spring. Shit! That was a doozy, thought mah gun was goin' ta burn my fingers off it got so hot.' Johnny could see Dwain was really getting into it.

'If you two ladies have finished gossiping . . .' Max's threat hung unfinished in the air as the boy followed Dwain over to the now open door.

Frank, I'm bleeding . . . Johnny plaintively croaked to his pilot, feeling the pain creeping along his left arm.

So? was Frank's less than helpful reply. Passing through the open door, Johnny could see Dillon had already removed the third clone from the proceedings and was standing waiting by the closed far door.

'Anyone noticed anythin', yet?' Dillon called out.

'No reaction from inside; looks like the SecCam hack's still working,' Max replied, then to all of them, 'Okay, you've all seen inside; this is how we do it. Dillon, you and Frank go down the left side, me an' Dwain'll take the right. We secure the main room, then you,' he pointed to Dillon again, 'go an' flush out the rest of the penthouse's rooms, ground upwards. You,' he pointed to Dwain, 'will clear the outside balcony, then stay with me in the main room: I don't want you outta my fuckin' sight, okay?'

Max waited until Dwain nodded an affirmation before continuing, 'And Frank,' he turned to the boy, 'you go right back to the top an' get that grey room open, then come back down, checking the rest as you go. I'll be monitoring you all on a visual when you're out of sight. All got it? Then let's go. And remember; I want this clean an' neat with no unnecessary violence!' He glowered at Dwain, before nodding to Dillon to open the door.

The four moved quickly into the main room, unnoticed by most of the guests below; the ones not dancing had their attention directed towards either the holo-display of the tower, spinning in the centre of the room, or beyond, to the tower proper.

Those standing on the balcony nearest the door the IS came through were too shocked to raise the alarm and meekly allowed themselves to be shepherded down the stairs by the men in black.

Half way down, Max located the source of the pounding music; a comparatively large Holo/Vid/Sat/Net micro system on a black slab of a marble table, next to a couple of other pieces of equipment. He gained the remaining guests' attention by unloading several rounds into it. The music immediately ceased, but somehow the holo-display visuals remained.

'This is the IS. The party is now officially over. Remain exactly where you are with your hands where they can be seen,' Max shouted, reaching the bottom of the stairs.

'Freeze, fuck face! You heard the man!' Dwain moved past Max towards the balcony doors, his attention on a large man still turning around. The man was reaching into his jacket pocket.

'DROP THAT FUCKIN' GUN, MOTHER!' Dwain shouted, leaping forward and whipping the barrel of his gun across the bridge of the man's face. The large man dropped to his knees, holding his face in his hands, the packet of cigarettes he'd just pulled from his pocket fell beside him.

'Do the balcony, Dwain,' Max said calmly, then to the unwilling audience, 'Okay, you get the idea now, I hope. Do exactly what we say, when we say it, and everything will be alright. Fuck up and you get hurt! Now, all of you, drop all your hardware where you're standing and move slowly over there.' He motioned with his gun towards the raised centre of the room and the quietly spinning hologram of the roof top.

Johnny watched Dwain disappear onto the balcony before Frank made him follow Dillon into the interior of the penthouse, past the shocked-looking caterers.

'Get the fuck over there!' he unwillingly barked at them, pointing behind him, towards Max. Johnny heard his ComLink buzz, and Dillon's voice followed.

'More cooks an' a guard comin' out, Frank. They're scanned as unarmed.'

As if on cue, half a dozen white-dressed men and women shuffled nervously into the big room. As they passed, Frank had the boy grab the last caterer by the collar of his smock, 'Nah, not you, or you,' he pointed at the Arnie guard in the tuxedo, 'I've got a little job for you both. Come with me.'

The man looked terrified and stared at him, questioningly.

What're you doing, Frank? Johnny asked. He didn't like the way

Killing

Frank was making him smile at the man. Frank didn't answer, just chuckled. The ComLink buzzed.

'What're you doing, Frank?' This time it was Max who asked the question.

Frank decided to answer Max, 'I'll need the guard to open the door, save me blasting it.'

'What about the cook?'

'Little bit of insurance, Maxie, just a little bit of insurance; I've no idea what's in this room and I want someone in front of me, okay?' Johnny heard Max grunt an affirmative, then pulled the caterer towards the internal lift and stairs, underneath the balconies. The lift door was open already, so they just stepped in.

'Top,' Frank had Johnny curtly bark at the lift's ice, and let go of the caterer. The caterer briefly looked at Johnny, then just stared nervously at the floor, visibly shaking. Johnny felt sorry for the man. He had a great deal of empathy for his situation but was also, he was ashamed to admit, quite relieved that Frank was taking protection of his body seriously. He was still a bit upset that Frank wasn't looking at his arm to see how badly he'd been shot.

The Arnie guard looked impassive and unconcerned, but Johnny wasn't convinced.

Just before the doors opened, Frank made the boy pull the caterer in front of him and as they opened, pushed him out first. The man stumbled a couple of feet then stopped and gazed sheepishly around, his shoulders hunched and hands covering his groin. Nothing happened to him. Frank pushed the guard from the lift, made the boy follow. Grabbing the caterer by the arm, they turned left and started to move carefully down the passageway. Johnny watched as a thermal scan sliced over his vision, the words NO PERSONS appearing in mid air briefly, followed by a quick stream of other "NO's", like aerial bombs, laser trips and the like.

Seems we're okay, at least until we open this door, Frank mumbled.

'You,' the boy pointed to the guard standing nervously behind him, 'open it.' He pointed to the door at the end of the corridor.

An Idol

'I, er . . . can't . . . er, sir,' the guard answered haltingly.

'Why not?' Johnny could feel Frank getting impatient.

'Mr. Alexander's the only person with the right chipset, sir.'

'Why didn't you tell me that before, stupid?' The boy shook his head at the man, as if he were an errant child.

Now, I wonder where the door's optic cables would run to? Johnny decided Frank was talking to himself, and remained quiet. He felt Frank reach onto his utility belt and snag a heavy baton-shaped thing. The boy offered it to the guard, 'Do you know what this is?' he asked the man.

'Er, yeah. Las cutter.'

'Clever boy. Do you think you could find the optic cables and cut them; they'll be somewhere around the door.' The boy asked the question in a friendly, conversational, manner.

'Er, yeah, sure.' The guard looked at the tool, 'You want me to try?' he offered.

'Wadda you fucking well think?' the boy screamed.

Max stood one side of the group of guests, guards and caterers, with Dwain on the other, next to a large pile of confiscated weapons. There were already over a hundred assembled and Dillon was still sending them more guests and "staff" from the penthouse's smaller rooms. Max watched Dillon's progress through the first floor in a virtual frame in front of him. Dillon was scanning each room using the penthouse's SecCam system and a thermal imager, in case anyone was hiding, then flushing them out and sending them down. Max was also watching Frank's attempts to get the shielded room on the top floor open, in another virtual frame beside Dillon's. Frank was about halfway down the corridor, watching, over the shoulder of the fat caterer, the security guard slicing chunks out of the wall around the door at the end. Max's ComLink beeped, it was Dillon.

'A couple more comin' down, Max. And they're certainly unarmed.'

Killing

Max turned towards the balconies and watched as a naked couple shuffled out to join the others. One of the couple was a young boy, perhaps no more than fourteen; the other was an older and much fatter man, maybe somewhere in his forties or fifties.

'Sick fuck!' Dwain called out.

The naked man walked directly over to Max, attempting to pretend his nakedness was immaterial and didn't affect his own stature and personal power.

'You! Are you in charge of this gross infringement of my personal rights? Have you any idea who you're dealing with? Do you know who I am?'

Max recognised the man as a relatively well-known Conservative politician and absently motioned with his left hand, turning off the virtual frames in front of him; he'd always found them distracting, the way they moved as you moved, only slower. He found it difficult to work when they were turned on. He then turned to face the man, removing his thick goggles.

'Whoever you are is immaterial!' He stepped nearer to the man and jerked his head forward, butting the naked man squarely on the bridge of his nose.

The politician dropped to his knees and briefly swayed like a drunk, before falling onto his face.

Max looked up, putting his glasses back on. 'I will not tolerate any dissent from anyone else. The next person so much as speaks without being spoken to will get an extra orifice. This is an IS matter and we are their representatives: you will do whatever we tell you. Understand?'

No one answered him directly, but Max could see from their faces that they believed him. He opened his mouth, about to add something else, when a loud explosion thundered above their heads. They all looked up, then ducked as debris sprayed over the main room.

Dillon pressed himself against the wall and buzzed Max, 'What's occurrin', Boss Man?'

'Dunno, it's Frank, but I've lost the visual so I dunno what the score is. Are you finished yet?'

'Nah, man. One more corridor before this floor's clear, and one to go. You want me to leave it an' check on the bang?'

Max paused a moment before answering, 'No. Continue your sweep. I'll check the situation, Dwain'll keep 'em quiet down here.'

Dillon clicked off and peered over the balcony. There was a load of burned rubbish strewn all over the big room and a couple of the guests seemed to have been injured by falling pieces of building, but otherwise nothing had changed.

He looked up and saw that the top balcony just above him was charred around the edges. Grinning, he activated his virtual controls, and sliced a therm-reading over his visuals and moved away from the balcony.

Two more rooms.

The first scanned empty on both visual and thermal, so he moved down the corridor, switching to the second.

Its Cam was out but he was getting a thermal of a figure standing by the door. He stopped, to consider the options for a moment, then walked directly up to the door.

Dillon squared up in front of it and holding his cannon in one hand, reached for the door handle with the other. The door opened before he even touched the handle. He had just enough time to realise that the figure that had opened the door, standing in front of him, was himself, before his gun was pulled from his loose, one-handed grasp.

A fraction of a second later, he was unconscious.

Max decided to take the stairs up to the sealed room. Or whatever was left of it. He decided stepping out of the lift without knowing who, or what, was left up there was a very bad idea and that the stairs would be a better option.

He bleeped Dwain after the first corner, 'Dwain, keep an eye on me. I'm going up the stairs.'

A small indicator appeared in the corner of his vision, indicating Dwain was jacked into his visuals.

He moved up the stairs, carefully but rapidly. He checked the first landing: nothing. Up again.

As he reached the second landing a door opened at the end of the corridor on his left. Max flattened against the wall, raising his gun. The figure stepped away from the door into the light, and Max relaxed. It was Dillon. Max's ComLink beeped.

'No one here, Boss Man. You want me to check upstairs?'

'No, you go down and make sure Dwain's behaving himself,' Max answered; then, 'You get this, Dwain?'

Downstairs, Dwain nodded. Then he remembered Max wasn't watching and answered, 'Yeah, sure, I heard. Tell him not to rush 'cause I certainly don't need no help lookin' after these people.'

'See you in a minute, Dillon. And call Control for backup, I don't like the way this is going.' Max waved briefly to the approaching figure, then continued his ascent. The soot-stained walls began after the next floor and Max had to be careful not to stumble on any of the fragments from the explosion.

The devastation on the top balcony made it difficult for him to see what exactly had happened at first. He couldn't see the gaping hole at the far end of the corridor where the door used to be, or the room beyond; it was all obscured by the watery haze of the penthouse's sprinkler system. Covering the walls and the floor around him, and stuck to the remains of the balcony wall behind him, were burnt lumps that, on closer examination, seemed to be some sort of meat.

Someone had obviously been very close to the explosion.

The first thing he really saw was halfway along the corridor, covered in assorted debris; a blackened corpse was spread across the floor.

As he got nearer to the body he could see the end of the corridor and the twisted room beyond. Burnt black and dripping with water, it was totally gutted, its contents shattered, giving no indication of its former use.

'You seein' this, Dillon? Shit!' He moved down the corridor, 'Frank, where are you?' advancing slowly. He paused for a moment and the obviously dead figure on the floor stirred slightly.

'Frank?' Max asked, almost dumbfounded as the corpse moved again. Still with his cannon trained on the far door, he went over to the prone figure.

The corpse was twitching, so Max bent down, dropped his gun and began to shift the largest pieces of debris.

Once cleared, he could see, from its size alone, that the body belonged to the caterer and was quite dead; the source of the movement came from beneath. Max, with an effort, flipped the body over to expose a barely conscious Johnny beneath. Max whistled then traced the wires from Johnny's head down to his ice and Frank's booster unit.

'Fuck, look at the state of him. Frank, what's happening? Talk to me.' Max found his own answer: Johnny had landed on his ice, smashing Frank's box into pieces, destroying the amplifier inside. Without it, Frank was stuck back at the academy, no use to anyone any more because he wasn't linked with Johnny's body.

Why he hadn't called back on normal channels and told Max that what had happened was matter for concern, though.

Max was also beginning to wonder why Control hadn't been in contact since the explosion, so picked his cannon up and touched the virtual activator on its butt, deciding to call in, when the shooting started.

The girl waited until the IS man reached for the handle of the door before swinging it open. His immediate expression indicated that the Smart Mesh woven throughout the fabric she was wearing was working well enough.

She grabbed the muzzle of his large gun with her right hand, easily twisting it from his loose grip, while she rammed the palm of her left hand into his stunned face.

The IS man was still dropping to his knees when she swung the stolen gun back towards him, cracking its stock down solidly onto his exposed skull.

Dillon slumped forward onto his face.

The girl tossed his gun into the bathroom behind her then quickly bent down and pulled his glasses off. She raised and touched them to the green glasses she wore. Her glasses made a slight, almost inaudible, bleep, then the words DOWNLOADING COMPLETED hung briefly in the air in front of her.

She threw his glasses away; the information and codes they had contained had been reloaded onto her own ice so she was now linked to the IS system itself and directly to the other IS operatives at the party. When they accessed 'Dillon', they'd get her instead.

She dragged the unconscious man into the bathroom and closed the door with her foot. Leaving him leaning against the toilet, she picked up her own gun and shot him in the face with a short burst of flachettes.

Dillon's head collapsed back in on itself as its contents fanned the wall behind him and his body went into spasms.

An Idol

The girl turned and looked at herself in the mirror; standing there was the large black man in a leather jacket holding a gun. She reached up to take the glasses off, and watched the black man do the same. As she took them off, he disappeared, leaving another reflection behind; a young girl in a shimmering gore spattered outfit holding a gun.

She started giggling and put the glasses back on.

The girl picked up his IS-issue cannon and thumbed the Virtual activator on its butt. Her fingers moved phantom keys for a few seconds as a window popped up before her.

It identified itself as Max's view, and he was walking up the stairs.

The girl turned the light off, and stepped out of the bathroom to meet him. As she closed the door, she could see Max watching Dillon close the door in the virtual image hanging in the air before her; the mesh of her clothes fooling Max's digitized vision.

She switched off his view as she turned to face him.

'No one here, Boss Man. You want me to check upstairs?' She spoke quietly, so only the small mic built into her jacket's hood heard her voice directly; Max was too far away. Her ice replayed her words through a sample of Dillon's voice, taken from the SecCam system earlier, then sent it to Max through the IS ComLink. She started walking towards him.

'No, you go down and make sure Dwain's behaving himself. You get this, Dwain?'

'Yeah, sure, I heard. Tell him not to rush 'cause I certainly don't need no help lookin' after these people,' Dwain answered from below.

'See you in a minute, Dillon. And call Control for backup, I don't like the way this is going.' Max waved briefly and was gone before the girl reached him.

She started briskly down the stairs, in the opposite direction.

Dwain sat in a large egg-shaped chair on a raised section of floor, with his back towards the balconies, watching his charges to ensure they didn't get up to any mischief, so he didn't notice the girl as she walked into the room. His cannon was resting on his knee, its muzzle pointing roughly between the two groups standing in front of him. One group, the larger of the two, contained the guests and bodyguards; they were standing on the largest raised dance floor.

All the bodyguards were standing around the edge of it, between Dwain and their employees.

The smaller group, on a lesser raised area to one side, consisted mainly of the catering staff and various other lackeys.

Both groups were facing Dwain, so they all saw someone enter the room. Those with Digi shades on, like most of the bodyguards, or those who were still wearing their image enhancers, saw the big black IS assassin stroll casually into the room.

The others, those who weren't wearing anything to digitize their vision, saw a young girl in a dayglo green outfit carrying a large gun walk into the room.

Dwain turned around to see what all the fuss was about. He saw Dillon standing there, an odd expression on his face.

'What's up?' he asked.

He watched Dillon grin, and aim the assault-cannon he was holding at the larger, more influential group of captives.

'What the fu–'

Dwain didn't finish his sentence, his voice died in his throat as the silent laser beam from Dillon's weapon cut through the bodyguards and into the guests behind them.

Open-mouthed, he sat transfixed, watching as the gun swung around at him, only just sprawling from the chair and out of the way of the deadly light, at the very last second. The chair fragmented behind him, spraying him with splinter shrapnel as he fell into a small cushioned recess in the floor.

Dwain lay there for a second, then spun around, drawing his hand-cannon; he'd lost his own larger weapon already. Aiming at Dillon's retreating figure, he caught a movement out of the corner of his eye; the bodyguards and some of the guests, those not hit by the laser arc, had reached their own discarded weapons pile and were rearming.

Once more, Dwain threw himself out of the way just in time. The first of their shots ripped into the cushions around him as he leapt. His roll took him behind a metal couch and he began returning fire from underneath it immediately, first aiming at legs, then the bodies as they fell.

His gun gave the fifty rounds left warning and he readied the new clip. The gun clicked out and he replaced the ammunition as he rolled away from the couch, then he was back on his feet, firing again.

He moved right, towards the outside balcony, using the raised sections of floor as cover, shooting as he went, and attempting to keep the group of panicking caterers between him and the now heavily armed former captives.

He tried to shoot between them but was only partially successful. The guests shooting back at him were even less accurate and the remaining caterers were soon chewed up by the crossfire. Halfway to the balcony, Dwain ducked behind a large treelike art installation and began to reload again.

'Dwain, what the fuck are you playing at?' Max was screaming at him through the ComLink, as the installation above him split apart and he threw himself onto his face.

When he uncovered his head, he realised that someone else was now firing at the guests again. They had stopped firing at him and begun running for cover or returning fire, or both.

Dwain stuck his head out from behind the wreckage and peered out, as if unable to decide whether to help Dillon or shoot him. Bloody bodies were everywhere and gunfire, smoke and screams filled the room.

'It's Dillon. He's gone loco. He was the one who started it, not me!' Dwain started to scream at Max, 'He lasered them an' then started shootin' at me. Shit! . . .' The laser swung towards him again. He dived back the way he'd come, sprawling across the slick floor and underneath the heavily dented metal couch.

He saw his own laser-cannon lying to one side of the wrecked egg chair, ten metres to his left. He went for it. Dillon's assault-cannon disintegrated the couch behind him, then started chewing up the floor as it followed him across the room. Then he had his big gun again; he turned and returned fire.

The heavy bark of the large bore weapon tore apart the first floor balcony, but Dillon wasn't there any more. Dwain spun around, legs firmly astride, and started shooting at the remaining guests, first still using the heavy point armalites the gun carried then the laser attachment.

Max heard the shooting start.

'Shit, Dwain's gone insane . . .' he said to himself, trying to contact Control. A virtual window appeared in front of him but instead of the face of Control, there was just static. No message either. Max was momentarily at a loss for what to do. He shut the window down. Someone was still firing and he could hear screaming.

He jacked into Dwain's field, just in time to see him firing at some caterers jumping around in front of him. He jacked back out and thumbed his ComLink.

'Dillon, what's going on?' he asked urgently, jacking into Dillon's vision field. He could see he was on one of the balconies and he was watching Dwain below killing the guests.

The raised dance floor and area around it was strewn with bodies and slick with the blood of the dying. Max saw that some of the guests were now armed and attempting to defend themselves.

'The guests have temporarily rearmed themselves, Boss Man, but as you can see, Dwain's coping with it,' he heard Dillon say sarcastically.

'How the fuck did all that happen?'

'Dunno, ask Dwain. He obviously couldn't control them. I jus' walked in an' people started shootin' at me!' Dillon sounded aggrieved.

An Idol

Max shut off Dillon's vision field and jacked back to Dwain.

'Dwain, what the fuck are you playing at?' Max yelled into his ComLink. Dwain didn't answer and after a brief bit of movement, he couldn't see anything at all.

The forgotten figure beside Max moaned and moved again. Max looked down at the boy's body; it was difficult to tell how badly hurt Johnny was because he was covered with blood and other, more solid, bits of the caterer.

Max turned off his window of Dwain's blank view and bent down. He grasped the boy by the lapels of his coat then pulled him to his feet. Johnny's broken IS glasses fell to the floor.

'It's Dillon. He's gone loco. He was the one who started it, not me! He lasered them an' then started shootin' at me. Shit! . . .' Dwain's voice broke off as suddenly as it started.

Johnny momentarily gained full consciousness, or at least enough to realise he was hurt and cry out in pain, then slumped against the old assassin. Max looked down and noticed a bone sticking out of Johnny's leg. He wasn't sure whether it was one of the boy's or one of the caterers. He hoisted the unconscious figure onto his shoulder then started back down the passageway, towards the shooting.

Max awkwardly jacked back to Dillon, in time to see Dwain in the room below turn and aim the assault-cannon at him. Max watched as Dillon threw himself backwards and the ceiling above him disintegrated. He switched off again.

The lift doors opened and Max walked out, carrying Johnny on his left shoulder, his gun held firmly in his right hand. He walked out into the large room and stared at the carnage before him. Dwain was standing in the middle of the wrecked room with a hologram of the Ministry of Truth tower spinning around behind him. He was taking casual shots at the balconies above, although no one was firing back.

Around him, lying on the floor, draped brokenly over the

furniture or splattered all over the walls, were the guests, bodyguards and caterers. Dwain was the only person in the room who was visibly still alive.

'Watch it, he's up there, somewhere . . .' Dwain motioned them to stay back, not taking his eyes away from the balconies above. Max ignored his gesture and continued into the room. He dropped the unconscious boy onto the nearest couch, walked straight up to Dwain and punched him in the face. Dwain staggered backwards, dropping the large cannon, the expression on his face one of shock rather than pain.

'Waddayadothatfor?' he blurted.

'Dillon couldn't have shot the fucking place up, you idiot.' Max stepped up to Dwain, and punched him again. Dwain fell over this time.

''Cause he's a sealed unit, totally wired up with inhibitors; he's programmed so he can only follow orders and no one fuckin' ordered this!' Max spat. Dwain opened his mouth to say something but Max got in first.

'I've had enough of your fuckin' gung-ho redneck shit to last me a fuckin' lifetime, you little arsehole, so . . .'

Dwain began to scramble to his feet, arguing back as he did so. 'So what are you– ' he began.

Max raised the hand-cannon he still held and grabbed Dwain by the collar at the same time. He pushed the muzzle of the gun into the protesting man's mouth and pulled the trigger.

The girl watched Max let go of the headless body and it slumped to the ground. She waited for him to turn around before stepping out of the shadows. He looked up and, seeing Dillon, shrugged.

'He was totally unstable, I can't work with people like that.' He shrugged again. 'Did you get through to Control? I seem to be cut off, or something,' he asked, activating his link.

'It won't do any good, Max,' she answered, 'You lost real contact with your keepers as soon as you entered the penthouse. Your glasses' emissions are being, ere, slightly adjusted before they're allowed to escape the field around this place.

'They think they're seeing what's going on but we both know how easy it is to create a totally different reality, don't we?' Max slowly turned to face the big black man, as the girl continued.

'Of course, there are other people watching a more accurate version of what's going on in here, like the Net and Sat companies who're hacking directly into the penthouse's SecCam system on our tip off. So I suppose someone at IS'll notice eventually, if they haven't already, but we've removed all the sound anyway, so there's no way you can tell anyone what's really happening.'

The instant Max's right arm twitched, she sliced him in two with the laser.

Johnny saw a big bright flash, then everything went first red, then deepest black.

Some time later he woke, but only briefly and in great pain.

The next time he woke, things were spinning and merging, past and present entwined in some great mockery of reality; a face, a name . . . mine? No, not important. Another name? Mine! Sort of . . . once, anyway. Dropping, sinking, away . . . from What? Not sure . . . it couldn't be important Crashing! real! The flash? no . . . later . . . Someone else that name? controlling me. Me? . . . The caterer who? . . . The ring spun a long way down . . . where's my board gone? I'll need it, this far up . . . Still rising again, weightless, free, just rising . . . MORE PAIN! . . and once again, darkness.

But not quite; there's something else with him, in the darkness. It's clean and edited and hard, like film, but distorted and extreme, like a dream; but not really as numb or unknowable as that.

It's a memory. A recent memory.

Back in the driving seat of the big black van, heading towards the Ring on auto.

When?

heading towards the Ring on auto today. It's today, and you're

Killing

in the IS now, remember? You've got a job to do.

What job?

you've got a job to do, and a big gun to do it with.

Who've I got to shoot?

a picture, in the air. A voice, from a girl next to it, saying, "Do you know who this man is?"

Yes! Yes, it's Vee! I know who he is! Bastard! Smug self-centred, rich and successful bastard. Is this who I've to shoot? YES! YES! YES! Oh joy!

you're leaping out of your seat, shouting. You hit your arms on the cramped cockpit roof. Some people are laughing at you, remember?

I . . . Yes. I remember

'Yes! We're gonna waste him!' Johnny exclaimed jubilantly. His fist hit the roof of the vehicle, jarring him back to his present reality. He glanced nervously around and saw Max staring at him in disbelief.

'Sit down now!' Max barked, totally grim faced. Someone behind him began laughing.

Control swam in front of his vision as he turned his head from side to side; she didn't look happy. He sat back down, and her face zoomed closer to his, her ice-generated eyes boring holes through him.

'Whatever you'll be doing tonight, which fortunately won't be much on your own, you certainly will not be shooting Vee!' Control sounded almost as angry as Max looked, and Johnny felt himself turn a deep crimson. He was also confused. What the hell were Government assassins going to be doing, then, if not assassinating Vee?

Control continued talking, directly to him it seemed, as if he were a small child or an errant puppy, 'In actual fact, your mission is the total opposite; your task is to preserve the life of Empti Vee at all costs!'

An Idol

Johnny slumped in his seat, wishing it would just open up beneath him and let him drop out of the vehicle and escape the steady gaze that bored into him. He listened disconsolately to the rest of the briefing.

'Our analysis of the current sociopolitical situation surrounding Vee indicates that his untimely death at the event staged tonight would cause a massive, OVERDRIVE-induced, civil uprising by approximately 30% of the City's population.

'This is only an estimate, based on the loose premise that most people watching will not be under the influence of the drug. Some sources suggest the figure could be much higher, up to 60% even.

'The extent of the damage caused by an uprising of even 30% is not accurately calculable; there are too many variables to consider, such as the initial strength of the drug, how long the drug's cerebral impact lasts, and so on. However, ice-generated models indicate that, at best, we'd be in for a week of total, completely uncontrollable chaos that would level a fair proportion of the City, at an incalculable cost. It would take decades to sort out and leave the City well and truly in the Third World.

'The worst scenario is that Vee's death tonight would cause the total collapse of our present society and with it the City and the Government and Corporations. We'd all be back in the Stone Age, almost literally.

'What effect Vee's assassination would have on a global level is anyone's guess. The world audience of tonight's concert is massive due to the free access Vee's media network is providing, and recent reports suggest that the OVERDRIVE problem experienced by other states is nearly as acute as ours. Every other country could find themselves in the same situation as us. So, as a nation, we wouldn't be too popular if we let Vee get so much as a scratch on him.

'Our Government and the Corporations are nervous and looking towards us at IS to sort it out. If we can continue infiltrating the One Tribe with our own undercover operatives we feel that we will be in a position to terminate Vee in a matter of months and be able to control and channel any subsequent fallout.

'Your job tonight, gentlemen, is to keep him alive until that time; certainly until he's finished giving his last public performance and everyone's gone home.'

Johnny sat there, open-mouthed; he didn't know how to react.

'Who are we protecting him from? Do we know, yet?' asked Max, professionally.

'Bet it's the fuckin' black Muslim fundamentalists again . . .' Johnny heard Dwain mutter in the back.

Control smiled before answering, 'Apparently, this time it's going to be the One Tribe,' Control paused, as if for effect, 'on the orders of Vee himself.'

Johnny's mouth gaped. He wasn't sure whether he had heard that properly, but didn't want to ask Control to repeat it.

'He fuckin' what?' Max had no qualms about asking.

'You heard correctly, Max. Vee, personally, has ordered his own assassination.

'It seems he believes he's going to be able to come back from the dead and lead the uprising his death caused, or something like that. IS psychologists believe he's quite insane, of course, but there are an unfortunately large number of gullible people out there who don't. You all know what your job is now. So go and do it.' Control and the virtual window disappeared, along with the memory.

Johnny opened his eyes in time to see a figure in green, standing in front of him. Her face was obscured by the hood of her coat, a veil and a large pair of green goggles underneath, but the gun she held, a large IS issue assault-cannon, was in full view. She shot a laser bolt at something behind him then turned her back on him and faced Edge Central through the rain and shattered window wall.

He stared numbly at her for a moment then reached slowly for one of his holsters, praying silently to himself that his gun would still be there and that his arm worked. It was, and it did. He slowly inched the cannon out of its clip and tried to sit upright. The effort was too much and he slumped back again.

What the fuck are you doing? he asked himself. He'd never killed anyone before, not until today anyway, and that didn't count; that was Frank's doing.

But the girl was going to kill Vee.

Let her. You wanted to kill him, anyway!

But what about what Control had said? Vee wants to be killed, and if he is, there'll be nothing left afterwards. Johnny didn't want it all to end. Sure, the City was crap, but it could be fun as well. And Vee wants to stop it all in its tracks . . .

Johnny raised the hand-cannon unsteadily and aimed towards her stationary figure. She still had her back to him and was staring out of the window towards the tower in the distance. Johnny took a deep breath, not sure whether he was doing this to save the City or just to get his own back on Vee . . . and fired. The gun jerked awkwardly in his hand and he dropped it.

Blood swam in Johnny's vision. He felt nauseous again and slumped back on the couch, breathing heavily. He shut his eyes, holding them tightly closed, trying to convince them to focus properly.

After several seconds he opened them again. The girl was standing in front of him, leaning on the large IS cannon. He'd missed. She was pointing a smaller handgun at him. Johnny thought about the gun he'd dropped, but only briefly. He gulped, closed his eyes again and waited for the inevitable to happen.

It didn't, but something else did.

'Nice shooting, Speed,' he heard her say.

He opened his eyes and looked at her. He hadn't missed; she was bleeding from just above the left knee, red staining and dulling the luminosity of her trousers as it seeped downwards.

'You nearly spoilt everything!' she laughed.

Johnny stared at her. He was too drained to even beg for his life, or realise she'd used his surf name and that he recognized her voice. He just watched as she slowly reached for the zip of her jacket, opened the hood and pushed up the veil and glasses just enough for him to see her face. His erratic heart missed a beat and he started to rise out of the couch, forgetting his injured leg.

'Mary! I . . . what . . . ARGH!' He fell forward onto his face in front of the couch as his leg gave away. He somehow managed to keep his eyes fixed on her smiling face.

'I know, I know, reunions can sometimes be quite painful experiences. I mean, look!' The girl motioned absently towards her bloodied leg, 'Still, where would we be without these little surprises? You look a little surprised, I must say.'

Johnny was still lying on the floor, staring at her, transfixed, his mouth hanging open. 'I, er . . . sorry, I didn't realise . . .'

The girl continued, 'Not as surprised as me, though. I really didn't expect any of this to happen. Still, I suppose I might as well make the most of it.' She reached into one of the jacket's pockets and pulled out a thin coil of cable, with sockets at either end. She threw one end to Johnny, keeping hold of the other, 'Plug that in, over there.' She nodded towards the penthouse's ice terminal unit next to the shattered sound system.

'I . . . um, Mary, er . . . my leg . . .' Johnny stuttered. 'I can't walk,' he added plaintively.

'Then crawl, you little shit, before I change my mind and waste you, here and now!' The girl screamed and fired the small hand-cannon at the ground, inches away from Johnny's face. The boy recoiled as the wooden floor splintered up at him. His self preservation instinct kicked in and he hurriedly snatched up the end of the cable she'd thrown him.

'Hurry up!' she added, pushing the hand-cannon back into her jacket. She balanced herself on one leg then raised the larger cannon, twisted it over and started unfolding its inbuilt tripod.

Johnny began dragging himself along the floor, trying to keep his weight on his left side, away from his injured and throbbing right leg. Each time he moved, the pain exploded afresh in his mind. His vision began to blur after only a few metres, and he paused.

An Idol

'I don't understand . . .' he croaked, and his voice faltered. He tried again but louder, 'I don't understand why?' He turned to face her, questioningly, trying to ignore the slick of blood he was leaving on the floor behind him and the shattered corpses around him.

'Why what? Why you're being made to crawl? I guess I like making people do things, especially if they don't want to,' she giggled, not bothering to look up from the gun she was adjusting.

'No, I mean why . . . shit, I mean I can't believe you're the one who's going to kill him. You always fancied him, I mean, but . . . I, er, how the fuck is it you, anyway? . . . What're you doing here?' Johnny was confused; there were so many questions hurtling around his head, he didn't know what to ask first.

She looked up and barked, 'Keep crawling, arsehole!' The cannon now had a spindly tripod underneath it and she was resting nonchalantly on it, fiddling with the end of the cable she still held.

Johnny turned reluctantly, and started towards the black slab table again, clutching the other end of the thin cable in his mouth. He had to use both hands to crawl over a cluster of bodies that were in his path. He tried not to put his hands in any of their open wounds or touch their now external internal organs, but it was inescapable.

'You're obviously not thinking straight, Speed,' he heard her say behind him. There was an edge to her voice he'd never noticed before and it really worried him. 'But apparently thinking was never your strong point, was it? Just plug the cable in like a good little boy, willya? And then shut up. I've got someone important to kill.'

Johnny finally crawled to the table, through a small lake of blood several inches deep, and pulled himself into a sitting position. He took the cable from his mouth, looked at the socket pin and then the black boxes in front of him. The sound system was shattered, so he pushed it backwards, away from the others. The box next to it had several sockets on the front but these were for smaller pins and try as he might, the pin he held wouldn't go in. He glanced at the next box; it didn't have any visible sockets at all.

Killing

'Turn the fucking thing around, stupid!'

He grasped the second box quickly, spinning it around on its rubber mounts; there was a big socket at the back with a cable already in it. He pulled it out and tried inserting the one he held. The pin slipped easily but firmly in and the thin cable lit up a luminous green.

'About fucking time.'

Johnny turned around, using the table to keep him in an upright position, and watched as the girl pushed the pin on her end of the cable into the side of her own neck. Johnny's hand involuntarily reached up and touched the dead cables hanging from his own neck, realization dawning.

'Who are you?' he asked, as the girl squinted down the sight of the gun.

'Can't you guess?' she answered.

Vee! The girl saw the boy slumped on the couch twitch, and his eyelids flutter.

Shut up, willya. I can't concentrate with your continual distractions. She felt herself, unbidden, press the trigger of the large cannon again, felt its slight recoil on her right shoulder and watched as she killed yet another person, took another life. So easily done.

But Vee . . . she tried again. She couldn't believe what she was seeing. Now, on top of everything else, this had happened.

He turned her around and walked over towards the outside balcony. *Look, it's nearly over. I'll give you your fucking body back soon, okay? Just don't distract me any more; this next bit'll be a bit tricky.*

But . . . There was the sound of a small explosion behind her, then sudden pain in her right leg. She screamed and watched as her body fell.

What the fuck? she heard Vee swear, as he spun her quickly to her feet.

I tried to tell you but you wouldn't listen!

Yeah? Well I've heard now! I'll sort it out, alright? He sounded mad and she felt herself reaching for the hand-cannon as he made her stand.

No! Mary screamed, *Don't! It's Speed. Please don't kill him, please, please, please . . .* She started sobbing uncontrollably as he levelled the gun she held at the prone figure. Johnny looked as if he'd passed out again.

What? She felt Vee pause.

Speed! It's Speed. Johnny. My Ex. I've told you about him – the surfer. Mary was frantic and began mentally struggling to regain control of her own body.

What's he fucking well doing here? Vee screamed at her, incredulously.

How the fuck should I know? Mary yelled back, *You're the one that planned tonight down to the last detail, remember? I'm just along for the fucking ride!*

Johnny's eyes flickered and opened.

I got one of the hackers to change his ID card; so he'd get in trouble with the law. I don't know how . . . she continued.

Yeah, yeah. I know that. You haven't done anything that I don't know about. Little shit must have been sectioned and drafted and somehow ended up here tonight! Well, I've always said that coincidences and shit always happen when you least expect them. She felt him shrug her shoulders, *Well say goodbye to him . . .*

The boy cowered away from the outstretched gun, pushing himself farther back into the couch. She felt her finger tightening on the trigger.

NO! DON'T! He's innocent! Nothing to do with any of this. You don't have to kill him . . . PLEASE . . . Let me have him.

'Nice shooting, Speed,' she felt herself say.

No one is totally innocent, Mary. You should know that by now. Just by being alive he's part of the problem. But I'll leave him for you, if that's what you really want, 'cause it ain't really his fault he's here; that's down to you so it's kinda right you should choose . . . Although I don't know what good a crippled surfer's going to do you after tonight. Fuck, he's just shot you . . . Are you sure you don't want me to waste him right now?

No, I want him.

Well, shut up and don't distract me, and I'll consider it.

'You nearly spoilt everything!' Vee made her giggle.

'Why are you going to kill yourself? I don't understand what good it'll do you, you won't be around to benefit. And why Mary . . ?' Mary quietly noted that Johnny had adopted his "superior" tone, the one he used when he was unsure of himself but still believed himself right.

'You are only alive because of a strange quirk of fate and the pleadings of a certain young lady, so don't push it, arsehole,' Vee made the girl say sweetly. Then in a more businesslike tone, 'The fact you understand so little is hardly surprising. And there's a lot to understand, so I doubt I'll have time to explain everything. For a start, I'm not thinking of myself, but the planet; it'll be a lot better off with less humans on it. And you're wrong, 'cause I will be around to see it. What else do you want to know? Why Mary, who you've just plugged into the mains? Well, it was a kind of a whim and a bit of an irreligious pun, really. I needed someone, she turned up, and I decided she'd do. The reason I needed someone else is simple: I've got to be somewhere else tonight but wanted to be here as well. I've had you plug her in 'cause one of us has to be plugged in at any one time to run the circuit. You see, me an' Mary are two halves of a closed loop at the moment I've been plugged in while she's been wandering around over here, under my complete control of course. Now I've got a few things to do with my own body, so she's plugged in so no one else realises what's going on. Was that simple enough for you?'

Mary looked at Johnny's baffled expression and would have shaken her head if she could.

Vee continued through her, 'Obviously not. Do you know what'll happen if I die horribly in front of all those people tonight?'

Johnny nodded, 'Uh . . . yeah, I think . . .'

'Good. Now, Mary, as you can see, is wearing some funky clothes. These clothes are made of SmartMesh and can fool any digitized image capturing equipment into seeing something else. So whoever is watching tonight's performance through the SecCams in here is going to see . . . Yeah, you got it! A large IS operative shooting the shit out of a party of rich dudes then blowing away yours truly. And, naturally, all on behalf of the Government.'

Tell him the best part, go on . . . Mary prompted. She felt herself swallow.

'But the best part is I'm not going to die. My body's fucked anyway; too many drugs and too much sun and poisoned food. And even if it wasn't, this planet of our isn't able to support human life any more. My soul, for want of a better word, is, as we speak, being digitized and captured on a multi-layered piece of software. All that's left is for me to cut the body out from underneath it. With no psychological umbilical cord holding me, I can escape, via the delightful Mary, into the Net to watch the chaos unfold.' Vee paused, then giggled out loud, adding, 'I might even lend a helping hand.'

'I . . . uh, don't understand . . . how . . .'

'We've both had some hardware installed, me and Mary. It's a bit like yours, but not as old. It's all internal, including the boosters. Mary's got some of it inside her: I've got the rest. I've been controlling her all night, sitting in a little room on the top of my tower. And she, like you, has just been along for the ride. Now the stage is set, I'm going to walk out into the open and make her shoot me. As she does, the hardware inside me will bounce the remaining pieces of the jigsaw of me directly to a receiver inside her. I'll all be in her then. But I don't want to stay there. I mean, what's the point in exchanging one piece of dead meat for another? The future, for however long that is, is going to be digital. And guess who's going to be there first?'

Killing

Johnny sat there, oblivious to the pain in his shattered body, and stared at the man inside the girl. He didn't know what to say, although it was obvious the IS psychologists were right: Vee was completely insane.

'Now you just sit there quietly, okay?' she asked, bending over the gun, one leg raised delicately off the floor. *And that goes for you, too*, Vee added to Mary.

Johnny sat, transfixed. Behind the girl he could see the spinning hologram of the Ministry of Truth. At first he thought it was on fire, but then he noticed that there were figures moving around on the top. They were shrouded by dry ice, which he had mistaken for smoke, and pulsing red and yellow strobe lighting that he had mistaken for the flames.

The only object totally visible was an old fashioned microphone which had been set up on the very edge of the roof. It was reproduced six more times on the VidWall down the entire length of the tower.

As the girl squinted through the gun, a figure emerged through the smoke and stood silhouetted against the lights. Johnny imagined he heard a distant roar, but wasn't sure, then the lighting on the roof changed and Vee stepped up to the microphone, fully visible, exposed, alone. Johnny watched, along with the rest of the world, as the image centred and zoomed towards him.

Vee raised his arms, and smiled.

The large cannon Mary held silently spat its thin beam of destruction and Johnny watched as Vee split in half, from his groin upwards. The two near equal halves fell apart, spewing intestine across the roof.

A microsecond later, the cable from Mary's neck turned a neon crimson, then back to green again. The girl pulled it violently from her neck, then stumbled and sprawled over the floor, knocking the gun over. For a moment she lay there, quite still, then her body started heaving, as if sobbing.

Johnny was trying to think of something to say that would

An Idol

comfort her when he realised she was laughing. She turned over, and looked at him, incredulously shaking her head.

'You really are a complete arsehole, aren't you, Speed,' she stated categorically.

The crippled couple staggered towards the lift, trying to support one another and the items they carried. She was using the large cannon as a crutch again, but it was awkward because of the black box she was holding under the same arm. The boy was trying to speak at the same time, but couldn't get the words through panting with the exertion of standing up.

'I . . . I thought . . . you were on . . . his side?' he eventually managed.

'I thought I was, but at the end of the day he just used me . . . worse than you or anyone else has. Shit! . . . You should have seen what he's made me do, tonight. No way!' Mary grimaced, but whether it was due to the pain of memories or her leg Johnny couldn't tell. He decided to change the subject.

'So what did I plug him into, then . . . if that's not . . . not the penthouse's ice?' He tried to indicate the black box she was carrying, but nearly made them both fall over by doing so.

The girl waited until they'd made it into the lift before answering, 'It's an isolated piece of ice, not linked to the Net. His mate Milton was keeping a digitized hacker in it, like a gold fish. It's a very expensive piece of custom gear. Fate is a strange thing, if you believe it. I'm not sure I do. I think I'm just lucky you're such an arsehole that you can't tell the difference between a normal ice terminal and this.'

'How come Vee didn't notice?' Johnny asked, sliding gingerly down the wall to sit on the floor.

'Too busy trying to do everything else. He'd turned off some of the feedback messages so they didn't distract him while he was shooting people. When you plugged the cable in, it activated 'cause it had found a power source and some vacant ice, but didn't say where the ice was or if it was linked to the Net or not. Vee didn't check, he just assumed you'd plugged the cable into the right box and jumped,' she answered, leaning against the door to stop it from closing.

'Why was he doing it himself? Why not get someone else to kill him?'

'I dunno. I think he didn't really trust anyone else to do it, and also wanted to get his own back on Milton, like, once and for all. He was mad, remember.' She tossed the gun crutch to him, and then the black box.

'What are we going to do with him?' Johnny caught the case awkwardly and put it next to the gun. 'I'm for kicking it off the roof, right now,' he added maliciously.

'No. I think he'll come in useful. I want to hang onto him for a while,' she said, distantly, as she began looking for something in her pockets.

'You look as if you still fancy him!' Johnny mumbled, dejectedly.

'Well, he was better in bed than you . . .' she said maliciously, then winked playfully to show she was only teasing him.

'What was he going to do in the Net?' This part of the plan seemed to have escaped Johnny.

'Same shit he's done in real life: cause trouble. I think he planned to turn himself into a virus or something.' Mary pulled out the hand-cannon, tucked it into her belt, then resumed the rummaging.

'So he'd have been immortal, then?' Johnny frowned, as if that made it worse.

'Huh!' she grunted, 'Only as long as there's electricity,' she looked at Johnny, 'which won't be forever, I can assure you. After tonight, I'll be surprised if there's enough juice left in the City to run a toaster!'

'What're you doing?' he asked. She pulled out the green goggles she'd been wearing earlier, and stepped into the lift.

'I want to see what's happening down in the lobby before we

get there. This is the only way out, so we'll just have to shoot anyone who looks like trying to stop us. It's my turn to shoot someone, anyway.'

The lift door closed.

'Which floor, please?' it asked pleasantly. Mary just smiled, and put her green goggles back on.

Siege Of Gresham – *Ray Murphy*

£7.95/$10.00 • pb •1 873176 05 8 • 144 pgs

A rollicking, hair-raising, manic mission across the abruptly blossoming war-zones of the urban northwest. A gang of thirteen Portland winos, would-be guerillas, have a score to settle ... and this time it's war. Their dark and perilous campaign picks up speed until it takes on a runaway life of its own. Isolation and fear forces bloody encounters with skin heads, crips and homicidal postal workers. A long history of disappointed desire becomes a symphony of murderous catharsis, building relentlessly to a dizzying conclusion. The lurid genre of sex and violence never appeared so vital.

The Diamond Signature – A Novel In Four Books & The Death Of The Imagination – A Drama For Four Readers
Penny Rimbaud aka J J Ratter

£6.95/$9.95 • pb • 1 873176 55 4 • 256 pgs

The first collection of prose (and a play) from the father of political punk. The first draft of *The Diamond Signature* was completed in 1974 and since then has been revised countless times. Always regarded as an organic work that could be added to or taken away from at will – several sections of it were adapted by CRASS, the anarchist punk band with whom the author was drummer and lyricist. Other sections have been liberally scattered through subsequent novels.

The Diamond Signature is what Penny Rimbaud considers his most important work. It formed the basis for the band CRASS, who literally revolutionised both punk rock, and politics in a blistering seven year career, which found them reviled by the mainstream, and revered by hundreds of thousands in the underground they helped to create. It is presented here together with his other significant piece of prose, *The Death Of The Imagination*, a new piece of work created originally for live performance.

The AK Mail Order Catalogue

AK Press is a workers co-operative that has been publishing and distributing fine independent, radical and revolutionary literature since the early nineties. To obtain the massive AK mail-order catalogue listing literally thousands of radical, hard to obtain books, magazines and pamphlets as well as t shirts, postcards and audio products please send a large SAE to:

AK Distribution , P.O. Box 12766, Edinburgh EH8 9YE
e-mail: ak@akedin.demon.co.uk

Residents in North America please send $1 to:
AK Press & Distribution
P.O. Box 40682, San Francisco, CA 94140-0682, USA
e-mail: catalog@akpress.org